MUSIC BEFORE MURDER

Jonathan Reuvid

Published by New Generation Publishing in 2023

Copyright © Jonathan Reuvid 2023

First Edition

The author asserts the moral right under the Copyright, Designs and Patents Act 1988 to be identified as the author of this work.

All Rights reserved. No part of this publication may be reproduced, stored in a retrieval system or transmitted, in any form or by any means without the prior consent of the author, nor be otherwise circulated in any form of binding or cover other than that which it is published and without a similar condition being imposed on the subsequent purchaser.

ISBN: 978-1-80369-745-1

www.newgeneration-publishing.com
New Generation Publishing

Cast of characters

Fullmere residents

Julian Radclive	*Author and editor of business books*
Gaby Radclive	*His wife, a retired market research consultant*
Georgina Delahaye	*Proprietor of a fashionable London escort agency*
Giles Delahaye	*Her son, an undergraduate at Cromwell college*
Aubrey Pinkerton	*Her tenant, an art dealer and self-styled connoisseur*
Lady Lucinda Mansfield	*Owner of the Eastwick estate and neighbouring farms*
Sir Percy Mansfield	*Her husband, a retired Commonwealth Office administrator*
Agnes Black	*Her maid of all work*
Silas Grimshaw	*Her estate worker*
Piroska Szabŏ	*An international concert violinist*
Barry Fullerton	*Landlord of the Eastwick Arms*
Emma Fullerton	*His daughter and girlfriend of Giles Delahaye*

Oxford Academics & Luminaries

Alexander Deakin	*Principal, St. Winifred's College, Oxford*
Theodora Deakin	*His wife and Director of the Clarendon Art Gallery*
Geoffrey Randle	*Master of Latimer College*
Hamish McAllister	*Bursar, Latimer College*
Jessop	*Head porter, Latimer College*
Valerie Wyngarde	*A working partner in the Clarendon Art Gallery*
Basil Gore-Smith	*Fine Arts expert at the Ashmolean Museum*
Christina Charteris	*Partner in the Clarendon Art Gallery*
Charlie Dibbs	*Arts Editor, The Oxford Guardian*

Other Attendees at Fullmere Festival

Bill Fentiman	*A solicitor and old friend of Julian Radclive*
Barbara Fentiman	*His wife and friend of the Radclives*
Joan Allnatt	*A concert cellist*
Werner Winkelman	*A concert pianist*
David, Max, Hugo	*Weekend guests at Fullmere Mill*
Trixie, Cheryl, Vanessa	" " " " "

The Police

Bernard Cartwright	*Chief Inspector, Oxford City Police*
Nigel Fellows	*Sergeant, Oxford City Police*
Duncan 'Digger' Mallory	*Inspector, Fraud Squad*
Trevor Wiggins	*Commander, Scotland Yard Murder Squad*
Sam Greenwood	*Inspector, Scotland Yard Murder Squad*

Also involved in London or Amsterdam

Robert Schindler	*Founder of Schindler Lyne, Julian Radclive's publisher*
Gerald Marl	*General Manager, Wigmore Escort Agency*
Cornelius Visser	*Commissaris, Amsterdam Police*
Van den Groot	*Fine art copyist supreme*

And in Hong Kong

Felix Blandford	*Fine art expert at Christie's*
Harry Foung	*Inspector, Hong Kong Police Force*
Li Peng	*Sergeant, Hong Kong Police Force*
Tao Qi Wei	*General Manager of QITIC*
Canning Kwok	*An entrepreneur of doubtful reputation*
Raymond Challoner	*Senior Partner, Challoner Chen*
Chen Yu Bo	*Raymond Challoner's partner*
Greg Barlow	*An Australian lawyer*

CHAPTER 1

Friday evening, 21 June 1996

"DON'T DO IT," Gaby called from the bedroom where she was applying her eyeliner. "I've decided that it's a bad idea. You don't want to look like a bandleader and give the wrong impression to the locals. Anyway, Bill is wearing a normal black one."

Reluctantly, I put my white dinner jacket back on its hangar in the dressing room cupboard. It was a perfect sunlit summer's evening and this was the first black tie event we were attending since we moved to Fullmere the previous autumn. I had thought that it would be fun to complement Gaby in her full length scarlet Gucci dress, a reminder of our more affluent days living in London . I was sure that she would make an impression and I had wanted to enhance her entrance. But, of course, she was right. Any appearance of being flashy would put off the farmers and landed gentry who were our neighbours as well as visitors from Oxford and further afield who might be attending the concert. I gave my silk bow tie a final tweak and slipped into my normal dinner jacket. Joining Gaby in front of her mirror, I kissed her affectionately on the neck.

"Will I do?" she asked standing up.

"No need to gild the lily further," I said.

At the age of fifty, Gaby was still an attractive woman. She wore her hair shorter now, blonde with any hint of grey carefully tinted out by the West End hairdresser whom she continued to visit monthly; the long-sleeved evening dress set off her slender figure seemingly unchanged over the twenty-three years we had lived together.

"You know very well that you look magnificent. I refuse to flatter you further," I said.

I took her arm, and we descended to the kitchen where Bill and Barbara Fentiman awaited us. Our oldest friends, they had sensibly helped themselves to drinks from the bottles on the breakfast bar with ice from the refrigerator for their large gins and tonic.

"Tell us more about what we're in for this evening," Bill said.

We'd known each other since we were at Oxford together and never lost touch; Bill had led a less adventurous life than me, combining the partnership in a prosperous legal practice in West Sussex which he had taken on from his father with commercial work as adviser to a carefully selected handful of City clients. The comfortable lifestyle had added weight to his upper body but he was still some way short of the padded jowls and pouches under the eyes accumulated by many successful members of his profession in middle age. By contrast, his wife had changed little over the years; tonight, encased in a flowered evening dress for the fuller figure with streaks of grey in her hair she was the same bubbly Barbara we had first met nearly twenty-five years ago.

"We can tell you more about some of the people you're likely to meet rather than the concert which is described as 'A Festival of Central European Music'; we understand that there will be pieces from Hungary, Poland and Czechoslovakia," I said,

"That sounds a bit heavy. Tell us about the people," Barbara asked.

"I'll give you a run-down on the leading players." said Gaby "starting with our resident celebrity, Piroska Szabó, the violin virtuoso and organiser of the Festival. She lives in a cottage across the Green when she's not touring in concert and we see her quite often. Piroska's lived in this country for more than twenty years since she left Hungary but her

English is sometimes impossible to understand. Great fun though and she always looks amazing."

I poured Gaby a glass of the Muscadet which I had chilled in the fridge and the same for myself. I knew that there would be drinks when we arrived and had decided to forego my usual whisky and soda. I let Gaby continue.

"I'll introduce you to the farmers and their wives as we meet them – all nice friendly people, but I never know what to say to the wives. Then there's Barry Fullerton, the landlord of the Eastwick Arms; he's doing the buffet this evening. Julian thinks he and Piroska are an item."

"What makes you think that, Julian?" Bill asked curiously.

"Elementary my dear Watson. On the two occasions we've been to Piroska's for a meal Barry has been in attendance as a guest; the second time he cooked the dinner," I said.

"Amazing, Holmes. A remarkable deduction," Bill declared in the same vein.

"Go on, Gaby, with your cast of characters," Barbara invited.

"The local big estate owner, Lucinda Mansfield, originally Lucy Lovell, and her husband Sir Percy Mansfield, who live at Eastwick Hall. We've seen them at one or two local events and are on speaking terms. They don't seem to entertain and we've never met them socially. He's much older than her and they've only been married a few years," Gaby said.

"I sense there's more of a story here," Barbara suggested.

"Yes, quite a tangled tale, but it will have to wait," I said. "Time we went if we don't want to be late. So finish up your drink, Barbara, like a good girl."

"Who is our host this evening? We ought to have a thumbnail sketch, at least," Bill said draining the last of his gin and tonic and tossing ice cubes into the kitchen sink.

Sensing that we were about to leave, our Labrador Fred who had been lounging on the kitchen window seat flopped to the floor and sat looking expectant. I had already fed him his evening meal before going upstairs to change and he had strolled around the garden to do what was expected of him.

"I saved the best to last," Gaby resumed. "Georgina Delahaye our glamourous mystery woman. She drives down from London every Thursday evening in her Bentley convertible and goes back on Mondays. Some weekends she has house parties with young tarty-looking girls and older men in her mansion and we hear disco music into the small hours. Rumour has it that Georgina owns a West End Escort Agency. The concert is in the grounds of her house."

"In other words, it's a high-class knocking shop," Barbara exclaimed with glee.

"A house of reported ill repute is all you can say without risk of slander," said Bill, ever the lawyer.

"Form your own opinions during the evening. Now we really must go if we want to talk to anyone before the concert starts," I insisted.

I shooed them out into the yard where the Range Rover stood waiting, gave Fred his expected outsize biscuit bone and locked up while Bill opened the double gates under the arch which gives on to the village street. There's just the one road through the sleepy village running between our house and the village green. An ancient oak tree stands in the centre of the green directly facing our dining room windows. At the far end in either corner there are two working farms and down each side are 17th century cottages, mostly semi-detached, built in local stone with thatched or stone-tiled roofs. I turned right out of the gates and, after a pair of semi-detached cottages, passed by the steps leading up to the churchyard and its simple Norman gothic church. Beyond, on the right, as we drove on was an open driveway leading to the Old Rectory, now occupied by the director of an exercise equipment business who commuted daily to his factory north of Stratford-upon-Avon. On the left-hand side were more cottages of the kind clustered around the Green without front gardens and one more imposing detached house which had seen better days and was currently unoccupied. Next on the right is the Eastwick Arms, which Barry Fullerton leases from the estate and, finally as we proceeded out of the village, a straggle of council houses built in the early 1950s as a part of the then government's drive to house families migrating from London and cities of the Midlands in the post-war period. They're not in keeping with the village but not too much of an eyesore; rendered in white, slate tiled and with neatly hedged front gardens. Many are lived in by a younger generation of old local families whose ancient cottages are now occupied by interlopers.

We drove on through open countryside for several miles until we joined a side road on our right which curled back downhill towards the bottom of the valley overlooked by Fullmere. My passengers chatted among themselves with Bill and Barbara comparing the patchwork of fields and spinneys with their own less rural West Sussex setting. A hand-painted sign pointing right proclaimed 'Fullmere Music Festival' in bold red capitals. We followed the sign through a stone pillared gateway on to a gravelled private road which took us into the grounds of Fullmere Mill. The area set aside for parking was closely packed but there was space for the Range Rover on a grass verge nearer to the house. Walking round one side of the building we found ourselves on a large well-cut lawn with the festival venue laid out before us.

---ooo0ooo---

The house faced west with the ground descending to a stream and overlooking a wood on the far side of the valley. To the right a large canvas marquee had been erected backing on to the stream where the concert would be staged. In the foreground, numerous tables and chairs were mostly occupied already by the fellow guests who had arrived before us. Closer to the house a range of trestle tables had been set up and covered with linen tablecloths. For the present it served as a bar with an array of ice buckets loaded with champagne bottles, glasses, bowls of nibbles and plates of canapes. Under the close supervision of a dinner-jacketed Barry Fullerton, a team of young waiters and waitresses were diligently refilling glasses and offering the canapes to seated guests and those standing in groups to socialise. They were dressed in white shirts and black trousers or skirts; the waiters wore black bow-ties to enhance the sense of occasion.

We helped ourselves to flutes of champagne and looked for our hostess. Georgina Delahaye had spotted us and detached herself from the group with whom she was mingling to greet us.

"Julian and Gaby Radclive," she said. "We've met, of course, in Piroska's house but this is the first time you've been here. Welcome to you and your guests. Thank you so much for coming."

I noticed for the first time that she had a discreet American accent: New England, I thought, but less brittle than Boston.

"We wouldn't have missed it for anything, Georgina," Gaby said. The two women scrutinised each other critically. Georgina's emerald green off-the-shoulder Givenchy with her copper-coloured long hair was a match for Gaby's Gucci; in truth they were both somewhat overdressed for this rural event – hardly an occasion for high fashion. Any tension that there might have been was dissipated as Piroska Szabŏ joined us. Her stylish showbiz attire trumped all competition: white satin trousers, a scarlet sequin jacket and T-shirt with scarlet patent pumps. It was her concert and she was to be the star performer. With her short curly hair and dark complexion, the effect was stunning.

"Dahlinks, *üdvoziom*," she welcomed us. "Introduce me to your friends; I was beginning to worry that you might not make it. We shall be starting very soon."

"In that case, I should be checking arrangements for the interval. We shall be coming out here again for supper if the weather holds. It's still light enough at nine o'clock these days," Georgina said and moved away, not towards Barry as I had expected but back to the group with whom she had been chatting before we arrived.

"And I must give last minute encouragements to my musicians," declared Piroska pointing to a table where a single man and two women of diverse ages, all formally dressed in evening clothes and looking uneasy, were seated. They were sipping champagne abstemiously and waved away the waiter who was offering to top up their glasses.

"Good luck, then; or how do you say 'break a leg' in Hungarian?" Bill asked.

"It's too difficult but thank you," Piroska said turning and then looking back over her shoulder. "Kéz-és-lábtörést. Do you think you can remember it?"

Bill shrugged and spread his hands helplessly. "What an amazing woman," he said as she moved away.

During this repartee I had been studying the group which Georgina had re-joined. At first sight they were an ill-assorted collection of attractive flashily dressed young women and an equal number of men of varying ages, two of them of a similar vintage to Bill and myself; their mood was decidedly jolly, fuelled by more frequent refills of champagne than normal concert-goers might be expected to imbibe. Barbara and Gaby were watching them too.

"Could this be one of her famous weekend house parties?" Barbara asked.

"Looks like it," said Gaby, equally fascinated.

"Well if it is, I know one of the men," Bill commented. "The one with his back to us, grey hair and balding; works for an investment bank which advises Konrad von Richthaven."

Any further speculation was interrupted by the ringing of a hand bell and a loudspeaker announcement summoning us to take our seats in the marquee. We had been allocated numbered seating in the third row of twelve chairs at the far side of the tent. Music stands and chairs for the quartet of musicians: pianist, cello, a second violinist and Piroska herself were positioned on a low stage backing on to the stream the other side of the canvas. As we sat, I felt a tap on my shoulder from the row behind and turned to see the familiar face of Alexander Deakin. I had met Alexander when I was writing a series of profiles of leading UK publishers for a magazine and he was Chief Executive of Oxford University Press. It was not a successful appointment for him; after two years of declining profits, he was quietly retired by the Vice-Chancellor and awarded his present incumbency as Master of St. Winifred's, one of the University's newer and less celebrated colleges. We had met him once socially in Oxford since moving to Fullmere at an evening lecture given by two of our academic friends on their return from a sabbatical spent exploring the Sahara. He was unexpectedly friendly.

"Shall we sit down together for supper in the interval," Alexander suggested. By his side, his wife Theodora, the leading light in the Clarendon Art Gallery, nodded her agreement.

"Let's do that," I said, including the others. "We'd be delighted if you would join our party."

We settled back in our chairs and there ws the expectant hum of an audience waiting for the curtain to rise. Of course, there was no curtain here tonight but the lights in the body of the marquee were dimmed while those above the stage were raised. However, there was one more intervention to come; a flap of the tent was raised and Georgina entered on the arm of a flamboyant figure: a willowy young man with wispy beard and flowing locks. It was her son Giles; he wore a large floppy velvet bow of the kind favoured by Edwardian Bohemians and a white silk blazer over dress trousers. Gaby and I exchanged glances; I was glad that my white dinner jacket was safely back in the closet.

---oooOooo---

The simple printed sheets we found on our seats when we took our places were headed "An Evening of Central European Music". I'm a philistine when it comes to classical music with a penchant for the baroque composers but the programme seemed exciting: from Poland pieces composed by Chopin and Paderewski; from Czechoslovakia by Dvorak and Smetana; and from Hungary Lizt and Bartok. In all there were to be eight pieces: four before and four after the supper interval ending with an aria from Smetana's *the Bartered Bride.* When Georgina and Giles had seated themselves in the front row alongside the more conservative figures of Sir Percy and Lady Lucinda Mansfield, Piroska stepped forward from her ensemble to the front of the stage.

"Good evenink. Tonight my friends and I offer you a *pot pourri* of Czech, Hungarian and Polish music – a soupçon of Central European musical culture. I shall not announce each piece; we shall play the pieces in the same order as the programme. But we begin with a song by Paderewski for violin and piano." For once, Piroska's English was almost perfect and I felt that she had rehearsed her opening remarks carefully. She signalled to the pianist, a mellow-looking man of middle age with rimless spectacles, who struck the first chord of the opening phrase on a Steinway Grand.

The string members of the quartet were placed in a shallow arc half-turned towards the piano but still facing the audience The lady cellist, a more forbidding figure in high-necked black dress and without jewellery was seated furthest from the pianist and the second violin, a much younger woman with lank blonde hair was positioned between them. Her dress was also severe but there were two strands of gold chain about her neck. For this first piece Piroska remained standing close to the piano with a matching scarlet silk scarf thrown over her shoulder where her violin rested to protect the sequins of her jacket.

The young violinist and the cellist played well but from the moment that Piroska first drew the bow across her Guarneri violin it was clear that we were in the presence of a virtuoso performer. Her playing had an attack and yet delicacy of touch which held her audience in rapt attention. There was warm applause at the end of this first piece; our appetites for more were whetted. The next piece was Chopin's cello and piano sonata in C minor featuring the cello with piano; it showcased the talent of the quartet's cellist with a warm and vibrant performance and complemented the first item from a Polish composer.

The third item was a show stopper of a different order: a song by Antonin Dvorak titled Sirotek (The Orphan). The singer was a tall, well-proportioned blonde sheathed in a white satin gown who had been sitting at the side of the stage; we realised we were in for something unusual when she loosened the long tresses of hair which had been coiled neatly on her head. As she came forward two waiters entered the marquee and placed before her a table on which they set a large enamel basin; into the basin they then poured water from a massive ewer before retiring. The music was slow and mournful, sung with increasing emotion by the soloist. Her song rose to a crescendo and she delivered an eye-popping climax by flinging forward her mane over her head and into the basin where she doused her hair vigorously. The audience sat in stunned silence as the music died away and the singer bowed her head. We started to clap uncertainly before applause swelled with a chorus of 'bravos' from the back where Georgina's house party were enjoying themselves with several bottles of champagne which they had smuggled into the tent. The singer smiled appreciation through her streaming hair before retiring; one of the waiters tended to her at the tent flap with a fluffy white towel.

Piroska stepped forward again with her fellow violinist to take us up to the interval. She had substituted her mellow Guarneri for a coarser instrument; with great verve they launched into a selection of Liszt's gypsy fiddler music from his Hungarian Rhapsody – foot-tapping stuff and a suitable prelude to supper.

"From now on," said Bill, addressing Barbara and Gaby "I shall expect you to sing whenever you wash your hair."

---oooOooo---

CHAPTER 2

Friday evening, 21 June

A WELCOMING AROMA of mulled red wine with cinnamon and cloves drew us to the steaming bowls of goulash. The trestle tables on the lawn had been set out with covered serving dishes while we were still in the marquee. There were stacks of plates and boxes of cutlery at either end with waitresses standing behind ready to serve us as we lined up. We secured a table for ourselves with six chairs; the Deakins joined us. Leaving Barbara and Theodora to secure our places, the rest of us joined the queues for food. Bill and Gaby lined up at the left-hand end; Alexander and I took the right. Covers were lifted from the chafing dishes revealing a rich, dark goulash, a variety of vegetables and a dish of macaroni. We were early in the queue and were soon served returning to our table with plates well-laden. The men carried two plates each while Gaby had grabbed six side plates, bread rolls and cutlery for six.

"All we need now is a bottle of Egri Bikavér," said Alexander as we settled, demonstrating his knowledge of Hungary's best known wine, commonly called 'Bull's Blood'. As if by cosmic ordering, or an act of telepathy a waiter appeared at the table bearing a bottle and six glasses.

"I think we may need another of these," I said as Bill charged our glasses and we each took a first swig of the dark red wine. In no time at all, the waiter returned with a second bottle and a conspiratorial wink.

The goulash was hot and spicey, the wine an excellent accompaniment and we ate our supper contentedly. Barbara and Theodora had been chatting animatedly while we were foraging and continued their conversation.

"You must visit the Art Gallery tomorrow while you're here. The gold jewellery we're showing now really is very attractive and I'm sure your husband would love to buy you something," Theodora said giving Bill a sideways glance.

"Your wife is propositioning my guests. Tell her to control her sales instincts for the evening," I appealed to Alexander, only half in jest.

"That's a lost cause, Julian. Theodora's gone commercial on me ever since she opened her wretched gallery. It seems to take up all her time these days, particularly at the weekend," he replied.

"In that case, we'll all come into Oxford in the morning," Gaby said.

"And Bill and I will leave our cheque books at home," I added.

I looked at Theodora more closely as Alexander changed the subject. She had developed a more predatory look since we had last seen her: the same expression that middle-aged wives of Oxford academics display as they compete for attention in the university's senior common room social circles. But, in Theodora's case, I sensed that there was something more; her vivacity seemed artificial. She was under tension and it was showing. In spite of her restrained unease, she was a handsome woman: a tightly curled head of dark blond hair caried high was offset by high cheekbones, dark eyes and a generous mouth.

"Are you able to relax now after the university goes down next week?" Bill asked Alexander politely.

"There's always a sense of anti-climax when the academic year ends although there are still viva examinations for those who sat Finals. However, I shall have a busy summer; next week I fly to Hong Kong to start a tour of Far Eastern universities to trawl for graduate students. So, I shall have my selling boots on too."

"Those students from abroad pay much more in tuition fees than UK undergraduates, don't they?" Gaby said.

"Indeed they do, which is why I'm getting my begging bowl out. Sadly, Theodora isn't coming with me; the College were prepared to pay her travel costs and she would do a much better job than me in wooing Asian academics."

"I couldn't possibly go with Alexander," Theodora interrupted rather too quickly. "It's the peak tourist season in Oxford and all hands on deck for the Gallery." I had the feeling that only one of them was too unhappy at the coming separation. I poured more wine to restore harmony.

We had finished our main course and a waitress appeared to take away our plates. She announced that afters were either trifle or apple strudel and invited us to help ourselves. This time the women set off to collect our desserts of choice, giving Alexander a chance to comment further on his trip.

"It really is rather tiresome of Theodora not to join me. It's not every day that the College agrees to pay for wives."

"I'm sure you'll both get over it," I said trying to be tactful but doubting my assurance as I gave it.

We were saved from further discussion by the sound of a disturbance which had broken out in front of the serving tables: an altercation between a large man, his back towards us, and one of the waitresses. From his shoulder-length black hair and the set of his shoulders I recognized the man as Georgina's tenant, Aubrey Pinkerton, a self-styled art critic and connoisseur. Gaby and I had come across him on two or three occasions; I had thought him arrogant and judged him a phoney. He was holding the girl in front of him by the upper arms and shaking her none too gently while shouting something; we couldn't distinguish what he was saying. Bill and I looked at each other and prepared to intervene. We were forestalled by Barry Fullerton, alerted by the commotion at the table where he was chatting with guests, who strode over and tapped Pinkerton on the shoulder causing him to turn. Barry spoke to him calmly, motioning him to move away. If he had hoped to defuse the situation quietly, he was mistaken. Reacting in fury, Pinkerton swung a vicious blow and connected with Barry's head knocking him backwards but not down. Barry rested on one knee for a moment to recover; then, shaking his head, rose to his feet and advanced with left foot forward and hands at waist height. Pinkerton squared up to his smaller, lighter opponent and aimed a second haymaker intending to finish him off. This time Barry was prepared; he blocked his opponent's second blow with his left forearm and drove a short powerful jab into Pinkerton's solar plexus. As the taller man started to double up, Barry delivered a left hook to his chin and finished the fight with a heavy right cross which knocked Aubrey Pinkerton out cold, felling him to the ground. He called two of the stronger-looking waiters over and instructed them. "Take this gentleman back to his cottage," he said.

With the incident at an end, the diners resumed their conversations. Most exhibited their normal English reserve, preferring not to acknowledge that anything untoward had happened; there was enthusiastic clapping from a few, in particular Georgina's house party, who were not embarrassed to show that they had enjoyed the spectacle.

"That was an impressive display of counter-punching," Alexander said.

"Par for the course," Bill replied. "The best since I last saw hm in the ring fifteen years ago when he was still in the army and was boxing for his regiment in the Southern Command tournament."

"How good was he?" I asked.

"No-one could touch him. He went on to become Army lightweight champion."

The waitress who had been assaulted was being comforted by Barry; she had her head on his shoulder and he was patting her back.

"That's Barry's daughter Emma. She's a pretty girl," said Gaby.

"Well, he certainly took good care of her," Barbara said approvingly.

We finished our dessert and were taking coffee when the handbell was rung, as before the concert, and the loudspeaker announced that the interval was over. The audience trickled back obediently into the marquee. As our table rose, Lucinda and Sir Percy Mansfield passed by; Lucinda addressed a comment to us.

"Not quite the thing," she said. "No mention on the programme of a cabaret in the interval." She was wearing a plain long black dress which suited her with a diamond and sapphire necklace; she looked cool and elegant and knew it. She managed to look faintly amused and condescending at the same time.

"Fullerton gave the fellah a good hiding; and quite right too," Sir Percy added. "By the way, Radclive," he went on "I want to talk to you about the memoirs I'm writing. Understand that you write for a living and thought you could advise me on choosing a publisher."

I felt that I was being approached as a kind of wordsmith tradesman; hardly flattering but not entirely untrue. I had long ago realised that churning out my kind of non-fiction was the last refuge of an unsuccessful businessman.

"By all means, if you think I could help." I didn't much like the man; his cultivated air of distinction and upper-class speech patterns was marred by eyes set too far apart and a thin-lipped ungenerous mouth. However, he had been a senior civil servant in the Hong Kong administration when Margaret Thatcher had struck her deal with Deng Xiaoping in 1987; so, he could have a tale to tell.

"You may come up to the Hall sometime; then you can tell me what you think." He spoke as if conferring some special honour.

"Give me a call after the weekend and we'll arrange something," I said, resolved to have the last word.

We trailed in their wake after allowing the house party to follow immediately behind. I noticed that Bill's investment banker and a striking girl with red hair had sloped off and were entering the house by a back door.

"Not serious music lovers, I see," Barbara observed.

"Perhaps they want an early night," said Gaby giving her an old-fashioned look.

---oooOooo---

The musicians had spent the interval together in the house, preferring to take their refreshment quietly together and to defer contact with their audience until after the concert. They returned to the stage when we were seated, this time without the singer in attendance. The second half of the programme opened with Dvorak's Opus 13/1 for violin, cello and piano which displayed each member's musical talent to advantage. Next up was a lively mazurka of Ligattii, a crowd-pleasing solo piano piece which showed off the player's skills, followed by Smetana's arrangement of *The Blue Danube*. Piroska's lyrical, soaring rendition of this romantic favourite brought a personal magic to the music, generating another round of warm applause. She came forward again to address us.

"Thank you so much. Sadly, it is already time for the finale to our concert in which you all have a part to play," Piroska announced. "My impressario and your hostess Georgina will give you your instructions."

Georgina took her place centre stage and the musicians stepped down with their string instruments; the pianist gallantly carried the cello for his fellow player and the four of them left the marquee. Speaking with charm and authority, Georgina gave the audience its marching orders.

"You've been a great audience. Now, we want you all to imagine that you are Hungarian peasants attending a village wedding. I guess that's a tall order for some of you," she said, directing her remark pointedly to the front row and the Mansfields in particular.

"And the wedding is taking place at the lakeside. The way is well lit and I'll lead you there. Just follow me."

She left the tent and turned right behind the marquee along the side of the stream until she came to a narrow bridge across with beacons lit on either side. It had been darkening rapidly when we came back after the interval; now at ten o'clock night had fallen and the only natural light was from a clear, almost full moon. We followed Georgina in single file across the bridge and then in pairs up some twenty shallow steps to the artificial lake which a previous owner had created. The torches were replaced by electric lamps up the sides of the stairs and around the nearside of the lake. The water level was above the height of the marquee and similar to that of the car park opposite where we had failed to find a space. The musicians were already grouped on a landing stage which projected over the right-hand side of he lake; the two violins and cello struck up and started to play more gypsy music as we gathered. It took some time for the audience to complete the short walk and we were closely packed along the lakeside when everyone had arrived. I estimated that the lake was about 30 metres across but was unable to reckon the length because there was no lighting to the left and what appeared to be a small island covered heavily in undergrowth intervened. We gazed ahead in anticipation not knowing quite what to expect.

The tempo of the music changed to the opening bars of the aria from Act 2 of Smetana's *The Bartered Bride* as billed in the programme. From the far side of the island a soprano voice rose, quiet at first and then swelling to full volume as a raft slid into view bearing the same statuesque singer in her white shift as before, standing proudly with her blonde hair fully restored to its former glory. Propelling the raft from the back with a punt pole was Giles Delahaye; in his role as gondolier he had discarded his white jacket and added a straw boater with ribbons. Perhaps his education at Oxford was not a complete waste of time, I reflected.

A faint mist rising from the water gave additional dramatic effect to the scene. Giles used the punt pole to keep the raft stationary mid-lake until the dying falls of the aria before steering it skilfully to the landing stage where he handed the singer up to the waiting pianist and safety.

"Our revels now are ended," Georgiana called, out quoting from the final lines of *The Tempest.* "There's a hot punch waiting for us on the lawn to speed you on your way."

We descended two by two, much as we had come, some steadying themselves with the handrail. Ahead of us I observed Theodora chatting to Lucinda Mansfield, an unlikely pairing, and Alexander Deakin to Sir Henry with stiff formality. The four of us were among the last to reach the lawn, where the linen-covered trestle tables were again in service, with tureens heated by spirit lamps from which waiters were ladling punch into glass tumblers. Returning to the table where we had taken supper with our glasses charged, we remained standing and were grateful for the hot drink as an antidote to what had now become a chilly night. Some of the ladies with bare shoulders and arms were feeling the cold; chivalrous partners were draping their jackets over those without wraps. The atmosphere was that of contented partygoers, rather than concert goers who had enjoyed a sociable evening together and were taking a nightcap before dragging themselves home.

Piroska and her band of players had joined the assembled company and were enjoying their glasses of punch amid the individual congratulations of many. Gaby, Barbara, Bill and I drifted among them and spoke to each in turn; charming and modest people, they told us that they played together regularly on the British concert circuit. The pianist was also Petroska's accompanist on some of her European tours and the second violinist her protégée; the cellist had known Piroska since her early days as a soloist and was one of her oldest friends. The singer was Polish and they had met quite recently when both were appearing at the same concert in Warsaw. I left Piroska to last and kissed her on both cheeks.

"You've given us a remarkable and truly memorable evening, my dear," I said. "It's the first time I've heard you play and you have a new member to your fan club."

"Drăgăm Julian. You're very sweet," she said hugging me in return. "Do you think we should give another concert next year?"

"Most definitely, Piroska. And if you could be persuaded to give a concert of German music I have a perfect location for you near Chichester at the home of a very rich Baron," said Bill appearing at her elbow.

"In that case, maybe we shall have two festivals next year: one here and one with your German friend in Sussex."

---ooo0ooo---

CHAPTER 3

Friday night, 21 June

THE CROWD HAD started to thin out as people slipped away and soon we were no more than a dozen diehards quaffing our second glasses of the heady infusion. I had lost sight of the Deakins until Alexander came up behind me sounding plaintive.

"Have you seen Theodora?" he asked. "I can't find her anywhere and it's time we went home."

I turned to face him and could see that he was in a state of some agitation.

"She was in front of us with Lucy Mansfield as we came down the steps. Have you asked her?" Gaby suggested.

"She says she hasn't seen Theodora since they reached the lawn together. Lucinda returned to the marquee to recover her handbag and Theodora wasn't about when she came out."

"Perhaps she went to the loo inside the house?" Barbara said helpfully.

"If you would like, Barbara and I will go inside to spend our pennies and you can wait here with Bill and Julian until we come back," Gaby said, taking pity on him.

Alexander looked grateful and muttered his thanks while the two girls sped off. They were gone longer than I would have expected; in their absence he tried to rationalise what might have happened.

"You could probably gather this evening that we've been arguing recently about the Gallery and Hong Kong. In fact, we're not in a very good place altogether," Alexander admitted mournfully.

I really didn't know him well enough for this kind of confession and felt embarrassed on his account. Bill tried to talk to him on university matters but was unable to distract him and received no more than a token response. Gaby and Barbara returned shaking their heads.

"There was no sign of her. We spoke to two of the house guests who've been around inside since we all returned from the lake and they were sure they had not seen her," Gaby reported.

"It's all very strange inside there," Barbara reported. "We looked downstairs a bit and the walls of the main reception rooms are painted dark red. It's a bit like the film set for a Hammer horror movie or, perhaps, ..."

Bill cut her off. "Barbara, that will wait until later. We need to concentrate on finding Theodora."

"Would you like us to assemble a search party? This is a big place and she might have wandered off and lost her way," I asked Alexander.

He welcomed the suggestion and I called Georgina over; she had been busy receiving thanks and seeing off departing guests including Piroska and her msicians. As soon as we had explained the situation she took charge and organised us into pairs: Barry and Giles were despatched to search around the lake; Graham Crouch, a local farmer, and the older of the five waiters were enlisted to inspect the back of the marquee and to patrol the far side of the stream; Bill and I were sent to look around the front of the house and the car park. While the lawn area remained well lit we had to set off into the dark; so we followed Barry's example and helped ourselves to two of the beacons which still provided a smouldering light. It was agreed that we should all report back within half an hour.

The frontage of the house was a mix of architectures: the centre section including the main entrance was Jacobean while the near wing with tall chimneys was composed of Tudor brick and the longer far wing was a later mid-

Victorian addition. The only car parked in front of the house was a Toyota people carrier; presumably the transport used to collect visitors from the railway station. We crossed the sweep of gravel and passed through a gateway in the yew hedge surrounding a rose garden which extended across the width of the Victorian wing and afforded a pleasant view in the foreground for guests staying in its upper floors. On the further side of the rose garden, a similar archway led into a stable yard where Georgina's dark blue Bentley convertible and a scarlet Alfa Romeo coupe were garaged. The outbuildings were single storey and quickly searched without result. From the yard a second driveway led up to the car park before merging with the main drive down from the entrance.

We returned to the rose garden and this time passed through a third gateway into the darkened area of a swimming pool. There was a building at the far end which housed changing rooms and the generator and electric pump which heated the pool. Bill found the switch and turned on floodlighting which illuminated the thirty foot pool, its coloured tiling and white loungers at either side with a springboard at the deep end. No expense had been spared in creating an outdoor playground for pampered guests. There were signs of recent occupation: empty glasses and a full ashtray on the low table between two loungers; damp towels flung untidily on the floor of the pool house. It was impossible to tell when the pool had last been visited; given the high standard of housekeeping which Georgina maintained, I suspected that two people had been there in the last hour or so – probably since the concert interval.

We moved on to the car park where the few cars of those who had not yet departed still remained. In the front row stood what were obviously the expensive vehicles of male guests who had motored down from London during the afternoon: two Porsche 911s, an Aston Martin and a Maserati Quattroporte. I guessed that one of them was the property of Bill's investment banker. That left the tenanted stone cottage of Aubrey Pinkerton behind the car park for our inspection. The ground floor was in darkness with light from only one upstairs room filtering on to the front step. We debated whether or not to disturb him; Bill thought that we should leave him alone to sleep it off. I saw no reason to give him special consideration and we decided that we ought not to leave any stone unturned. I pushed the doorbell and, when that failed to produce a response, applied the door knocker while leaving the bell depressed. After a good ten seconds an upstairs window was flung open and Pinkerton's tousled head appeared.

"What the hell do you want?" he asked.

"A woman's gone missing and we're part of the search party," I explained.

"None of your bloody business or mine if some silly bitch has wandered off."

"Have you seen anyone moving around up here? A middle-aged blonde lady, the wife of an Oxford College principal. Perhaps she rang the bell to ask for your help?"

"I don't have anything to do with academics' wives – avoid them like the plague. Now, go away and let me go back to sleep," Pinkerton said and slammed the window shut. This time he turned off the light.

"Did you notice that he seemed completely sober?" Bill asked. "Remarkable powers of recovery."

"Yes, but still a bad-tempered slob," I said.

---ooo0ooo---

Having completed our fruitless search we returned to the back lawn where Alexander was being comforted by Gaby and Barbara. Graham Crouch's sweep along the river bank had been similarly abortive. We had to wait another ten minutes before Barry and Giles joined us. Barry was hot but unruffled; Giles was dishevelled, his trousers wet below the knee. While Barry circumnavigated the lake, he had punted the raft back to the island; attempting to step on to dry land while holding the raft steady he had lost his footing and dropped his beacon into the lake. Without light his subsequent search of the islet had been cursory. Nor had Barry found anything. Between us we had discovered no trace of Theodora or indication of where she might have strayed. The search party had failed.

"We can search again in daylight but there's nothing more to be done tonight," Barry concluded.

Alexander had become increasingly downcast. "We can't just give up," he said. "There must be something we can do to find her."

"There were half a dozen other people from the University here this evening. If Theodora was really annoyed, she could have taken a lift back with one of them," Georgina suggested sensibly. She had a list of the attendees with her which she passed to him.

"There's a couple here we know quite well, the Hendersons; he's a senior editor at OUP, one of my appointees."

"There you go. You'll probably find her waiting for you when you get home. They left quite soon after we all got down here," Georgina said.

"That's certainly a possibility. It wouldn't be the first time she's dumped me at a party," Alexander conceded, a ring of hope in his voice. "If she's not there, I'll ring Paul Henderson first thing in the morning. They may have put her up overnight. And if she's not with them, what should I do then?" His mood darkened again.

"If she's not been with the Hendersons, you telephone the Oxford police immediately and report Theodora missing. And then you call us," I told him firmly.

"But the police won't do anything until she's been missing twenty-four hours."

"In a case like this of someone disappearing in identifiable company, they'll act immediately," Bill assured him.

Alexander pulled himself together and set off for the car park; we watched him go, a lonely figure comforted by no more than a ray of hope.

"I hope we're not going to be overrun by a police investigation," Georgina said voicing her concern.

Gaby sympathised, saying what the rest of us were thinking. "I can see that could cause you embarrassment, Aside from all this, it was a fabulous evening, Georgina. We'll call you, in any case, after breakfast."

---ooo0ooo---

We took our leave and drove the short journey back to the village. Fred greeted us with enthusiasm all round. I gave him a leisurely stroll in the garden while Gaby put on the kettle. Like a black shadow he was indiscernible among the bushes except when the beam of my flashlight caught him passing from one to another. At this time of year he loved the garden at night; in particular he had developed a fascination for natterjack toads as they hopped out of flowerbeds on their way to the shallow lily pond where they bred. From bitter experience Fred had learnt that licking them was a painful mistake; so, he watched with respect and, I thought, possibly counted them.

There was a mug of tea waiting for me when we returned. It was well past midnight. Barbara and Bill were seated on stools at the breakfast bar with theirs and Gaby on the kitchen window seat facing them where I joined her. She had changed into her pink towelling bathrobe and Fred arranged himself between us with his head on her lap. They had already started to review the evening. We agreed that Piroska's talent was awe-inspiring and that the concert had been a musical success. The hair-washing singer had provided a touch of unintended comedy in the first half but her closing aria from the lake had been *a coup de theatre*. We went on to discuss people and personalities. Fuelled by her glimpses of the ground floor decorations, Barbara was in no doubt that Georgina was operating something more than a high-class dating agency.

"It's not just a country retreat. It's well-appointed weekend love nest with hot and cold running harlots," she said.

"Georgina's good fun," Gaby countered. "She's a very stylish lady and a superb organizer. I like her."

"I agree with Gaby," said Bill. "I like her too. She spared no expense tonight and did Piroska proud. If she turned her mind to it she really could be a successful impressario; she certainly brought a festival flavour to the concert."

"Of course, the catering arrangements were down to Barry Fullerton – under Georgina's direction, no doubt. The mulled wine afterwards was a perfect ending," I said adding my endorsement.

"And Barry provided the cabaret for the interval. That can't have been part of Georgina's masterplan," Barbara commented.

"I'd like to know more about the relationship between the appalling Aubrey Pinkerton and his landlady. He popped up like the demon king in a pantomime. He was so out of tune with everyone else there," Bill reflected.

The conversation moved on to other people we had talked to or noticed in the course of the evening. "What did you think of the gentry who favoured us with their presence?" Gaby asked.

"A toffee-nosed pair," was Barbara's verdict. "But you said there's more to tell."

Gaby obliged with the background story. "Lucinda Mansfield, or Lucy Lovell as she was, has lived up at the Hall most of her life. Her mother Belinda was a gypsy taken up by Charles Eastwick after he inherited the family estate.

He never married and Belinda became his live-in housekeeper. The villagers who lived here then say that Lucy is his daughter. He paid for her private education and she spent her holidays here with him and her mother. By all accounts he was a fair landlord and everyone speaks well of him; the estate included most this and three other villages and all the farms surrounding them. However, the income from sitting tenants was slender so that by the time he died at the age of sixty-seven most of the farm buildings including farmhouses were in need of repair. He left a rather unusual Will; Julian knows the details."

"Charles Eastwick may have been a bit eccentric but he was no fool," I explained. "He recognized that the estate was no longer financially viable. So what he did was to grant each of the four major tenant farmers the right to buy their freeholds in the Will at a price equal to the capital gains tax liability on the probate value of the farm. In this way he hoped that his sole heir would be able to mortgage the rest of the estate to pay the remaining tax due and to carry on farming. His appointed sole heir was his Ward Lucy," I explained.

"And is that what came to pass?" Bill asked.

"Yes and no. The four farmers did what was expected. Without any more rent to pay, they had no difficulty in raising funds; you met one of them just now – Graham Crouch. He was the first and the other three followed his example. But Charles Eastwick would have been disappointed. Lucy didn't want to be a farmer. She engaged a beady land agent who consolidated the most productive farmland remaining into a single home farm with a manager and set about selling off the rest of the estate – not just the farmland but also most of the village houses and cottages. In this village, for example, which is the nearest to the Hall, she took in everything but twenty acres of mainly water meadow and sold them off with this house to the local solicitor who lived here before us until we bought it from him last year."

"Go on," said Barbara pouring herself more tea. "Do you have any biscuits?" Gaby pointed her towards a tin of chocolate digestives; she selected one for Bill too.

"Well, now she had a fine house, a manageable estate and money but she wanted something more: social status. She was well educated, good-looking, young and wealthy; she started riding to hounds with the local Hunt but the County set still didn't accept her. She needed something more: a title."

"And along came Sir Percy?" Bill suggested.

"Exactly. Percy Mansfield took early retirement at sixty, about five years ago. He was the senior civil servant in Hong Kong at the time and had disagreed with the way the Governor was amending unilaterally provisions of the Basic Law negotiated by Margaret Thatcher with China's paramount leader, Deng Xiao Ping, in advance of the handover to China. He was awarded his knighthood for services rendered but also to avoid any opposition by him in public. He came back to England a widower and rented one of Lucy's cottages to base himself near Oxford. Lucy snapped him up and, bingo, was transformed into Lady Lucinda Mansfield overnight."

"Not exactly a love match but a perfectly respectable marriage of convenience. Lucy gets what she wants and Percy gains a rich young wife and comfortable security for life," Gaby concluded for me and reached for the biscuits.

"And that brings us back to the Deakins and Theodora's disappearance. I do hope that Alexander finds her waiting for him when he gets back to Oxford," said Barbara.

"I don't think that's at all likely." said Bill. "for two reasons: first, however much you are at odds with your husband, it's one thing to stalk off in a huff at a drinks party in central Oxford; quite another to abandon him without warning when you're twenty miles outside the city."

"And your second reason," I asked.

"The Hendersons. Alexander and Theodora were with us throughout the interval. They could have met up on the lawn before the concert started, but I don't think so. When we returned to the marquee for the second half, I saw them wave to two couples in the rows behind theirs; they were the sort of acknowledgments one makes to someone you haven't spoken to previously."

"In that case, where do you think she is?" Barbara persisted.

"I don't have a good feeling about this," Bill was uncomfortable and answered sombrely. "Either still up at the lake or somewhere downstream."

I recalled the bedraggled Giles Delahaye on his return from scouring the lake. Perhaps, if he had not dropped his beacon, he might have found her on the island. Perhaps Barry had missed something during his search of the perimeter. As if by telepathy, Gaby said:

"At least Giles came up to scratch. I didn't know he had it in him."

"It shows how deceptive first impressions can be," Barbara agreed. I thought that said it all and probably applied to at least one other of the evening's concert goers. There was nothing more to say on the subject for now. Gaby thought otherwise.

"Never judge a sausage by its skin," she said, decanting Fred from her lap and leading the way upstairs to bed. We followed.

---ooo0ooo---

CHAPTER 4

Saturday, 21 June

WE WERE WOKEN at seven o'clock by Fred as we were about to take our early morning cups of tea in bed. It was his daily routine to wake us at that hour having seen us safely up to bed the previous night before retiring himself to his sprung dog bed in the utility room. Sundays were the exception when he gave us an extra hour's lie-in before jumping on the bed and delivering a wake-up lick. I marvelled daily at his built-in alarm clock. Gaby had promised to telephone Georgina after breakfast but she was spared the call when the bedroom 'phone rang while I was shaving.

"It's Georgina," she said as I lifted the receiver. "I've just heard from Alexander Deakin. Theodora wasn't there when he got home and she didn't leave here last night with the Hendersons. He was going to call the Oxford police next. How long do you think before they turn up?"

"At a guess, I would say by eleven o'clock. That's all bad news," I said. "I'm afraid you'll have them all over you. Is there anything we could do to support you?"

"I was going to ask you," she sounded apologetic "do you think your friend Mr. Fentiman could give us some guidance about what to expect and what we should do? One of my house guests, Hugo Bassinger, knows him in the City and says that he's strong on sound practical advice. Is that too awful a thing to ask?"

"You'll have to ask Bill yourself. If you hang on I'll call him to the 'phone" I wiped shaving soap off the receiver and shouted for him. He appeared quite quickly wearing a polka dot silk dressing gown. "Georgina wants to ask you something," I explained and handed him the receiver. I could hear her giving him the same story ending with her request for help.

I half-expected Bill to say 'no' nicely but curiosity overcame his professional reluctance. "I'm happy to give you general advice on how to handle the police, Georgina, but I'm not a criminal lawyer. If, for any reason, you were to be arrested I would find one of the best in London to look after you."

There was a further question from the other end and I heard the name 'Barry.' "Yes, it would be a good idea to ask him to come over. Whoever's in charge will want to question him as a material witness. But no, don't ask him and your son to start searching again up at the lake; the police will want to conduct any further searches themselves. Julian and I will be over straight after breakfast."

Barbara and Gaby were disappointed that our plans to visit Oxford had been disrupted. "Why don't you two go anyway," I suggested. "You could visit the Gallery and see if you can find any clue why Theodora seemed so troubled last night. We'll try to be there around midday and, if not, meet you at The Trout at Wolvercote for lunch."

Bill and I had finished our breakfast by nine-thirty and set off promptly for Fullmere Mill leaving our wives to drink more coffee before driving into Oxford. "I didn't expect you to agree to this," I said as we drove out of the village, waving a greeting to our churchwarden Raymond Bates who doubled as Clerk to the Parish Council.

"I confess to curiosity and since we are going to be material witnesses ourselves, having spent the interval with Thoedora and Alexander, I thought it would be good to be in from the start. We were also probably among the last to see her coming down from the lake," Bill replied

As we reached the mill entrance we found Giles taking down the Festival notice and I slowed the Range Rover to speak to him. "You'll find my mother in the rose garden. She's waiting for you there," he told us.

---oooOooo---

We sat in wicker armchairs in the rose garden which Georgina Delahayehad set out for our meeting. Already the day was heating up; Bill and I sat in our shirtsleeves. Georgina was wearing a leopard print silk shirt and white jeans with gold sandals. She appeared composed but I could detect that, underneath the sunglasses, she was less at ease. Four chairs were arranged in a semi-circle with a low table before us on which cups, saucers and a cafetiere were laid out. The fourth chair was already occupied when we arrived by Hugo Bassinger.

"Thank you, Bill, for coming. I know it's an imposition but can you give us some idea of what we can expect from the police?" Georgina said, pouring us our first cups of coffee.

"I'll do my best but remember that I don't have experience of missing persons investigations," Bill replied. "However, I would expect that the first to visit this morning will be the Inspector who has been given responsibility for the incident with his sergeant. They will form an overview of what happened last night and scope out the situation here on the ground. At this stage they won't be focussing on suspects; what they will want is circumstantial accounts of how the evening played out and you will be able to give them the facts. Simply answer the questions factually and thoroughly but don't offer any opinions."

"And then, he'll take our addresses and telephone numbers and we can leave when we want to?" Hugo Bassinger asked.

"So long as this is a missing person case, yes."

"But what if they find her dead?" Hugo persisted, putting into words what we were all thinking.

"Then things become more complicated for everyone – particularly if she were found here. Once the investigation becomes a murder inquiry, the police have to interview everyone who was here last night and that will take time. Their first objective is to identify those who could help them with the investigation and to eliminate everyone else from the inquiry."

"How on earth will they do that? There were more than eighty people here including the staff," said Georgina.

"Well, one way would be to call everyone back for a reconstruction of events from start to finish," I suggested.

"You've been watching too many detective programmes on television," Hugo scoffed.

"Actually, police procedure as shown on episodes of Midsomer Murders is not too far from reality," Bill said.

"In that case," Hugo declared "I shall leave my home address and telephone number and drive back to London with Trixie for the rest of the weekend. They can interview me there, if they wish."

I looked at him lolling indolently in his wicker chair and decided that he was of that City stockbroker type still surviving after the Big Bang whom I dislike most. He wore a navy blue towelling robe, Flip Flops and displayed bare white knees when he crossed his legs. Sounds of splashing and laughter from the other side of the yew hedge indicated that other members of the house party, possibly including Trixie, were already desporting themselves around the swimming pool.

"That would be a very foolish thing to do," Bill drawled in reply. If you want to eliminate yourself from the inquiry you should not attract attention to yourself. Leaving without permission could be construed as running away."

"That's absurd. The Oxford police couldn't possibly consider my returning home as a suspicious act. You said yourself that you're not experienced in this kind of matter. I think you're just speculating," Hugo Bassinger sneered.

"Then, let me speculate further," Bill continued. "If this turns into a murder inquiry and the local police don't have any lead within two or three days, it's likely that Scotland Yard will be called in. And if that happens, everyone not explicitly ruled out will be interviewed intensively again. The Murder Squad leaves no stone unturned and you might find a knock at the door embarrassing. Does your wife know you're here?"

Hugo coloured heavily and his expression was that of a spoilt child about to throw a hissy fit. "Susan and I have a very open marriage. As a matter of fact, she's in Hampshire this weekend, staying at her hairdresser's country bolthole."

"Tell me," said Bill quietly deploying his forensic skill "How did you pay for your weekend here?"

"By American Express – not that it's any business of yours" Hugo replied, starting to lose his temper.

"Your personal credit card, or the bank's?" Bill asked with icy calm. "Because, if you said the bank's, the Murder Squad might find that interesting as evidence of character and could turn up at your office instead of your home."

"In that case, I would ask you, Fentiman, to represent me as my lawyer." His temper restored, Bassinger was again supremely confident. Bill's response took him by surprise.

"In which case, I would say that I couldn't act for you, Basinger. Since we have a client in common, there would be a clear conflict of interest."

"But there is no connection between this incident and von Richthaven," Basinger protested.

"Indeed not; nor should there be. If the worst happens and the search for Theodora hits the Red Top headlines with your name attached to the story, the Baron may ask me if you, and indeed, your bank, should continue to be his financial advisers."

There was little doubt among those of us listening what Bill's advice would be. As put-downs go, it was a conversation-stopper. Hugo Bassinger rose to his feet with a mask of stone. "I shall make my own decisions as events unfold," he said.

Gathering his towelling robe about him he attempted a dignified exit in the direction of the swimming pool; in his flip-flops he could manage no more than a stately shuffle. Georgina, who had been observing the exchange with barely disguised amusement, added her contribution.

"I hope you won't be so dismissive, Bill, if I ask you to act for me? Konrad von Richthaven has never availed himself of my services," she said.

"Let's cross that bridge when we come to it," Bill replied.

---oooOooo---

As if on cue, a crunch of tyres on gravel announced the arrival of newcomers. Enter the police. The flashing of warrant cards was superfluous. "Detective Chief Inspector Cartwright," the older man announced "and this is Detective Sergeant Fellows. I think you know we're here to pursue inquiries into the disappearance of Mrs. Theodora Deakin." Then addressing Georgina "Are you Mrs. Georgina Delahaye, the owner of this property?"

Georgina nodded and the Chief Inspector turned his gaze to Bill and myself. "And who might you gentlemen be?" he asked. I took it upon myself to answer for the two of us, declaring who we were and adding that we were probably among the last to have seen Theodora the previous evening. DCI Cartwright was an admirably methodical man of a gloomy disposition, beetle-browed and grizzled with a military moustache, who believed in putting first things first. He asked for a tour of the concert site and a summary of the proceedings. Georgina led him around the side of the house to the lawn where Barry Fullerton and some of his crew were tidying up. The marquee was untouched; the contractors, she explained, would be coming on Monday morning to take down and remove the tent and chairs. Barry had started to remove the supper tables and chairs which were Eastwick Arms property; he planned to take them away later in the back of his Landrover. Until then they were being stacked against a wall of the house. Notepad and ballpoint at the ready, the fresh-faced Detective Sergeant trailed in his DCI's wake with Bill and I bringing up the rear.

The Chief Inspector was at pains to establish a detailed timeline for the whole evening from the arrival of guests and pre-concert drinks, through the first half of the concert, the interval and second half including the times of the audience transfer to the lake, the time spent there and the return of audience and musicians to the lawn for the punch. With some assistance from us on the timings, Georgina gave a clear account with as much detail as he required for what Cartwright described as 'his first pass'. We climbed the steps to the lakeside whre he surveyed the scene gloomily.

"The first thing we need to do is to carry out a daylight search of the grounds," he announced. "Go back to the car, Fellows, and organize a search team for this afternoon. We'll need eight, I reckon, and a frogman in case we have to drag the lake." The Chief Inspector was seized with a sudden fit of sneezing. "I suffer from hay fever in the countryside at this time of year," he said reaching into a pocket of his jacket for a decongestion sniffer.

We returned to the lawn. "Leave those tables and chairs there against the wall for the time-being, please," Cartwright demanded. "You may be sure, Mrs. Delahaye, that if she's here on your estate we'll find her by the end of the day." Then, as if arranging snacks for a cocktail party: "Otherwise, I'll order a fingertip search for tomorrow around the lake."

"Is there anything you would like to ask us while we're here, Chief Inspector?" Bill ventured.

"You said, Mr. Radclive, that you and Mr. Fentiman were among the last to have seen Mrs. Deakin. Can you elaborate?" Cartwright asked.

I told him that the Deakins had been sitting in the row behind us and had joined us and our wives at the same table for the duration of the supper interval. No. They had not mingled with anyone else then and had been with us when the bell sounded for the second half and the Mansfields passed by our table. I added that they were behind us when we all went up to the lake for the finale and that afterwards we had descended immediately behind them with Theodora chatting to Lady Lucinda and Professor Deakin to Sir Henry. The Chief Inspector considered my account carefully.

"And how was Mrs. Deakin during supper? Would you say that she and the Professor were relaxed and in good spirits?" I had the feeling that he already had an answer to that question from Alexander. Remembering Bill's earlier caution, it seemed safer to pass the question to him for the appropriate response; so I nodded in his direction.

"Generally, we were all conversing happily and relishing the first half performance of the concert. However, it would be fair to say that the Professor and Mrs. Deakin were at odds over his forthcoming visit to Hong Kong. He wanted her to accompany him and she felt obliged to stay in Oxford to manage her art gallery," Bill answered in measured tones.

"Was this the sort of disagreement that could have flared up into a more serious row later in the evening, prompting Mrs. Deakin to storm off by herself?" Cartwright pressed him.

"No, Chief Inspector. I would say that it was the sort of well gnawed bone of contention between couples which continues to be nibbled at for some days later," Bill replied.

"Very colourful, Mr. Fentiman. That's consistent with Professor Deakin's account."

The Chief Inspector smiled mournfully and continued. "There's nothing further that I need to ask you gentlemen about just now. I may need formal statements later. I shall need to know where we can reach you."

"I live in in the centre of Fullmere on the Green at Home Farm; Mr. Fentiman and his wife are staying with us until tomorrow evening," I said.

"So, you're a farmer?" Chief Inspector Cartwright asked.

"It's no longer a working farm and hasn't been one for many years. We have a garden and about twenty acres which we let off for grazing," I answered. The Chief Inspector sniffed disparagingly and took another pull on his nasal sniffer.

---oooOooo---

CHAPTER FIVE

Saturday afternoon and evening, 21 June

IT WAS CLOSE TO midday and too late to meet Gaby and Barbara in Little Clarendon Street; so we drove direct to The Trout. I took the third exit on the roundabout at the top of the Woodstock Road down into Wolvercote and then along the Godstow Road at the end of the village through to the inn. We left the Range Rover in the car park across the road from the pub. Gaby's electric blue Subaru was not yet there. On the way over neither of us had much to say about the situation at Fullmere Mill.

"Chief Inspector Cartwright seems a safe pair of hands," I remarked.

"It may need more than that if they find Theodora on site. I tried to say the minimum about her quarrel with Alexander, but I felt at the time that there was something else that troubled her in connection with the Gallery – some other reason why she didn't want to leave Oxford," Bill said.

"Do you think Georgina will be able to drill some common sense into Hugo and the rest of the house guests?"

"She'll be fine. Georgina's a tough cookie," was Bill's verdict.

We ordered our pints at the bar and sat on the stone wall overlooking the stream which, flowing along the length of its frontage, made The Trout one of the most popular haunts for students and dons on summer evenings. Today it was not particularly busy and there was no difficulty in reserving a table for when the others arrived. We enjoyed the sun in our faces and reminisced contentedly about our own days at Oxford when we had been regular visitors.

"Do you remember the night you jumped in off this wall?" Bill asked. "We all thought you were crazy and might get drowned."

"I did it for the money. You put up ten pounds between you as a wager. In my financial state, the bet was irresistible," I said.

"But you could have still drowned. The stream was fast flowing."

"That wasn't the problem. But I hadn't bargained for the weed; not something to be done again," I agreed.

We didn't have long to wait. The growl of the Subaru Imprezza's twin exhausts shattered the lunchtime calm. We heard it turn into the car park and two minutes later Gaby and Barbara joined us; hot and breathless they pleaded for Pimms. When we were seated at the table and thirsts were quenched we decided to order our food before exchanging notes. Bill and I collected smoked trout and cheese ploughman's for all from the bar with a second round of drinks. We were requested to tell our tale first and we related all that had occurred at Fullmere before hearing the girls' account. Their reaction to Hugo Bassinger's conceit was identical: "A chateau bottled idiot" was the consensus. Gaby labelled him "Hooray Hugo" and the nickname stuck over the coming days. Barbara thought that the Chief Inspector seemed "avuncular"; Gaby was less sure and thought that he and his sergeant were not in the same league as the fictional Morse or Lewis.

It was their turn to give us an account of their visit to the Clarendon Art Gallery. Gaby started off and Barbara added her comments as she went along. "It's about halfway down Little Clarendon Street from the St. Giles end on the right-hand side. There's a decent shopfront window with pieces of their current exhibition of pottery and ceramics on show. Inside there's a single ground floor room with more of the same on plinths and stairs down to the basement - no upstairs. There's a desk and chairs at the back of the room."

"On the walls there are carefully lit paintings and prints: still life and, more prominently, sort of neo-cubist abstracts, I suppose," said Barbara. "I didn't like most of them. In a funny way the modern art seemed very dated." She returned to her smoked trout ad forked a piece into horseradish sauce before poppig it into her mouth.

"Downstairs was more intersting," Gaby continued. "Some rather attractive engraved and cut glass: a claret jug, salad bowls, vases and table decorations. Also the jewellery: gold and silver rings, necklaces, earrings and bracelets, many set with semi-precious stones. Some of them I really liked, particularly a necklace of gold and amethyst beads. Then, at the far end of the basement, partitioned off, there is an office area where, presumably, the administration and book-keeping takes place."

"What are the prices like?" I asked, cutting a wedge of Stilton from my ploughman's plate to eat with French bread.

"There were no price tickets on the exhibits; just a card naming the artist and a description of the piece. Some of the cards upstairs and in the window have red stickers to show they have already been sold," said Barbara.

"It's one of those places where they price according to those asking the question and their assessed depth of pocket as much as the product itself," Gaby added cynically.

"Were any of Theodora's partners there?" Bill asked.

"Valerie Wyngarde was in charge. She's a full-time working partner - in the gallery five or more days a week. She was expecting Theodora to join her at midday and then relieve her for the afternoon," Gaby said.

"Had she heard that Theodora is missing?" I wondered.

"Yes. She had a call from Alexander shortly after she opened to tell her. So she called in a post-graduate student called Nancy who helps out when required; Nancy was on the front desk when we arrived," Gaby replied.

"Rather a floppy girl with a fringe but nice enough. I shouldn't think she's much of a saleswoman though," Barbara commented.

"Did any other people come into the gallery while you were there?" I asked.

"Two couples and a single woman wandered around but they didn't request prices on anything in the half hour that we spent looking ourselves and chatting with Valerie," Barbara answered.

"Little Clarendon Street gets a fair amount of visitors in the summer months but it's not exactly in the city centre. The gallery would do better if it were located on the High, Broad, Cornmarket or even the Turl," Gaby said, anticipatig my next question.

"And what did you make of Valerie herself?" Bill questioned changing the subject.

"A willowy blonde in her early thirties with strange eyes - no way of telling whether she is looking at you directly or right through you when you talk. Quite an engaging personality, though, but her hair was a mess," Barbara answered.

"With a little effort and the right makeup and clothes she could be quite glamorous," Gaby added. "Her husband's a mining engineer; he's abroad much of the time, advising mineral extraction companies on their new developments. I agree with Barbara about her eyes. I think she might be on drugs."

"We also met the third partner, Catherine Charteris," Barbara resumed. "Very briefly. She floated in - breathless and stylish in a lavender boiler suit and high heels with a trailing crepe silk scarf like Isadora Duncan."

"But not in an open sports car, I hope," commented Bill spreading Branson pickle on the last piece of his French bread and adding a chunk of cheddar.

"It was quite clear that she is not a working partner," Gaby confirmed. "She only dropped in to 'borrow' a rather spectacular gold and coral necklace to wear tonight at some dressy party that her mother is giving out at Eynsham. It seems that she uses the gallery as her personal lending library for jewellery."

"From what you tell us, there seems to be no compellng reason why Thoedora should feel obliged to stay in Oxford to tend the gallery rather than accompany Alexander to Hong Kong next week," Bill concluded.

We drained our glasses and decided not to take coffee. "What do you have in mind for Barbara and Bill this evening, Gaby?" I asked her.

"Dinner at home; I bought lobsters in the covered market this morning and I thought I'd cook them Thermidor."

"What a treat. Just the four of us, or are you asking anyone else?" Bill asked.

"We've enough lobster to invite Piroska and any of her musicians who are still around to come over." Gaby answered. We all thought that an excellent idea.

We walked over from The Trout to the car park. Bill elected to take a white knuckle ride with Gaby in the Subaru Imprezza while Barbara preferred the solid comfort of the Range Rover with me. As we opened car doors, she had a sudden thought.

"There was something else at the gallery," she said. "When Catherine opend the door to the office in the basement I caught a glimpse of a painting propped aganst a filing cabinet. It looked like one of those 17th century Dutch interiors - you know, black and white tiled floors and a succession of rooms in perspective. It seemed rather out of keeping."

"How very interesting," said Bill calling out from the passenger door of the Subaru as he climbed in.

---ooo0ooo---

We drove back to Fullmere; as we re-entered the village we noticed a police car parked outside the council houses on the right hand side. When we arrived at Home Farm, Gaby and Bill were already in the kitchen with the kettle on. I walked through the dining room to my study and saw the answerphone light flashing. There was one message timed ninety minutes earlier from Georgina asking me to call her back as soon as possible; I did so.

"Julian, hi, I'm glad you're back. They've found Theodora' body up at the lake - at the back of the island in the reeds. I had to identify the body when they brought her down and that was pretty grim. But there's more awful news," Georgina said.

"That's bad enough but not entirely unexpected, I suppose. What more could there be?" I asked.

"There's another body - one of the young waitresses. Whoever killed her stuffed the body under the stage from outside the back of the marquee."

"That would explain why there was a police car outside one of the council houses just now when we came through the village. What is the Chief Inspector going to do next?"

"He's calling everyone back who was at the Festival tomorrow morning for a re-enactment. You'll get a telephone summons during the evening; I had to give him the telephone numbers of all those who bought tickets. It's what Bill expected when he was talking to Hugo earlier," she said.

"The poor girl. She must have seen the murderer going up or coming back from the lake. Of course, we'll be with you tomorrow to give our support . Try to get some rest yourself if you can calm your guests down; it's bound to be a traumatic day for you and Giles," I cautioned.

I returned to the kitchen and told the others what had happened; their reactions echoed mine.

"I saw the Bennett girl there last night as one of the waitreeses with Emma Fullerton. It may have been her,"

Gaby said. "I'll go round there tomorrow and see if there's anything I can do to help her poor mother."

"Meantime, why don't you ring Piroska and invite her for this evening," I suggested.

A series of Hungarian squawks on the line onfirmed that Piroska would be delighted. The Polish singer and her second violinist had taken a mid-morning train to London; her cellist, Joan Allnatt was staying the weekend and her pianist, Werner Winkelman had moved down from the Eastwick Arms for the night. She had been wondering what to do with them for the evening and the dinner invitation solved her problem. The police had telephoned her just before Gaby called; so she was already alerted to the summons to attend the re-enactment. They hadn't seemed too concerned that two of her group had already departed.

"Fred needs a good run over the fields," I announced. "Will anyone join us?" Barbara stayed to help Gaby prepare dinner while Bill decided to accompany me. We changed into boots - I had an extra pair of wellies in Bill's size - and set off. The sight of his choke lead was enough to energize Fred from apparent sleep in an instant and he bounded ahead of us to the top of the garden and through the field gate when opened into the meadow. The top third of our field is flat and is inhabited by cattle from one of the farms across the Green but beyond it descends quite steeply to the water meadow below. A stream flows across the property from under the road on the right through to the adjacent fields on the left. We took a direct route down to a stile at the bottom left hand corner where we were joined by Fred who had beaten the boundaries scouring the hedges unsuccessfully in the hope of flushing out rabbits.

Climbing over the stile into the next field we followed the line of the stream which turns left at the far end where it is joined by a second stream coming down from the Eastwick estate. Shortly before their confluence our stream is crossed by a shallow ford where there were tracks of heavy tyre treads from a Landrover or some similar four-wheel drive vehicle. Bill and I continued our walk along the near bank of the enlarged stream without attempting to cross; it was too deep now for our boots. The uninhibited Fred splashed happily to and fro' chasing moorhens and grebes from the reeds; they were careful to keep just out of his reach. We strolled on through an open five-bar gate into the next field. The tyre tracks stretched ahead of us alongside rhe stream.

"Where do we end up eventually if we follow the river bank?" Bill asked.

"The boundary to Georgina's property after about forty minutes. And, if we walked on we'd come out below the lake on the opposite side of the stream to the Mill gardens," I told him.

"No need to walk if you took your Land Rover up to the boundary. So, it's entirely possible that Theodora's assailant came along here and hid up at the back of the lake before she returned after the concert," Bill mused. "Where do you think these tracks came from?"

"Well, the first few fields are still part of the Eastwick estate; so, the vehicle could have entered the field from a gate off the top road. But these tracks are old; we've had no rain in this part of Oxfordshire for the last ten days," I told him.

"If there's an entrance from the top road and the gate was not padlocked, anyone who knows the neighbourhood could have driven down here last night," Bill persisted.

"That's pretty far-fetched. Much more likely, surely, that the murder was committed by someone who atteded the festival."

"Nevertheless, we can show that the killer could possibly be an outsider. I rest my case," Bill said in his best courtroom voice. "....for the time-being," he added smugly.

---oooOooo---

It was time to return to Home Farm to prepare for our dinner guests. I called Fred who emerged from the stream dripping wet; he joined us and shook himself vigorously soaking Bill's trousers. We turned back and took the same route home. The church clock struck six as we crossed the stable yard; we had been gone rather more than an hour. In our absence Detective Sergeant Fellows had telephoned with our summons to attend the onsite reconstruction in the morning. Gaby reported that he was obviously speaking from a standard script and sounded hard pressed to work through his list of attendees; he had seemed pleased to cross another one off his quota of calls without having to answer questions.

Fred devoured his evening meal of tinned dog food and grains with gusto and retired to his bed for a nap. I put out glasses and selected our drink for the evening: two bottles of Macon Villages to accompany the lobster and champagne for pre-dinner consumption. I placed a teaspoonful of cassis in each champagne flute and the Lanson Black Label in the refrigerator pending our guests' arrival; a glass or two of Kir Royale seemed like a good way to dispel any gloom that the murders might have cast over our gathering.

Piroska arrived promptly at seven-thirty with Joan Allnatt and Werner Winkelman. There had been time to bath and change and we were dressed in the Oxfordshire summer version of "smart casual": slacks or loose skirts and silk tops for the ladies; chinos, open-necked shirts and linen jackets for Bill and me. Piroska was similarly dressed but Joan wore a more formal flowered dress; Werner was embarrassed by being overdressed in a dark suit and tie. It was still a glorious summer evening; so we opened the French windows in the drawing room and took our drinks on the terrace. Gaby served smoked salmon on blinis covered with cream cheese, a perfect accompaniment to the Kir Royale. To begin with conversation was a little stilted but soon flowed freely. Gaby and Bill broke the ice by congratulating the musicians again on their music which we had all enjoyed the night before. I commented on Piroska's clever selection of the programme which had displayed their talents so well and Barbara asked each of them what were their next engagements. I refilled everyone's glass. Joan would be playing chamber music in a string quartet at a series of Oxford Music concerts at the Sheldonian theatre throughout much of the summer while Piroska was embarking on a month's concert tour in the United States in a week's time with Werner as her accompanist. Her final engagement was booked for the Hollywood Bowl after playing in Boston, New York, Philadelphia, Chicago and San Francisco. "What a tour," Barbara gasped. "You'll need a good rest when you get back here at the end of July."

"You must know Oxford well, Joan," Bill commented.

"Yes, indeed. I was an undergraduate here at St. Winifred's more years ago than I care to remember," Joan replied. "I've kept in touch quite regularly and attended last year's September Gaudy."

"Did you meet Alexander and Theodora then?"

"Alexander was presiding at the top table but not Theodora. The Gaudy was for alumni and members of the Faculty exclusively; no husbands or wives included."

"Julian and I were at Latimer together; so we're equally familiar with the University," Bill told her.

The four of us reminisced about Oxford while Gaby and Barbara repaired to the kitchen. We agreed that University life was not what it used to be - "A sure sign of advancing years," Joan joked.

Dinner lived up to expectations. For our starters, and as a prelude to the lobster Gaby had prepared avocado pears stuffed with prawn cocktail, awaiting us in our places at the dining room table. The lobster thermador served in the shells with its succulent mustard, tarragon and gruyere cheese sauce and parmesan sprinkled on top: a half lobster each with the meat from the eighth half shared between them was a culinary delight and repaid the careful preparation. There were no vegetables, but a green salad with French dressing was offered either as a side dish or separately after the lobster. Inevitably, the conversation strayed to the events of the previous evening. Gaby told Piroska and the other two musicians how the Deakins had joined us in the interval and relayed the gist of what was said over supper including their differences over Alexander's forthcoming visit to Hong Kong. Neither Piroska nor Werner showed much interest as they concentrated on their lobster, but Joan paid closer attention to Gaby's account between mouthfuls.

"I suppose you get a quite different perspective of audience reactions from the stage during the performance," Bill enquired directing his question at the three of them in general.

Piroska was the first to answer. "I make a point of never studying the audience at my concerts. It is a distraction from my playing," she said.

"For me, it is no good. It is all a blur," Werner announced. "I am very short-sighted and cannot see much further than the keyboard and the people I play with." He shrugged his shoulders but did not seem regretful and selected a forkful of his remaining lobster. I poured more Macon into his almost empty glass.

"Then I am the exception," Joan Allnatt declared. "I always study the audience intently during the pieces when I am not playing."

"Then you must have picked out Alexander Deakin siting directly behind us," I said.

"Yes, and I assumed that the lady at his side was Theodora. I realised I had seen her in Oxford before."

"And where was that?" Gaby asked.

"Last autumn at the Holywell Music Room. I was playing Bach in a quintet - a much smaller audience there, of course," Joan added.

"So, her husband was not there or you would have put two and two together at the time?" Barbara queried.

"It was the week before the Gaudy; so I hadn't yet met Alexander and I assumed that they were partners if not husband and wife. They certainly seemed very close from their body language. But he was quite different in appearance from Alexander, a large heavy-featured man with shoulder-length black hair. I thought at the time that they were rather an ill-matched couple."

"That's interesting," Bill said thoughtfully. "Maybe the Deakins' marriage was under strain anyway."

"The same man was there last night," Joan added, helping herself to the green salad. "He came into the marquee through a flap at the back of the tent just before the interval; he walked up behind Mrs. Deakin and whispered something into her ear before walking out again. I didn't see him anywhere in the second half during Werner's solo when I had another good look at the audience."

I replenished all our glasses with the rest of the Macon Village while Gaby served dessert: a summer pudding with ice cream which was a suitable contrast to the richness of the lobster. There was cheese on offer to follow which no-one wanted, much to Fred's disappointment; he was always hopeful for a small chunk or two of cheddar when the opportunity arose.

We took our coffee and Bendicks mints at the table with liqueurs: Cointreau or Grand Marnier for the ladies, Hine brandy in balloon glasses for Werner, Bill and myself. None of us were able to put a face to the waitress who was also murdered; aside from Emma Fullerton suffering the unwelcome attentions of Aubrey Pinkerton they had remained anonymous throughout the evening. Gaby thought that it might have been the Bennett's daughter from up the road but couldn't put a name to her.

It was pitch black when the time came for Piroska's party to leave amid thanks and pecks on cheeks all round. Piroska had forgotten to bring a torch with her; so I took our flashlight from the study and escorted the three of them across the Green to her cottage and waited while she fumbled for the door key from her handbag. "I become *zsenilis* before my time," said Piroska, her last word before letting them in.

Back in the house Gaby and Barbara were still putting plate, glasses and crockery in the dishwasher. I found Bill out on the terrace enjoying the night air with his brandy in one hand and one of my best cigars in the other. I selected a Bolivar for myself from the humidor, clipped and lit it before joining him. We sat companionably in silence for several minutes with the balmy scent of night-scented stock and honeysuckle competing against our cigar smoke. Bill was the first to speak.

"Of course, the musicians were indoors throughout the interval," he reflected. "So, Joan wouldn't have witnessed the fisticuffs ...."

"And wouldn't have recognized the awful Aubrey from his shoulder length black hair," I finished for him.

"You catch my drift," Bill said.

"As always," I agreed.

---ooo0ooo---

CHAPTER SIX

Sunday morning, 23 June

CHIEF INSPECTOR CARTWRIGHT and his team had prepared thoroughly for the mass gathering of all Festival attendees. Tables and chairs had been replaced on the lawn in their original positions. As we arrived, we were each assigned a number and checked off on the clipboard lists which Sergeant Fellows and a police constable were holding. We were then told to sit at the same tables as for supper on Friday night. When we were all registered the two policeman toured the tables marking on site plans where each of us was seated. At each table they left blow-up photographs of Thoedora Deakin and a girl named as Molly Bennett. Gaby had been right about the identity of the murdered waitress.

The two empty chairs at our table were where Theodora and Alexander had sat, the one now dead and the other excused the pain of attendance. Not everyone was seated. Barry Fullerton and his staff stood together in front of the trestle serving tables. Georgina and Giles Delahaye were at one side, close to the two tables where the house guests were located, dressed in casual clothes except for Hugo Bassinger who was wearing a sober City suit and tie. Looking around, I could see that there was no common order of dress; some were wearing what might have been their gardening clothes, others the more formal uniform which the rural middle classes normally reserve for attendance at Church of England Sunday morning services. No doubt they would have preferred to be singing hymns or listening to lessons read badly by churchwardens. Piroska,

Joan and Werner stood together at the entrance door to the house. No-one looked comfortable or relaxed, least of all Aubrey Pinkerton; he had been the last to arrive from the direction of the car park and was standing awkwardly near to Georgina and Giles.

The stage was now set for the Chief Inspector to address the assembled gathering as he strode to the centre of the lawn. A quick tug at his moustache and he launched into a prepared speech which he delivered without notes.

"Thank you, ladies and gentlemen, for joining me this mornng. I know that you all have better ways of spending your Sundays but two women were killed here on Friday night shortly after the end of the concert which you attended, probably before you left to go home. We need your help to get a clear picture of the sequence of events from the interval though to the time that you descended from the lake to take a hot toddy on this lawn. The photographs which my colleagues have handed out are of Mrs. Theodora Deakin, who was killed up at the lake, and of Miss Molly Bennett, one of the waitresses who served you on Friday evening. She was murdered, we think a few minutes later, down here at the back of the marquee. One of my team will be coming round your table again and will ask you whether you spoke to either or both victims or had any previous contact with them. If you did, you will be asked to stay behind when we have finished and to be interviewed then or later. To complete our understanding of everyone's movements, we shall proceed from here into the marquee where you will be required to sit in the same seat that you occupied at the concert and your positions will be logged. Finally, we shall ask you to evacuate the marquee and take the steps up to the lake and then down again, in the same order that you can remember from Friday. Are there any questions?"

DCI Cartwright had spoken with authority and admirable clarity. There was only one question, from Hugo Bassinger who did not attempt to conceal his underlying impatience.

"What happens, Chief Inspector, when we have completed your play acting?" he asked.

"Those of you who have nothing to tell us about either victim will be free to leave," Cartwright replied patiently.

"Does that mean that you will have eliminated us from your inquiries?" Bassinger persisted.

"It's too early - Mr. Bassinger, isn't it ? - to make any presumption."

By the time we had completed the police routine it was well past midday. The majority of those attending departed in time for their Sunday roasts or other delights; only a handful of us were left: Georgina, Giles, Barry and Emma Fullerton, the Mansfields, the Hendersons, the Oxford Guardian reporter and, of course, ourselves. The waiters and waitresses other than Emma were dismissed after names and addresses were taken. I noted that Joan Allnatt had not mentioned her previous sighting of Theodora at the Holywell Music Room; nor, more interestingly, had Aubrey Pinkerton declared any relationship with her. Having been questioned already on Saturday morning, the Hendersons were also released.

Chief Inspector Cartwright came over to our table and I introduced him to Gaby and Barbara. He sat himself down at our table and addressed them.

"I've already had an account from your husbands of your contact and conversation with Mrs. Deakin. I've heard about the disagreement with Mr.Deakin over his trip to Hong Kong. Do either of you have any further impression of her state of mind on Friday evening?" he asked.

Barbara and Gaby looked at each other and it was Barbara who replied.

"I thought she was a deeply troubled woman. Something more than a husband and wife spat about accompanying him."

"Some underlying issue to do with her Art Gallery. I can't be more precise than that," Gaby added.

"And after you descended from the lake, you didn't you see or speak to her again?" They both shook their heads.

"Thank you. In that case, I have nothing more to ask you at present. If you think of anything else, please call me; and I can always reach you in Fullmere, with Mr. and Mrs. Radclive, can't I?"

"One question for you, Chief Inspector," said Bill. "Can you tell us how Mrs. Deakin was killed?"

"It will be common knowledge tomorrow after my morning press conference; so I will tell you now in confidence, Mr. Fentiman," Cartwright replied. "Theodora Deakin was bludgeoned to death at the back of the lake with some heavy club, possibly the punt pole."

"And the poor girl who was a waitress?"

The Chief Inspector didn't dodge the question.

"Molly Bennett's throat was slit by a thin, very sharp blade. then she was stuffed under the stage."

"Do you think she was killed because she saw Mrs. Deakin's murderer returning from the lake?" I asked.

"That is one line of enquiry we shall be pursuing," Cartwright agreed but would be drawn no further.

---ooo0ooo---

On the way back to Home Farm, Bill and Barbara debated when they would return to Sussex. Gaby suggested that they stay another night and travelled up to London in the morning. In the end it was decided that Bill would take an early Monday morning train from Bicester in time for a 10.00 a.m. meeting in London and that Barbara would take a later train so that they could travel home together in the afternoon.

It was too late for lunch; we spent the rest of Sunday afternoon with the newspapers spread out in the drawing room, lounging on sofas and comfortable chairs until Fred reminded us that it was time for his walk of the day. As

Fred became more insistent Bill flung down the sports section of The Sunday Times and returned to our dinner conversation of the previous evening.

"I wonder if Joan told the Chief Inspector that she had recognized Aubrey Pinkerton as Theodora's companion at the Holywell Music Room concert last year," he pondered.

"Let's ask her," I said and went to the telephone.

"She's no longer here," Piroska said when she answered. "I took her and Werner direct to the station when the police told us we could go. Can I help?"

"I wanted to ask her if she identified Aubrey Pinkerton to the police this morning as the man she saw with Theodora at her Oxford concert last September."

"Oh, I don't know. We rushed off in the car as soon as the Chief Inspector released us. So, maybe not. Do you want to ask her yourself?"

"No, it's none of our business, Piroska, but she may have to report the link later as the police investigation continues."

"As soon as she does, that puts Pinkerton in the frame as a suspect," Bill said when I repeated Piroska's remark.

The four of us set out together with Fred on his lead and best behaviour, walking this time on the road past our field and across the bridge, then up the hill. We crossed the main road at the top and through the gateway over a cattle grid on to the Eastwick estate proper. I released Fred who bounded off towards a wood on our left while we strolled up the drive, an avenue bordered by stately elms, in the direction of the Hall. One of the pleasanter social contacts since we moved to Fullmere had been an informal visit by Lucinda Mansfield soon after our arrival to tell us that we were welcome to wander in the grounds whenever we chose - not exactly an act of *noblesse oblige* but rather civilised. After a quarter of a mile the house and stable block came into view and we paused before turning back. The frontage of the house looked over to our right; it seemed to be early Victorian but built of Cotswold stone rather than brick. The stable block seemed larger than the house and encompassed a vast courtyard, out of proportion to the house. Apparently, we were told, the original much bigger Hall had burnt down in the 1840s. The present building was less imposing but happily the architects had used stone from the first building so that the resultant structure, although less imposing, was almost attractive.

"It's a bit of a disappointment, isn't it," Barbara commented.

"It's not too bad inside," said Gaby. "The reception rooms are of a decent size and ceiling height but you have to enter the house through the stable yard and kitchen quarters. Really, the whole house needs redecorating and they say in the village that the roof is in poor condition."

We retraced our steps but before we had gone far our progress was halted by an approaching car from the main road. A green Volvo estate with a roof rack came abreast of us, having slowed down to pass. There were dents in the offside front wing and rear door; a visit to the carwash was overdue. The driver was Aubrey Pinkerton; he must have seen who we were but gave no acknowledgment and drove on stony faced.

"What on earth is he doing here? Any relationship with the Mansfields seems unlikely," Gaby exclaimed, echoing all our immediate thoughts. I made a mental note to find out when I was summoned by Sir Percy in the coming week to talk about his planned book.

There was no need to call out for Fred or blow the dog whistle which he always ignored; he was waiting for us as we approached the entrance gates. Sitting at the side of the drive, he looked pleased with himself, a dead rabbit between his paws.

Back at Home Farm again, without the rabbit, it was time for a first drink: gins and tonic for Barbara and Bill, Chablis for Gaby and a large Ballantine's and soda for me. Gaby produced smoked salmon on cream cheese and blinis as for the previous evening. Having not eaten since breakfast, we were more than ready for sustenance and the smoked salmon stimulated appetites.

"There is the small matter of supper," Gaby announced. "There's very little to eat in the house. I can offer spaghetti Bolognese or bacon and eggs, or I could open a tinned ham. Otherwise, we could go out."

"Dinner on a Sunday at the Eastwick Arms, if any, won't be up to much. What about a takeaway?" I suggested.

"So long as it's not pizza," said Barbara firmly.

"Perhaps we should have kept Fred's rabbit," Bill commented.

---ooo0ooo---

We settled for curry and I telephoned through our order to the Indian takeaway in Brackley: chicken Korma for Barbara, Jalfrezi for Gaby, lamb Rogan Gosh for Bill and lamb Madras for me. I added pilau rice for us all and side orders of poppadom, bhajis, samosas, dahl and chutney for starters. Half an hour later, after feeding Fred (wild venison according to the label on the tin), I drove into Brackley to collect. Outside the takeaway I recognized Giles Delahaye's scarlet Alfa Romeo in the car park opposite; Emma Fullerton was standing by the passenger door. She was wearing the student leisure uniform of unzipped black leather biker jacket over white T-shirt, faded blue jeans and Doc Marten boots. With her long chestnut hair she was a pretty girl; she could have stepped out of a crowd scene in "The Wild One". Marlon Brando would have found her irresistible, I thought. Presumably, Giles who was inside collecting their order did too.

I walked over to her. "Hello, Emma. Friday evening turned out to be pretty horrific. You must still be shaken. Are you alright yourself?" I asked.

"I still can't believe that Molly was murdered. We went to school together and she was always good for a laugh. But thank you for asking, Mr. Radclive," she replied.

"Julian, please, "I said. "If you don't mind talking about it, when did you last see her after the end of the concert?"

"Molly and her boyfriend Ted - one of the waiters - wanted a fag and set off to light up on the far side of the marquee; but Dad called him back to help move tables. So, she went on alone. There was no-one with her." Emma bit her lip and it was clear that she was on the verge of tears.

"You had an unpleasant experience yourself in the interval," I said changing the subject. "Aubrey Pinkerton must have been drunk to attack you like that. Was it very frightening?"

"Actually, it wasn't. It was rather odd; he wasn't even drunk," Emma reflected. "It was creepie - almost as if he was play-acting."

"But your father dealt with him very firmly. That wasn't play-acting, surely?"

"No, that was for real; Dad doing his mother hen bit. Really cool."

"Really cool," I agreed.

The door of the Indian restaurant opened and Giles emerged carrying several large boxes and a bag. He was surprised to see me chatting with Emma. "Hello, sir, are you here for a curry too?"

I commented on the size of his order and he explained that it was not just for the two of them. They were collecting for parents as well and returning to the Mill where they would be eating together with them and Piroska whom Georgina had invited over. I opened the car door for Emma. "Good night - Julian," she called as Giles drove off; he looked at her questioningly.

---oooOooo---

CHAPTER SEVEN

Monday, 24 June

WE WERE UP early on Monday morning for Bill to catch the 8:05 train from Bicester direct to Marylebone; I left the house with him at 7:35 after he had snatched a hurried breakfast. On the short drive to the station I related to him Emma's comments on Friday evening's events having decided against sharing them the evening before.

"Aubrey Pinkerton will certainly provide Chief Inspector Cartwright with a second line of enquiry," Bill said.

"The first being Alexander Deakin himself, I suppose, following the precept that in any murder enquiry the spouse is the most likely perpetrator," I added.

"Quite so. And, when Pinkerton comes under investigation, the spotlight will inevitably fall on Georgina as his landlady - if not by the police, certainly by the media who will have a field day on her rather risqué business activities."

"That seems unfair, even if she is bound to receive some attention anyway as the hostess of the Festival," I protested.

"Who said that the Red Top tabloid Press is ever fair, particulary in the case of a page-turning murder story," Bill said, more as a statement than a question.

"If it blows up will you be able to advise her?" I asked.

"I'd like to but I need to know how Georgina operates her escort business here and in London. Would you see her in the next few days and probe gently for details? I ought to have the back story of her activities in America too before I take her on," Bill replied.

I agreed to do what I could although I didn't much relish the role of inquisitor. However, I liked Georgina and knew that Bill could provide her with the necessary bulwark if she became a subject of public interest. Bill already had his return ticket; so, I dropped him off at the station entrance and watched him take the footbridge and wave cheerily at the top before turning round the Range Rover and heading home to my own breakfast.

What other lines of enquiry would there be for the police? Could someone have driven over the fields on Friday evening, as Bill had suggested, and entered the property along the stream? It sounded far-fetched but there was one way of finding out if it was at all possible. When I reached Fullmere I drove straight through the village towards the Hall; on reaching the main road opposite the entrance I turned left and stopped on the grass verge by the five-bar metal gate giving access to the field which slopes down to the stream. There was no padlock on the gate but, of course, that proved nothing. I wondered if and when Chief Inspector Cartwright would consider this alternative method of accessing the Mill.

---ooo0ooo---

The rest of Monday passed without incident. Barbara took an early afternoon train to London; Gaby dropped her at the station and then went on to Banbury to food shop for the week in Sainsburys. I applied myself to editing articles for a new issue of *Managing Business Abroad* and the mundane task of reminding those contributors who had not yet submitted of their month-end deadlines. Of the twenty who had agreed to write only a dozen had delivered and I still had my chapter to write on the global economy and foreign trade. Mid-morning there was a call from Robert Schindler my publisher and I accepted his invitation to meet him on Thursday. He wanted to discuss the publishing programme for the next twelve months, in particular the opportunity for a third edition of my China book which continued to sell well in North America as well as in Europe.

Mindful of Bill's request, I picked up the telephone again and dialled Georgina's number. There was no reply; she had probably left for London and wouldn't be back much before the next weekend. I telephoned Piroska instead and asked if she had a London number for Georgina. She gave me the office number for the Wigmore Escort Agency, her business name, and I called that next. It was answered by a pleasant well-educated female voice; I asked for Mrs. Delahaye taking care to say that I was a friend rather than a business acquaintance. When Georgina came on the line she sounded pleased to speak with me.

"Julian. How nice to hear from you. Are you thinking of joining my club?" she asked.

"Consider me an honorary member, Georgina, and probably Bill Fentiman too. He thinks you may need his help in the coming days and he's asked me to find out more about you before he commits his law firm," I said. There was no point in prevaricating.

"I don't plan to be back in Fullmere until Friday. What's made Bill believe that I may need support?"

"He thinks that, as the police open up their lines of enquiry, Aubrey Pinkerton will be on their shortlist; because he lives on your estate you could suffer unwelcome publicity by association. I think so too," I said.

Georgina hesitated for a moment. "I guess you guys may be right. I'm happy to spill the beans about myself. Will it wait until the weekend?"

"Better not," I replied. "Look I'm in London on Thursday. I could come and see you in your office."

"That would be great. Come to lunch," she suggested.

I told her that was not possible since I was lunching with Robert and we agreed that I would come over to her office in Wimpole Sreet at around three o'clock. I thought that lunching with Georgina would have been more fun but, occasionally, work comes first.

By the time Gaby returned laden from Sainsbury's Fred and I had taken our daily ramble across the fields; we were ready for a drink. It was another sunny evening so that five-thirty found us on the terrace, glasses in hand. Gaby had visited Olive Bennett, Molly's mother, on her way home to pay her respects and commiserate; not surprisingly, Mrs. Bennett was still grief-stricken and Gaby was unable to give much comfort. We were discussing last Friday yet again when the telephone rang. The voice was familiar.

"Radclive, Percy Mansfield here. You said you would advise me about publishing my book. Perhaps you would come up to the Hall now and have a word," the voice said. The tone was peremptory and there was no mention of a drink. No good reason not to comply but I didn't care to be summoned like the butler.

"That's not possible, Mansfield," I replied "but midday tomorrow would be convenient."

Plainly Sir Henry was used to having his own way and didn't like being crossed. I could hear him harrumph down the telephone. "Very well then; tomorrow at twelve o'clock," he said and the line went dead.

"Not a great start to the relationshp," Gaby commented.

---oooOooo---

I continued to struggle with my business book editing for the first part of Tuesday. "Why is it," I asked myself aloud "that lawyers write so badly - overlong sentences and no punctuation?"

"Simple," said Gaby flitting through the study with a feather duster. "It's all those years of writing contracts with relative clauses and no commas."

"You're probably right but that's no excuse for them anymore. Contracts nowadays are all based on word processed documents which they take off the shelf and tickle up", I answered.

"Are accountants any better?" she asked.

"On the whole, yes. Addicted to bullet points but mostly dull as ditch water."

"You don't seem to be enjoying this book much," Gaby observed.

"Too many editions and increasingly difficult to find good authors and sponsors but it does bring in the money. So, long live *Managng Busines Abroad*," I agreed.

I persisted in my labours until shortly before midday when I drove out of our yard and turned left up towards Eastwick Hall. As I crossed the main road on to the cattle grid at the entrance, I noticed a tractor emerge from the unpadlocked field; I was unable to see who was driving. Parking in the Hall's vast stable yard at the rear of the house made our more modest yard seem like a postage stamp. The left hand side comprised of a bank of stables with a groom's cottage at the entrance; the right hand side was more open and included what I took to be the estate manager's office and a single storey wooden building resembling a cricket pavilion. The house itself formed the far side of the yard with a single large oak door and iron bell pull. Its sound reverberated within the house when I rang. There was no answer; perhaps this was one of those country houses were visitors are supposed to walk in and announce their presence.

"Hello there," I called out as I opened the door and stepped in. The stone-flagged kitchen in which I found myself was enormous. To the right under the widow was a series of Belfast sinks and draining boards. No evidence of any dishwasher here except for the black clad figure of an elderly, white-haired woman bent over the furthest sink preparing vegetables for the evening meal. She seemed to be hard of hearing and did not raise her head from her labours in response to my greeting. I recognized her vaguely as a village resident but could not put a name to her. There was a proportionately huge table in the centre of the kitchen and a four oven Aga; I noticed some concessions to modern living in the form of a washing machine and spin dryer on the far side of the room and kitchen furniture with work surfaces, drawers and cabinets alongside. A somewhat spartan way of life but not entirely medieval, I concluded.

The kitchen gave on to a long corridor leading to the front of the house from which Lucinda Mansfield emerged. "Black," she shouted at her retainer "you can go home as soon as Silas returns with the tractor. He'll give you a lift down to the village."

Turning her attention to me, she said "There you are. You'll find Percy in the study waiting for you. I'll show you the way."

Lucinda led me down the corridor, past a front staircase and through a pleasant drawing room overlooking a front lawn and a small lobby containing an alcove with drinks tray, arriving finally at the entrance to a panelled library which served as her husband's office or study. Today she was dressed in jodhpurs and hacking jacket over a polo necked cashmere pullover; the riding clothes suited her slim figure well.

"It's Julian Radclive for you, Percy," she announced. "Give the poor man a drink."

Sir Percy Mansfield rose from his ormolu decorated Napoleon III writing desk to receive me in country gentleman mode. He was wearing a rather loud windowpane tweed jacket, grey flannel trousers and scuffed suede brogues. "You'll take a glass of sherry," he said "and you too, Lucy, I dare say," delivered more as an order than an invitation.

He removed three glasses from the drinks tray and a bottle of San Patricio which he poured carefully. My opinion of him rose slightly; there had to be some good in any man who offered his guests Garvey's stylish fino instead of the vinegary Gonzales Tio Pepe. Mansfield returned to his desk and motioned me to sit in the chair before him. Lucy took a first swig and retreated to the drawing room. He handed me a plastic folder of typewritten loose pages.

"There's a synopsis of the complete book here and the first twenty pages of text. Tell me what you think," he said.

I scanned the numbered pages of text and read the synopsis more carefully. The book, it was apparent, would be a personalised account of Hong Kong politics in the Thatcher and present government periods highlighting the *real politik* of the UK's relationship with China and serious errors of judgment which the Governor and British government had made since the joint declaration. It was highly critical of both. The text read better than I had expected; Percy Mansfield's prose style lacked inspiration but grammar, syntax and spelling were sound. With decent editing I thought that the material was publishable.

Mansfield had started to fidget. "Well, what's your opinion?" he asked querulously when he could contain his impatience no longer.

"I'm happy to show this to my publisher when I see him on Thursday," I said. "Robert has an appetite for the controversial and, if he believes a book will attract attention, he'll want to publish. I think you could produce a well-written text without being libellous but are you sure that you want to publish?"

"Of course, I'm sure. D'you think I'd have asked you to come up here and talk about the book if I wasn't serious? What's putting you off?" He pronounced the last word as 'orf' in the upper class style of speech adopted by diplomats and aspiring gentry.

"Only that the Foreign Office won't take kindly to grave criticism by one of their own. And you can't expect the last Governor to like it much either."

"Bugger the lot of them. They can't touch my pension and I don't expect any further preferment. Publish and be damned, as they say."

It dawned on me then that Percy Mansfield's retirement may not have been entirely voluntary. They may have thought that the trappings of a knighthood and probably full pension would be enough to fob him off so that he would fade into obscurity, but they had misjudged their man. The memoirs were to be a bitter act of vengeance.

"So long as you're prepared for any counter-criticism, I have no objections," I replied. "In fact your account of events and reactions is entirely congruent with what Chinese government sources were saying to me at the time during my fairly frequent visits to the mainland." I handed the file back to him.

"What on earth were you doing there?" Mansfield asked sharply, like a man whose estate has been invaded by a trespasser.

"Negotiating joint ventures in the eighties and, after Tiannamen Square, setting up the first edition of my China book with a Chinese co-editor," I told him.

"Then I suppose you may know what you're doin'," he said grudgingly.

Percy Mansfield returned the file to me. "Show it to your publishing friend. If he likes it he can make me an offer. I shall need the file back when you return from London." No word of thanks and no offer of a second glass of San Patricio.

"If Robert is at all interested, he'll take a copy and make his mind up in the next day or so before inviting you to meet him."

We left it at that and I returned to the drawing room leaving Sir Percy to contemplate his literary aspirations and, no doubt, refill his glass.

Lucy Mansfield was sitting languidly on a sofa, glass in hand, the leader page of *The Times* open upon her knees with spectacles perched on her nose. "Shall you be able to find a publisher for Percy's book?" she asked putting down her paper.

"I think there's a very good chance. It's sufficiently controversial to attract readers from the chattering classes. They enjoy personal criticism of government ministers past and present," I replied.

Lucy rose to her feet. "More sherry?" she said, retrieving the bottle from the drinks tray and refilling both our glasses. She noddel towards the fireplace and asked "What do you think of the painting?" Above the Adam-style carved mantelpiece was a striking oil painting of a horse in a handsome gilded frame. The horse was a deep chestnut bay with a docked tail standing in an open field close by a tree.

"It looks well there. Is it valuable? I know absolutely nothing about animal art," I said.

"That's the point. I want to know what it's worth. With the docked tail and anatomical accuracy it could be eighteenth century, even a Stubbs, in which case it's worth quite a bit. If it's nineteenth century it could be by any one of a number of painters and worth much less."

"Is that important to you?"

"Yes, I want to redecorate this room and Percy's study. You probably noticed that the paper in there is stripping off the walls - damp probably - and not much better in here. I hate it looking shabby. If the painting is worth a lot, I'll put it up for auction."

I looked at the painting again. The brushwork was fine, but it didn't have the warm glow of eighteenth century pictures painted outdoors which I associated with Gainsborough and others. I couldn't see a signature. Perhaps, it needed cleaning.

"Shall you have it authenticated by a professional?" I asked.

"I wanted to have a sighting shot at it first, before going to Christie's or Sotheby's. In fact," Lucinda Mansfield confessed "that's what I was talking to Theodora Deakin about when we came down the stairs from the lake last Friday."

"And what did Theodora say?"

"She suggested that I invite Aubrey Pinkerton to give his opinion and offered to ask him for me. So, when we were all together again on Sunday I asked him myself and he came up to have a look that afternoon. He wasn't very encouraging; not really his field he said. He suggested that I have the painting cleaned before showing it to an expert and offered to arrange it for me."

"Why don't you take it to the fine arts panel of experts at the Ashmolean? At least they'd give an informed opinion," I said.

Before she could comment further, we were joined by Sir Percy who emerged from his study looking disagreeable.

"What are you doing still here?" he demanded inhospitably.

"Julian is being very helpful to me too. But we mustn't keep you from your lunch," Lucy answered.

"My pleasure," I said putting down my glass. She accompanied me down the corridor to the kitchen and the back door.

"You mustn't mind Percy. He misses not having people to order about and treats visitors as a substitute," were her last words.

Back in the stable yard, the tractor was parked near the entrance and an elderly estate worker, whom I recognized as Silas Grimshaw, was herding Mrs. Black into an ancient Ford Cortina before returning to the village for his lunch. Returning to Home Farm I found Gaby hoovering upstairs; in Olive Bennett's absence we were without daily help. She switched the vacuum cleaner off and I carried it downstairs for her with Fred following close on my heels. Over our kitchen lunch I gave her my impressions of the Hall and related the individual conversations with each of the

Mansfields. She was more interested in the exchange with Lady Lucinda.

"So that explains what Aubrey Pinkerton was doing up there on Sunday," she said.

"But why make a point of telling me that he had been recommended by Theodora and the nature of their relationship?" I asked.

"Perhaps because he told her that he passed us on his way there and she wanted to tell us that there is no relationship." More food for thought.

---ooo0ooo---

CHAPTER EIGHT

Wednesday, 26 June

OVERNIGHT WE HAD made a firm resolution to stop trying to play detectives. I would have my meeting with Georgina Delahaye so that Bill could help her if necessary but that was it. Leave it to Chief Inspector Cartwright and the police; any interference by us would be unwelcome, we told ourselves. Snuggled up in bed and enjoying a leisurely love-in we looked forward to normal life resuming in the morning.

Our good resolution lasted until precisely 10:30 on Wednesday morning when a Jaguar XJS coupe swept into the yard. I was at my desk making a start on my introductory chapter for *Managing Business Abroad* and Gaby had walked up the village to see if she could find someone to stand in as our daily until Olive Bennett felt able to return to work. I waited until the doorbell rang and there was a knock on the front door. I was confronted by a very familiar figure. It was almost two years since I had collaborated with Duncan Mallory on our book about international crime and he hadn't changed in any discernible way. Inspector Duncan 'Digger' Mallory of the International Bureau of the Fraud Squad, was always a natty dresser with a taste for the better things in life. Today he was wearing a pristine white raincoat over a dark suit and tie with highly polished black semi-brogues. With his trademark heavy horn-rimmed spectacles and wavy blonde hair, cut longer than might be expected of a senior policeman, there was a marked resemblance to the young Michael Caine.

"Wotcha, Julian. How's the word factory?" he greeted me.

"Duncan," I said glancing at the flashy car "Nice wheels. I can see that the world is treating you well. Come on in. It's a pleasant surprise to see you again."

I put on the kettle and we settled ourselves comfortably in the kitchen. As I completed the task of coffee-making, Gaby returned.

"Guess what. The Digger's here," I shouted. Duncan stood up and they hugged affectionately like the old friends they had become since our paths first crossed in the matter of a false stock market prospectus issued by one of her former market research clients long before we left London. We had enjoyed several sociable evenings since with him and whatever girlfriend he had in tow at the time.

"What's brought you here to rural Oxfordshire this sunny morning?" I asked. "I know you too well to imagine that it's only for the pleasure of our company."

"That too, of course," Digger replied "but you're right. I'm in the early stages of an art fraud investigation involving at least one Oxford College. I need a bit of insider information."

"You have our undivided attention," I assured him. "We had our own taste of murder with mystery this past weekend and we'll share that with you after you tell us your tale."

"My investigation arises from the forthcoming sale at auction in Hong Kong of a Dutch 17th century oil painting which appears to be the same as a painting by Pieter De Hooch in the ownership of Latimer College. It's listed in the sale catalogue as 'school of Vermeer' but the dealer who alerted us thinks that it's the De Hooch original. Before I start interviewing people at the College, I'd like to have some feeling for the art scene in Oxford and college collections in general," the Digger explained.

"There's not really much of an art scene in the University - certainly not in paintings and other fine art - but, of course, rare books are a preoccupation of many academics with priceless tomes in the Bodleian and in college libraries. Some permanent collections of valuable paintings are held in the Ashmolean Museum which also hosts visiting exhibitions of work from all over Europe. As for the colleges individually, some of them have the odd Old Master left to them in a Will or by bequest. None of them, except perhaps Christchurch which is particularly well-endowed, has what you would call a collection," I said and added that I had a very imperfect knowledge of the subject. "Incidentally," I admitted "Latimer is the college that Bill Fentiman and I both attended."

"What about art dealers and auction houses?"

"None of the big houses have offices in Oxford. One of the third tier holds auctions there or in Banbury but the lots are often from country house clearances; very rarely does anything go for more than four or five thousand pounds. There's only one gallery of any consequence, the Clarendon Art Gallery, but it deals in modern art: pottery, ceramics, jewellery and a few paintings. The leading partner who owned and managed it was one of the two murdered at the concert last Friday night."

Gaby had been listening intently to our exchange and interposed her own question.

"Duncan, what is the subject matter of the painting?" she asked.

"The picture tells the story," he said withdrawing an illustrated sale catalogue from an inside pocket. The photograph showed a well-dressed lady seated at a tsble in an inner room of the house looking though an outer hall to the front door which a housemaid has opened. A gentleman in a hat is standing outside with hands on hips and a small black and white dog is watching him.

"That looks like the painting which Barbara noticed last Saturday in the back room of the art gallery basement,"

Gaby exclaimed. "We'd better tell you all about the weekend's happenings."

We gave Duncan Mallory a full account of the Festival evening, our separate visits of Saturday morning and Chief Inspector Cartwright's re-enactment of the concert proceedings on Sunday. He listened with increasing interest, paying particular attention to our interval conversation with Theodora and Alexander Deakin and Gaby's description of the gallery. By the time we had answered his questions it was well past midday and Duncan suggested that we take a snack with him at the pub. He said that he would spend the night locally and Gaby invited hm to stay with us.

"Not allowed according to the rule book. I have to stay in a hotel – not in a possible witness's private house," he said regretfully.

And so we did the next best thing and booked the Digger in for the night at the Eastwick Arms on the understanding that he would dine with us that evening. We checked him in with his smart pigskin overnight bag, introduced him to Barry Fullerton and lunched on sausage and mash at the otherwise unoccupied bar. Over lunch, we discussed how he would spend the afternoon.

"My first port of call must be DCI Cartwright at the county police station in Kidlington, a matter of courtesy since I am on his patch. Besides, he might have found out more in his investigations over the last two days which could be relevant. Then, I'll pay a first call on Latimer College to see what they know about this painting. Who do you think I should ask for?"

"Go to the Porter's lodge and ask for the Bursar who's responsible for the building, all its fittings, furniture and anything else the college owns," I answered ."At some stage I want to visit the Clarendon Art Gallery, but I don't want to alert the management yet in case they're involved in this business. It may be difficult to call there in a private capacity without attracting suspicion."

"I've got an idea which might help," said Gaby. "Why don't I call Alexander and offer my services to substitute for Theodora at the gallery until they can find a permanent replacement? I would be protecting his interests and at the same time I could do some detective work to see if they've been up to something."

"That's brilliant, Gaby, but are you sure that you want to get involved in this?" Duncan cautioned her.

"Definitely. I'll call him this afternoon and, if he agrees, ask him to set it up with Valerie Wyngarde to meet her at the gallery tomorrow morning," she confirmed.

With that agreed, the Digger set off for Kidlington in his Jaguar XJS while Gaby and I walked back to Home Farm.

---ooo0ooo---

Chief Inspector Cartwright's lot was not a happy one. He was under pressure from his immediate superior Superintendent Desmond Bland, himself harassed by the Chief Constable, to make an arrest and yet there was no one against whom he had sufficient evidence to detain. In turn, the Chief Constable was nudged daily by the Vice Chancellor of Oxford University to bring the matter to a speedy conclusion. The unresolved murder of the wife of a Head of House reflected badly on the University's reputation and was already a front-page topic for the national Press.

There were two credible suspects: the husband and the self-proclaimed art expert. Alexander Deakin might have some kind of a motive but no obvious opportunity. Aubrey Pinkerton had opportunity but no discernible motive. He had some contact with Theodora Deakin at her gallery but Cartwright could had not found evidence of any kind of relationship between them. Pinkerton's opportunity was grounded in the fact that it was possible to reach the lake from his cottage without crossing the lawn and the report of

Radclive and Fentiman that he had been sober when they visited him in the hour after the primary victim's disappearance. In fact, there were plenty of others who had opportunity in theory but no connection whatsoever with her. This morning, five days after the murders – one must not forget the girl whose killing he had treated as collateral damage – the Chief Constable had ruled that if there were no arrest overnight he would call in Scotland Yard.

The visit from Inspector Duncan Mallory of the IFIT that afternoon was therefore a not entirely unwelcome diversion from his gloom. They had not met previously but were at ease with each other almost immediately. Having exchanged notes on their respective investigations they debated whether there might be a connection between the murder of Theodora Deakin and Mallory's suspected art fraud. One piece of additional information from Mallory was of interest to Cartwright: the apparently close relationship between Pinkerton and the primary murder victim noticed by Joan Allnatt at the Holywell Music Rooms the previous autumn. Aubrey Pinkerton was now firmly in the spotlight and gave the Chief Inspector enough circumstantial evidence to bring him in for questioning. Aside from that, there were no obvious links and the two policemen agreed to keep each other informed of their progress. Before departing Duncan took directions to the city centre location of Latimer College.

---ooo0ooo---

With his limited familiarity of Oxford he drove up The High towards Carfax and took a left turn down Alfred Street. On reaching the gates to Christchurch Peckwater Quad, he turned left again down Merton Street and reached his destination. Like most Oxford Colleges, Latimer is built round two quadrangles; it is the next college along from Corpus Christi and backs on to Port Meadow. Having parked outside with the near certainty of attracting a parking ticket, Mallory entered through a postern in the massive front door and found himself in the entrance lobby to the front quad flanked by the Porter's lodge. He presented himself at a side window where he was confronted by a small elderly man, balding and with horn rim spectacles like himself, dressed in a blue serge suit and tie,

"I would like to speak with the Bursar," he said.

"A very busy man, sir. I doubt that he will see you without an appointment," came the reply.

"Just call him now, please," Mallory replied wearily passing his card through the window. "I'm sure that he will see me."

The porter stiffened, picked up the house 'phone and dialled a three digit number

"I've someone here from the police who wishes to see the Bursar, Margaret. Will you check that he's free," he asked and. after a short pause, I'll send him up then." He called to his assistant inside the lodge. "Eric, take this gentleman up to the Bursar's office." A slight emphasis on the word 'gentleman' indicated his lack of respect but was not quite sufficient to be taken as a personal insult and Mallory let it pass. Whether the porter's dislike was of the police in general or particular to Mallory was unclear.

The youth Eric emerged from the back of the lodge. Tall of stature and spotty of face with dank black hair, Eric was at least properly dressed in black trousers with a white shirt and stringy black tie. With a perfunctory "Just follow me, sir," he set off to the near left- hand corner of the front quad, through a short stone flagged passage lit only by daylight at either end and into the rear quad which they circled clockwise past the College Chapel. Then turning left through a narrow archway they arrived at the door of a more modern annex with letterbox, bell push and knocker. The outer office was occupied by two middle-aged women, the one gaunt, bespectacled and severe in appearance, the other rounder, with grey hair heavily permed and a cheerful expression to whom Mallory offered another of his cards; the boy Eric, having performed his duty left without further word. "I'll take you through to Mr. McAllister immediately," she said rising to her feet and waddling the inner office door on which she knocked lightly before entering. "Inspector Mallory for you, Mr. McAllister," she announced handing him Mallory's card.

"Hamish McAllister." The tall figure who rose from behind his desk advanced towards Mallory with hand extended. McAllister invited his visitor to be seated. "How can I help you, Inspector Mallory? I see from your card that you come from a Scotland Yard department with which we don't normally have contact. Has one of our students got himself into trouble?"

"I've no doubt that you may have students in trouble with the Oxford police for minor offences but not with the Fraud Squad. I'm here about something quite different - a suspected art fraud of which Latimer College is a possible victim. At this time my investigation is in its very early stages and I shall appreciate your discretion.," Duncan Malllory replied. He surveyed the man opposite – a Scot by name with more than a trace of Highland lilt, tweed suited, wearing the tie of a well-known regiment and of a similar age to Julian Radclive; a military man rather than an academic and more likely to take a practical view of problems arising within his responsibility.

"That's intriguing, Inspector. If it concerns property of this College, the matter falls under my jurisdiction in the first instance and I can guarantee my confidentiality. However, I am accountable to the Master and shall need to keep him informed if your suspicions have substance," McAllister cautioned.

"Understood," Mallory said. "On that basis, I'll tell you all that I know before asking any questions." While McAllister called for mugs of tea from Margaret on his intercom, Duncan gave him the same detailed briefing that he had delivered earlier to Julian and Gaby. He concluded the account by passing the Hong Kong auction catalogue to McAllister.

"My first question is whether you recognize this painting?" he asked.

"It looks identical to our De Hooch hanging in the Latimer Senior Common Room, but it's described here as 'school of Vermeer'. What does that mean?" McAllister answered.

"It means that either your painting or the one in Hong Kong is a copy."

"Well, I can show you ours while you're here. It was delivered back to the College on Monday."

"Delivered back! Did someone take it from you; where had it been?" Mallory asked sharply.

"No, it wasn't stolen. We sent the picture away to be cleaned three months ago; it has just been returned to us. It looks much fresher – you'll see for yourself."

"Where did you send it for cleaning then?" Duncan took out his notepad.

"The Clarendon Gallery arranged it all for us; they handled the collection of the picture from the College, its safe shipment to a specialist restorer in Amsterdam and then the return shipment and delivery. All very efficient."

"In that case, I need from you the name, address and telephone number of the painting restorer and a copy of their invoice which they have no doubt sent."

"I canna do that, Inspector." The Bursar looked embarrassed and his Highland burr became pronounced. "The whole operation was undertaken by the Clarendon Gallery as the College's contractor and they did a guid job for us," he explained.

"Show me the Clarendon invoice, then," Mallory asked.

"I could telephone them now, the while you're here, and ask for the name and contact details of the restorer," McAllister offered.

"On no account should you or anyone else call the gallery about this or any other matter while I am investigating," Mallory insisted. "If there is something amiss, we need to discover how and to what extent Clarendon Gallery is involved."

He turned his attention to the invoice dated 24 June. It was a simple enough document typed on Clarendon Gallery headed stationery and addressed to the Bursar, Latimer College. The detail was sparse, on two lines with a single item for VAT added to the total. "To: Professional cleaning of Pieter de Hooch painting - £4,790; packaging and shipment to Amsterdam and return - £630; underneath the sub-total of £5,420, then figures for VAT and the Total."

"I shall need to keep this for a time; you may wish to take a photocopy for your records and I will write you a receipt," Mallory said. "Now tell me how the painting was delivered on Monday."

"I canna do that either. It was left at the Lodge during the morning and the Head Porter, Jessop, brought it through to me around midday. It was packed in plastic bubble wrap; we took it through immediately to the Senior Common Room and hung it in its usual place so that it was there for the Fellows to see at lunchtime," McAllister replied.

"Perhaps we could take a look at it now and then I will question Jessop on my way out."

Hamish McAllister led him back into the front quad to the left hand corner beyond the entrance to Hall where they ascended a single flight of stairs to the Fellows Dining Room and Common Room. At this time of day the area was empty except for one elderly Don asleep in a sofa corner with a copy of the Manchester Guardian spread out on his knees. The De Hooch adorned the centre of the back wall; it was properly lit by it own picture light and looked in mint condition, fresh as the day it was first painted – whenever that might have been, Mallory mused. They stood together in front of the picture; it was manifestly the same subject in the same detail as the auction catalogue photograph.

"How does this relate to the painting in the Hong Kong auction?" McAllister asked.

"The obvious explanation is that your painting was copied by an expert in Amsterdam while it was being cleaned," Mallory began.

"And the copy is being auctioned in Hong Kong next month?" McAllister continued for him.

"Or the original is now in Hong Kong and the copy was returned to Latimer College. I'm not an art expert and I can't tell you whether this is your de Hooch or the copy" Mallory concluded.

The Bursar looked distressed. "We shall have to authenticate this painting immediately," he cried. "I'll consult with the Master and we'll call for an expert from Christie's or Sotheby's on 17th Century Dutch interiors to give an opinion."

"Please leave that to me, Mr. McAllister. The Yard has its own art experts which it uses regularly. I'll arrange that for next week if you and the Master will attend."

"Is there anything more advice you can give me, Inspector?" McAllister asked.

"Don't be in a hurry to pay the Clarendon Gallery invoice," Duncan said.

---ooo0ooo---

Leaving the Bursar to report to the Master, Mallory returned to the Lodge where he found the Head Porter pinning new notices up on the undergraduates' board.

"Ah, Mr. Jessop," he called out "may I take up a few minutes of your time?"

The Porter turned towards him. "You may want to move your motor car first, Inspector," Jessop said. "You seem to have collected a number of parking tickets," he added with some satisfaction.

"As expected, Mr. Jessop," he answered. "What is of more consequence is the package you received at the Lodge on Monday morning shortly before noon. Can you tell me who delivered it and how it was recorded. Did you receive it yourself?"

"I received it myself from a large man with long black hair. He arrived in an old green Volvo estate car with a roof rack which he parked outside the gate where yours is now. He wasn't here long enough to pick up a ticket."

"Did you log an entry in your day sheet? If so, did he sign the entry and did he ask you for a receipt?"

"We don't keep a register and we don't issue receipts. The undergraduates are always leaving things here for collection during the day. Are you telling me how to do my job, Inspector ?" Jessop asked querulously.

"Not at all, Mr. Jessop. It is entirely up to the College how to handle its own security," Mallory answered taking notebook and pen from his pocket. "I'm only noting what measures you take to safeguard Latimer College's valuable property." Jessop bridled at the implied criticism while Duncan put away his pen and the notebook with its blank page.

Duncan Mallory returned to the Jaguar, took the sheaf of parking tickets from under a windscreen wiper and walked up to the female warden who was now clocking cars across the street outside Merton. Flashing his warrant card he handed the tickets over to her. "Collected in the normal course of duty. I don't think we need to waste police time on these, do we?" She looked daggers at him and tore them into small pieces. "At least, you're not paid piecework" Duncan comforted her.

---ooo0ooo---

CHAPTER NINE

Thursday, 27 June

THE NEXT DAY I took a cheap day return to Marylebone arriving in good time for my meeting with Robert Schindler at 12:30 p.m. at his Charlotte Street office. The previous evening, the Digger had filled us in on his visit to Latimer and Gaby had confirmed that she was all set to start part-time attendance at the Clarendon Art Gallery in the morning. Between them, they decided that Duncan would give Gaby a clear run for detective work at the Gallery before he arrived after midday. Having listened to Duncan's account of his conversation with Jessop, Gaby and I were confident that it was Aubrey Pinkerton who had delivered the painting.

The modest offices of Schindler Lyne are halfway up Charlotte Street and occupy three upper floors in a 19th century building. Now in his late seventies, Robert was a well-respected publisher of academic and business books, having founded the firm with his partner Simeon Lyne in the 1950's. The first title, a directory of university degrees and courses had been commissioned and edited from his kitchen table. Simeon had died from a massive heart attack in the early 1960s leaving Robert to build the business on his own. Over the years he had accumulated a core staff of seasoned editors and collaborators to become a doyen among independent business book publishers. He had cultivated a reputation as a tough critic with a mordant wit who ill tolerated the many charlatans inhabiting the world of publishing and was a scourge of authors who served up ill-written or specious texts, but his bark was worse than his bite. Under the daunting crustiness he encouraged new authors, was a loyal partner and had a nose for commissioning books which sold – the ultimate test of the successful publisher. I had written and edited for him for nearly ten years since I had interviewed and written a profile article about him for a magazine. Surprisingly, Robert had liked my article and, on that slender evidence, invited me to commission and edit a book about business opportunities in South Africa. One thing led to another and here we were, seven years later, with many other titles under my belt, including a second edition of the South Africa book and the first edition of my China book which had achieved bestseller status. In the interval I had become a fully-fledged associate of Schindler Lyne and I was here today to discuss my publishing programme for the next twelve months.

At reception I was greeted warmly by the redoubtable Velma, receptionist and Robert's personal gatekeeper who had been with him ever since she arrived from Grenada as a young immigrant in the 1970s. Velma waved me through. "You know your way, Julian. He's expecting you."

As usual, Robert was crouched over his desktop computer at the far end of his top floor den editing the manuscript of an academic whom he had commissioned personally to write a biography of past prime ministers. He waved me to the comfortable sofa nearest to me while he finished the page with several highlighted corrections, pressed 'save' and logged off. "The first book he's written for us," he explained as he joined me on the sofa. He was as spry and attentive as ever. He wore his full head of grey hair long, not quite curling over the collar of a grey herringbone sports jacket, his perennial publisher's uniform.

"How's the new edition of *Managing Business Abroad*," he asked abrupty. "It's due next week, isn't it?"

"Almost there. One late submission, quality generally good, most chapters readable and a couple are quite attention grabbing. The complete text will be with you by 8th July," I reported.

"What's next. Where do we go for honey?"

"South Africa, perhaps. Now that Mandela's fully up to speed, the outlook's changed but I no longer have any strong connections at South Africa House here in London. Definitely time for a new edition of the China book and I have a new author to offer you who wants to write about the Hong Kong handover."

"Sounds like you have enough to earn your lunch. Why don't you tempt my palette next door?"

'Next door' was Robert's favourite Italian restaurant, Bertorelli's, still owned and managed by the family; it was four doors down Charlotte Street on the same side of the road. We repaired there after telling Velma that he would be out for the next two hours. Seated at his usual table at the back of the restaurant we ordered antipasto and a bottle of Villa Antinori before moving on to *osso bucco*. Over lunch we discussed new projects. On the train journey that morning it had occurred to me that it might be interesting to attend the auction of the De Hooch lookalike painting on 10th July and that, since most of the sponsors and advertisers who had supported previous editions of the China book were located in Hong Kong, a case could be made for going there to solicit repeat orders. While we enjoyed the succulent lamb shanks of the osso bucco I made my pitch to Robert, citing a target of £20,000 for promotional advertising income against £25,000 last time.

"Why less this time?" he asked

"There's one dissident who wasn't satisfied with the first edition outcome and I can't be sure of a replacement or any more paying contributors."

"And what would be the cost of your little jolly?"

"A budget of £5,000 for travel and accommodation for the week," I quoted.

"I'll think about it," he said. "Now, tell me about your new author."

We moved on to a full discussion of Percy Mansfield's proposed memoirs and I gave Robert the copy of his outline which he scanned quickly.

"That could sell well, if he comes up with something reasonably objective and not just a rant against the last Governor. What are the chances of that?" Robert asked.

"Well, he's certainly an embittered man but he's intelligent enough to know that he has to avoid libel; a careful editor should be able to minimize the risk Still, you'd need to have the firm's lawyers read the manuscript through for clearance."

"If we do the book, I'd expect you to be the careful editor. After all, he's your chum and lives on your doorstep," Robert suggested.

"He's certainly not my chum," I protested. "He's a pompous, conceited ass."

"That's why you'll be an appropriate editor," he replied loftily.

"Not very flattering, Robert Why don't you ask Percy to lunch and make up your own mind?"

We completed our meal with the famed Bertorelli *cassata siciliano*. As he paid the bill Roger turned to me: "Edit Percy Mansfield's memoirs, Julian, and you may tell Velma to book your flights."

---ooo0ooo---

A discreet brass nameplate at the side of the black front door confirmed that I had arrived at the address of the Wigmore Escort Agency when I reached Wimpole Street just after 3:00 p.m. Most of the almost identical late Georgian buildings in this and the equally decorous Harley Street which runs parallel house members of the medical profession from private clinics and the consulting rooms of eminent physicians and surgeons to psychiatrists and the occasional less reputable but fashionable dietician. The expensive motor cars parked outside proclaimed the prestige and well-heeled status of the inmates.

The contrast with Robert's offices in Charlotte Street was marked further after the entryphone buzzed to give me access to an elegant black and white tiled hall. There was a fine curved staircase at the rear and, in the foreground to one side, a reception area comprising of a massive antique boule table which served as desk with two telephones and a vase of apricot-coloured roses. Behind the desk sat an attractive blonde woman in her late twenties in a summer dress which matched exactly the colour of the roses. Open-faced with catlike green eyes she wore a double string of cultured pearls about her neck. The sort of girl, I thought, that any nice young man would be comfortable taking home to meet mother. A place card in front of her confirmed her name as Veronica Phillips. She lifted the receiver of the white telephone and announced "Mr. Radclive is here to see you." The cut-glass accent suggested past attendance at Cheltenham Ladies College or Westonbirt.

Georgina Delahaye appeared on the staircase above me. "Hi Julian, come on up," she said welcomng me warmly. "Veronica, ask Annie to rustle up a pot of tea for us in my office."

Panelled double doors at the head of the staircase gave on to Georgina's elegantly furnished first floor office. Two pairs of full-length casement windows overlooked Wimpole Street with brocade curtains in celadon green. The wallpaper in Regency stripes of old rose and grey and a Georgian bureau and chairs grouped on one side of the room completed the formal decor. Georgina led me to comfortable armchairs with a coffee table between and a clear view through sash windows. Today, she was wearing a black Armani trouser suit with scarlet pumps which matched perfectly the colour of her lacquered fingernails and lipstick. No sooner had we seated ourselves than a discreet tap on the door heralded the arrival of our tea tray.

"Tell me, Julian, what you and Bill need to fend off the press pack and TV when news of the murders goes public. How do you think they'll attack?" she asked pouring tea into Ainsley bone china cups and passing one to me.

"I'm no expert in this area, Georgina, but I imagine that they'll focus on you and categorise the escort agency as a disreputable, shady business trading in girls. If the Red Tops get really vicious, they'll probably try to characterise it as a kind of 'Rent-a-tart' outfit and your house parties in Fullmere as 'dirty weekends'."

"As bad as that? Then, I need to tell you exactly how Wigmore Escort Agency works. Too late to change the name I'm afraid – I know that it sounds suggestive."

"Yes, Bill wants to head them off at the pass by showing that they will enter libel territory from the outset at their peril," I said confirming her grasp of the situation. "Tell me how the agency operates and your part in its direction."

"Wigmore is a limited liability company which I run as a registered Club. I own ninety per cent of the shares and am executive chairman. The minority shareholder and only other director is Gerald Marl – I'll introduce him to you while you're here. Club members are either companies or institutions and private individuals, mostly people who entertain on a grand scale. The corporate members need to hire good-looking respectable young ladies for particular occasions to help entertain unattached guests. Individual members are mostly single men of substance who need attractive companions to accompany them to social events in the public eye, such as Ascot or the parties thrown by corporate members, where it is more noticeable to arrive single. The corporate members include embassies, multinational companies and film studios, even government departments and publishing houses. In fact, we are providing a team of girls for a cocktail party at the French embassy this evening."

"A case of carrying coals to N|ewcastle, one might say," I quipped. "Where do the girls come from?"

"Most of them are single girls in boring office jobs who want to supplement their incomes and socialise. Some of them take up membership themselves; they're still paid for the assignments they accept. We never employ hookers or personality girls – the ones that decorate automobiles at photoshoots and motor shows," Georgina explained.

"So, they're respectable girls. What's your business model? How does it work?

"Typically, a client, like the embassy tonight, books four or more girls on a fixed hour contract – say, three or four hours for a reception - and pays up front. If the event overruns in time, we bill them the next day. Alternatively, if a corporation hires a girl to accompany its Chairman to a business convention in the South of France, the contract provides for specific hours of duty requiring the escort's consent to any variation. All her travel and accommodation expenses are paid by the client and sometimes there is a clothes allowance so that she can dress appropriately. The escort receives from us thirty per cent of the fees charged after the event."

I decided to probe further as any competent newshound would.

"What happens if one thing leads to another and the client or someone the girl meets at a reception takes her off outside the hours of contract and she is required to act outside 'the normal course of duty'?"

"I guess that's the crunch question that anyone would ask," Georgina acknowledged. "Of course, that happens quite often and the girl has two ways to go. Either she can agree and it's up to her what kind of deal she makes. We are not involved and want no part of any additional payment or she can give him the breeze We avoid any charge of 'living off immoral earnings' which is the rather cute way you guys put it over here."

"And if he continues to 'force his attentions on her', to use another good old English phrase?"

"He's banned. We have a very strict code of conduct to which members sign up. In the case of an individual member, he's blackballed. If the offender works for a corporate or institution which is the member, it gets a second chance. But if it happens again with another employee, the employer's membership is cancelled. Two strikes and they're out."

"And how often does that happen?" I persisted.

"With individual members, hardly ever. They know the rules and stick to them. Corporate members and institutions are another matter. There's often some wise guy who decides to try it on. So, warnings are quite frequent. Second strikes, not often. Most recently, we had to cancel the membership of a Middle East embassy."

"That sounds unquestionable good practice. But what about the weekends at Fullmere? Even the locals are curious about your visitors, and last weekend's batch are sure to attract scrutiny," I asked.

"They're all club members and paying guests. Sometimes a male member pays for a girl if they've met before, like Hugo and Trixie. And to answer your next question before you ask, if they hop into the sack together while they're staying, that's entirely their own business. If there are no more questions, time for you to meet Gerald." And so saying, Georgina dialled in an internal connection and invited him to join us.

I hadn't known what to expect. Gerald's appearance was entirely in keeping with the surroundings. Of above average height, his slender frame was dressed in a tailored double-breasted grey flannel suit with highly polished black Oxfords, a striped shirt and an Old Harrovian tie. It was difficult to judge his age. His thin straw-coloured hair was carefully combed; he could have been in his late forties or a younger man with a world weary face. Either way, his manner was friendly and his manners superb.

"How nice to meet you, Julian. Georgina tells me that you are coaching her how to ward off the vultures," he said.

"I don't think either of you need much coaching," I replied. "You seem to run an immaculate establishment."

"There's not too much that happens here. Most of the action takes place at clients' locations. We have a club room across the hall where members can meet up and have drinks with each other - no non-members admitted - and there's a dining room downstairs leading off the foyer where corporate members can host private luncheons or dinners for their clients and visiting VIPs whom they want to impress. Naturally, they hire agency girls with good social skills, quite often members themselves, to make up the numbers."

"So, you have kitchen and in-house catering staff? That must add to your overheads," I commented.

"Not at all. We don't serve food on a daily basis. There's a kitchen but we use outside caterers for all special events," Gerald replied smoothly.

"And upstairs. This is a big house; do you offer accommodation for members and their guests?" I suggested.

"No way," Georgina interjected. "This is not a cathouse."

"Nor house of ill repute," Gerald added. "The floor above is where I live and the top floor is Georgina's flat."

"And our appartments are strictly off limits to members," Georgina insisted.

The three of us walked across the landing to the members club and rest rooms which occupied the rest of the floor. They were decorated and furnished with the same impeccable taste and afforded discreet comfort equivalent to any prestigious West End club, the kind where fathers put their sons down at birth for future membership. At the far end of the clubroom was a well-stocked self-service bar.

"It operates on a 'slate' system," Gerald explained. "Members enter what they have helped themselves to in the logbook and sign each entry. At the end of the month we bill them individually."

We returned to Georgina's office and the elegant Gerald excused himself. "Is there anything more that Bill Fentiman needs for his briefing?" she asked pouring me a second cup of tea.

"Only the back story. Where you're coming from and why you started up the agency here in London?"

"The full story would take us all evening; so, I'll give you the concise version. When my husband, Bart Delahaye, died suddenly he left me the estate on Long Island in the Hamptons which he owned, but not the appartment in Manhattan which was on a company lease. He was a partner in a realtor outfit which specialised in upmarket East Side real estate and made big bucks. So, we lived high on the hog and there was little in the bank when he went. Who would expect a fit guy in his late forties with no history of illness to drop down without notice? The partners paid me his share of profits for the current year, but that was it. I had enough to live on for a year or, maybe, two in the high cost house in the Hamptons but, aside from that, I was in a jam. I didn't have the investment capital to turn the estate into a country club without taking in a partner and I didn't want to do that. So, I had to think up something else, What could I do?"

Georgina's question was rhetorical but I prompted her all the same by nodding to show my interest. "How then did you solve the problem?"

"I'd been working in the theatre when I met Bart. I'd played a few small parts in Broadway productions but no big breaks. To keep myself in the money I had become a party girl in the intervals as a freelance escort working with the big agencies. One night we were seated next to each other at a fund-raiser in the St. Regis hotel where one of Bart's clients had taken a table. He was a guest and I was cannon fodder to make up the party. We hit it off immediately and within a week or so became an item. Bart was ten years older than me but when you're in your twenties the age difference doesn't matter a damn. Three months later we were married and beginning to mix socially with the Manhattan 'A' list. After 12 years we were living the good life: weekdays and nights in town and weekends in the Hamptons, often with house guests to keep us amused; our son Giles was in private school and we took holidays in Europe. So, setting up my own escort agency was a no-brainer. I had a network of high rollers: bankers, heads of multinational corporations, embassy heads, media top executives and partners in service consultancies. I recruited them as clients offering membership of my exclusive Long Island club. They generated all the demand for escorts I could manage. The supply side of the market was more of a problem."

"You mean the escorts. How so?"

"Oh, there were plenty of girls eager to escort. The problem was quality. Actresses resting were usually okay but most catwalk, fashion magazine or artists' models couldn't cut the mustard with the clients. They expected escorts who could hold an intelligent conversation - not chicks who looked good but were dumb. And girls with office jobs wanting to moonlight preferred to hire themselves out to the big established agencies rather than a two-bit out of town broad. However, I got over that one in time by paying above-market rates and throwing in opportunities to network at weekend parties out at my place in the Hamptons." Georgina had warmed to her story as she continued to reminisce.

"What about your Long Island neighbours?" I asked her. "How did they react to the weekend invasion of uptown glamour girls?"

"The neighbours were fine. The cops were less happy; they suspected I was running a cathouse. I got over that hurdle by giving complimentary membership to the local sheriff's office."

"Not enough hassle then to prompt you to relocate here. Sounds like you had built a good business. What made you decide to move?"

Georgina looked at me thoughtfully while she decided how to answer my further question. There was some hesitation before she replied. Perhaps she was deciding how far she could trust me.

"As you say, after three years I had a long list of regular clients and an inventory of classy and scandal-free escorts. The agency had a high reputation for integrity and exclusiveness. Then it all went sour; the Mob tried to move in."

"They made you an offer you couldn't refuse," I suggested.

"You got it," she said. "They saw the agency as a market for drugs and the blackmail of clients who played away from home and got themselves into trouble. They offered me protection at a crippling price or a partnership deal which would allow them to peddle their rackets."

"So, you walked away?"

"I did rather better than that. I cashed in my chips," Georgina stated proudly. "I closed the agency, told my international clients that I would be starting up in London and sold the house and land to a real estate developer. He built two blocks of luxury condominiums in place of the house and trebled his investment, and I walked away with enough to begin again and buy myself a country pad in he UK. So, here we are today and you have the story."

"That's enough," I agreed. I put down my cup and saucer carefully and rose to my feet. "Thank you, Georgina. Some time, you must tell me about the teething troubles of the start-up here to satisfy my curiosity, but I can guess much of it. Bill thinks that an arrest is likely before the weekend; so, it will be good if you are back at Fullmere when the balloon goes up."

Georgina stood up too and assured me that she intended to drive down the next day with Gerald to give her support and to ensure that that there would be no-one at Wimpole Street if the Press decided to camp on the doorstep. I was pleased that she was prepared for trouble and had thought it through. And yet, as I descended the broad staircase and passed by the reassuring figure of the wholesome Veronica on my way out, I had a nagging feeling that Georgina's account of how she had come to relocate in London was incomplete.

---oooOooo---

CHAPTER 10

Thursday, 27 June

DUNCAN MALLORY'S and Gaby's days were no less eventful than mine. They set off at much the same time: the Digger to check in at Kidlington police station and Gaby to arrive at the Clarendon Art Gallery by 10:00 a.m. when it opened.

When Digger Mallory pulled in at the police station he saw that the visitors' parking slot which he had occupied the previous day was now taken by a highly polished black BMW 7 series saloon. Upstairs he found that Chief Inspector Cartwright already had a visitor. Seated behind the DCI's desk with Cartwright relegated to a visitor's chair opposite him, was one of Mallory's Scotland Yard colleagues whom he liked least, Commander Trevor Wiggins of the Murder Squad. Apparently, the Chief Constable had reneged on his promise to delay overnight before calling in the Yard.

"You may come in and sit down, Mallory. DCI Cartwright has just been telling me that you are swanning around here," said the Commander.

Duncan did as he was told and took the second visitor's chair alongside Cartwright. The two men surveyed each other across the desk with ill-concealed distaste. Foxy-faced with pointed ears and ginger hair swept back from his forehead, Wiggins exuded the self-importance of a man vested with unexpected authority and enjoying it. Mallory was his usual well-dressed self with horn-rimmed spectacles which helped to give a misleading impression of bland indifference.

"We need to understand each other from the start," Wiggins said flatly. "This murder case takes precedence over your investigation. So, you will not trample over my turf by interviewing anyone who is involved in my case. Is that understood?"

"Understood, sir, but the two cases may overlap," Duncan replied evenly.

"Explain to me, how a case of double murder at a concert can possibly be connected to the suspected theft of a painting from an Oxford college."

"Well, Commander, I have firm evidence that the Clarendon Art Gallery is involved in sending college artworks to Amsterdam for cleaning and that, in one case at least, the picture that was returned may be a copy of the original. I expect to establish that in the next few days and you know already that the main murder victim was a partner in that art gallery. I also have evidence that one of those around and about at the concert was a friend of the victim and involved in handling the suspected fake."

"That's rapid progress since you were here yesterday afternoon, Mallory," commented Cartwright in the first words he had uttered since Duncan had entered the room. "And the man you refer to as the handler is presumably Aubrey Pinkerton who is high on our list of suspects for the murder?"

"Yes, Chief Inspector. I was planning to interview Pinkerton later today after I've visited the Gallery," Duncan affirmed.

"You'll do no such thing," Wiggins retorted with a vulpine grin. "You will only interview my suspects with my permission and, if granted, you will be accompanied by my sergeant Meadows."

"In that case, sir, would you make Sergeant Meadows available to visit Pinkerton in Fullmere this afternoon," Duncan asked respectfully but stone-faced behind his spectacles.

"That won't be necessary." This time the Wiggins grin was almost wolfish. "We shall be bringing him in for questioning later today - and, before you ask, Inspector, you may not attend the interview."

"Thank you, sir. I'll continue to pursue my enquiries in Oxford," Duncan Mallory said, acknowledging the instruction and rising to leave the room. There was nothing more to be said.

DCI Cartwright caught up with him as he reached his car. "I'm off the case, Duncan, but I'm around if you think I can help you with yours. You might like to know that Wiggins is calling a Press Conference for 10:00 a.m. tomorrow. I think he intends to keep Pinkerton in overnight for further questioning."

"Thank you, Chief Inspector. From experience, the Commander likes to extract the maximum personal publicity from all his cases. It's not always productive."

"I'll try to pick up the pieces, if it falls apart," Cartwright assured him.

---ooo0ooo---

Gaby's morning was less abrasive. She reached Little Clarendon Street just after 10.00 a.m having parked the Subaru in the meter-free Park Town. On the short walk across she rehearsed in her mind the plan of action she and the Digger had hatched. Her objective was to discover the address in Amsterdam where the Clarendon Art Gallery sent paintings for cleaning before Duncan's arrival at the agreed time of 12:30. He wanted to avoid asking a direct question which could alert the Gallery and the Amsterdam copyist before he could arrange for a raid on the premises. They had agreed a series of coded responses. On his arrival, Gaby would say "Is there anything particular which might be of interest to you?" and Duncan would answer "Jewellery for my girlfriend, perhaps." To which, there were alternative responses: "If you're looking for diamonds or precious stones, we may not be able to help you" which meant that she had failed; in the alternative, if she had found the address, "I'm sure you can find something she would like" would signal that she had been successful. In either case, she would follow up by inviting him to view the gallery's collection downstairs and it would be up to the Digger to decide how to play it.

Valerie Wyngarde greeted Gaby rather coolly. "Alexander says that you want to help. What do you think you can do? We can't afford to pay you anything, you know," she said.

Gaby had prepared herself for a less than enthusiastic response. "I've run my own business as a market research agency; so, I'm good with people and I can manage the books and accounts of a small company," she replied. Valerie's interest quickened.

"What kind of time could you spend here helping out?" she asked.

"I had in mind six hours a day for three days a week. It won't replace Theodora's input, I know, but I thought it would help to fill in."

"Would you be willing to work two of the days on the floor which would give me some time off and one day on the books and accounts which Theodora used to look after? But I can't believe you would do this for free," Valerie said doubtfully.

"Not entirely, no; although it would take me out of the house which is the main attraction. How about paying me commission on everything I sell on my two days a week with customers - say, at 10 per cent?"

"I'll have to check with Catherine, the remaining partner, but that sounds reasonable. We could try it for a month."

"Why not. Let's give it whirl. Ready to start," said Gaby.

For the next hour a more animated and friendly Valerie took Gaby through the exhibits giving her the background on each artist: an assessment of those who sold well already, those for whom she thought the Gallery could create a market, those who were pleasant to deal with and those who were demanding and continually caused difficulties. She also explained the terms of business between gallery and artists. They agreed the offer price between them - usually that suggested by the gallery; the standard deal was that the artist would receive 50 per cent of the actual sale price within thirty days of customer payment. Exceptions to the rule were made in the case of best-selling artists whose work was also on offer at other galleries; to limit competition the Gallery sometimes cut its take to 40 per cent, on occasion to as little as 35 per cent.

During this induction Gaby took time to examine Valerie's appearance and mien and to re-assess her previous judgment. She was dressed more stylishly today in a blue denim jumpsuit which suited her willowy figure and her blonde hair, formerly straggly, was swept back behind the ears and secured with a ribbon at the nape of her neck. Altogether more attractive Gaby decided, although the usual impenetrable stare was turned on in her direction whenever she asked a question. She still suspected that Valerie was a drug user but her pupils were less dilated; maybe she had been abstemious over the weekend.

Shortly after midday the doorbell in the front showroom rang while they were still in the basement. "Why don't you have a look at the records in the office while I deal with the visitor," she suggested and hastened up the stairs. This gave Gaby the opportunity she had been waiting for. The office space was cramped: a desk with word processor and telephone, a shelf full of ring binder files and just one chair. On the back wall of the office was a small safe with combination lock. Gaby sat down, ignored the word processor and reached up for the purchases ledger and daybook. Starting with the ledger she quickly identified four entries under the name "Johannes Van den Groot" BV in the past three months. She took a pad and pen from her handbag and wrote down the details, then looked for an address book which she located in a drawer of the desk where she found the postal address and telephone number of Van den Groot in Amsterdam. Her next task was to identify the Colleges which had commissioned the Gallery to have paintings cleaned, requiring a further search in the sales daybook over the same period. There was no time to do this before she heard Valerie returning from the shop above; so she placed the address book back quickly into the drawer where she had found it.

Valerie was in a good mood having sold a large piece of pottery which Gaby had thought particularly unattractive. She placed the invoice flimsy on the spike for entry later into the sales daybook. "That's a good contribution to the week's takings," she said and looking sideways at Gaby "without any commission to pay."

There was another ring on the bell and this time the two of them went upstairs. The newcomer was the Digger, arriving precisely on his appointed hour. They allowed Duncan to wander around for a minute or two before Valerie signalled to Gaby to step forward and address him.

"Good morning. Is there anything in particular which might be of interest to you?" she asked, launching into the rehearsed script.

"Jewellery for my girlfriend, perhaps," Duncan replied by rote.

"I'm sure we can find something she would like downstairs," Gaby affirmed leading him to the jewellery display. Valerie did not follow them down.

While they were still in earshot she added "There are three or four pieces here which I wouldn't say 'no' to myself," and passed him the page from her pad with the contact details for Van der Leiden.

Duncan went through the actions of looking carefully, handling several pieces and making appreciative comments.

Finally, after pondering for about five minutes he announced that would bring his girlfriend in with him to choose for herself. "Will you be here on Monday if we come in at about the same time in her lunch hour?" he asked as they returned upstairs. Gaby assured him that she would make a point of being there and asked him for his name.

"Damian Mumford," he said and left the Gallery after nodding to Valerie.

"I can see that you know how to talk to customers. Good to ask him for his name; they only give it if they're serious," was Valerie's verdict.

Soon after Duncan's departure Valerie asked Gaby if she was happy to hold the fort while she "nipped home" for an hour, explaining that she lived less than ten minutes walk away in Jericho, just across Walton Street at the end of Little Clarendon Street. Of course, this suited Gaby perfectly and she resumed her search as soon as Valerie had left. The sales daybook revealed what she was looking for; over a nine month period there were entries for three Colleges: Curzon, Hereford and Latimer. The amounts charged varied between £5,000 and £10,000. The most recent entry for Latimer was dated 4 June and matched the copy invoice which Duncan had taken on his visit there earlier in the week. There was a pattern of approximately ten day intervals between Van den Groot billing and the next Gallery invoice to a College. Worryingly, there was no correlation between the fourth entry for Van den Groot on 25 June and any College. Gaby deduced that there was a painting in transit from Amsterdam for a fourth College which had not yet reached Oxford. Aside from that loose end her mission was accomplished and, when Valerie returned after 2:30 p.m. she decided that she would go home, promising to return in the morning.

---ooo0ooo---

CHAPTER 11

Thursday 27 and Friday 28 June

WHEN I REACHED HOME that evening, I found Gaby and Duncan Mallory engrossed in conversation. On the return journey I had composed in note form a report of my meeting with Georgina Delahaye to be delivered verbally on the telephone to Bill later. My first priority was to give Fred a run in the field to make up for a mouldy day. He was not a dog to bear grudges and 20 minutes of hyperactivity chasing and retrieving sticks was enough to restore his spirits. It was a splendid summer's evening but a bank of black clouds on the Northern skyline suggested that the good weather was going to break soon.

We returned to the house and I poured myself a large Ballantine's in a tall glass with ice and soda water before preparing Fred's tea of tinned meat and dog biscuit which he consumed methodically with evident satisfaction. Joining the others on the terrace I refreshed their glasses from a half empty bottle of Chablis and settled down to compare notes. They were pleased with themselves at the fruits of their time spent at the Clarendon Art Gallery. Duncan had already capitalised on the information that Gaby had gathered. He had alerted his opposite number in Amsterdam, Inspecteur Visser, who had arranged to raid the premises of Van den Groot BV in Herengracht the following day as soon as Duncan Mallory could join him. Duncan had booked himself on the first flight to Schipol. The priority was to secure whatever original canvases there might be in Herengracht before trying to match them up with the paintings from Oxford colleges that had been sent to Amsterdam from the Gallery.

Meantime, while Duncan was there, Gaby would attempt to discover the destination of the outstanding shipment in transit from Van den Groot invoiced to the Gallery on 25 June. It was agreed that she would cofine her investigations to a further search of the books without questioning Valerie Wyngarde. That would wait until the original canvases had been secured.

After dinner Duncan returned to the Eastwick Arms for an early night and his drive to Heathrow in the morning and I called Bill Fentiman to give him my report. He heard me out to the end before asking a single question.

"Do you think Georgina was telling the truth throughout?"

"About her escort agency here in London, yes. I'm less certain about the back story in America. I don't think she told any untruths but she showed some hesitation before she embarked on her 'concise version'. I am uneasy that it may not have been the whole truth, that there was something missing," I replied.

"Then I'd better check it out in New York. I'll call Bernie Klein, the attorney with whom I work on the Baron's businesses over there. There's time to put in a call to his office now."

"That's good," I said "because the balloon will probably go up here tomorrow. Commander Wiggins is keeping Aubrey Pinkerton in overnight and holding a press conference in the morning."

---oooOooo---

After Bill rang off we returned to the subject of the Oxford art frauds and discussed how we might determine whether the paintings which had been brought back by the Clarendon Art Gallery were the originals or copies, without involving formal validation by a London auction house. Gaby remembered that Barbara had a cousin whose son had trained with Christies and was last heard of as a resident expert at the Ashmolean Museum; so Gaby telephoned back to Sussex and spoke this time to Barbara. She was pleased to have a gossip and to divulge his name as Basil Gore-Smith.

The next morning was dull and drizzly, and I volunteered to drive Gaby into Oxford before going on to the Ashmolean to look up Gore-Smith and, hopefully, arrange for him to visit Latimer College with us over the weekend. I dropped her off at the Gallery and parked the Range Rover on a meter in The Broad before walking across to the Ashmolean where I asked for directions to Basil Gore-Smith. They called him from Reception and he invited me to come up to the top floor where he met me at the lift gate. A tall, stooping young man with a receding chin and a lock of blond hair flopping over his forehead, he led me to his shoebox-sized office. There was just enough space for the two of us to sit opposite each other with his back against the desk and mine against a filing cabinet with our knees almost touching. Sunlight from the direction of Beaumont Street was filtered through the grimy panes of a single sash window and did little to brighten the miserable workspace. He looked at me expectantly and I gave him the relevant part of the story to explain why I was there.

"And so you can see that we have a dilemma. Is the painting to be auctioned in Hong Kong or the canvas returned to Latimer College a fake and which of them is the original de Hooch?" I said, summing up where we were.

"Of course, they could both be copies," Gore-Smith drawled languidly.

"The first thing we can do is narrow the field," I replied. "Would you be willing to help, Basil, by giving an opinion on the painting now at Latimer?"

His interest quickened . "Will there be a valuation fee?" he asked.

"Not for this first appraisal, I'm afraid. We just need your personal informed opinion this time. As the investigation continues there may be other colleges with pictures cleaned recently through the same channel who will need something more formal."

"In that case, I shall have to visit Latimer outside working hours. When would you want me to do it?"

"I shall call on the Master after I leave here and suggest he invites you to view over the coming weekend."

Basil confirmed that he would be available most of the time and I hastened across to Latimer College, feeding my parking meter illegally and striding up the Turl, across the High and down past Oriel College under the lowering gaze of its Cecil Rhodes statue. Jessop was on duty at the Lodge. He recognized me from my last attendance at a college gaudy and I requested him to ring the Master and ask if he could spare me a few minutes of his time. Five minutes later I was seated comfortably with a glass of Madeira in my hand in the Master's rooms where he gave his weekly tutorials in Greek philosophy.

"This is an unexpected pleasure, Julian. What do you have for me?" he asked.

Geoffrey Rundle, the Master, was an imposing figure. With his full head of white hair, an actor's profile and actor's gestures, female students found him fascinating; male students were less certain. I thought him a poseur but enjoyed his company.

"I've come about your De Hooch, Master," I said bluntly.

"You sound like the man who's come to service the boiler. What is your interest in our painting?" He looked at me down his Roman nose with his chin raised slightly and took a sip from his glass.

"I've been recruited by Inspector Mallory to help in his investigations of art frauds here in Oxford. We became friends several years ago working together on a book about fraud to which he contributed as a co-author. He visited your Bursar yesterday and I'm sure you have been briefed."

"Yes. It's very alarming. Hamish McAllister has given me a full report and I understand that if it is our painting on auction in Hong Kong next month, we can hope for it to be recovered."

"That's right. In the meantime, I think we can establish whether or not the canvas returned to the Bursar is a fake or the original. We could bring an expert here to have a look, if you like."

"So long as there's no publicity. Who do you have in mind and will your Inspector Mallory attend at the same time?"

I explained that Basil Gore-Smith was willing to view and give an appraisal this weekend and, if we arranged his visit for Sunday, Duncan Mallory would almost certainly be available. The Master was intrigued by the news that Duncan was busy in Amsterdam raiding the offices of Van den Groot.

"How very dramatic, Julian. What exciting lives you all lead. Shall we say midday Sunday after chapel?"

---ooo0ooo---

Time to see how Gaby was getting on. I alerted Basil to the plan for Sunday and repacked the car at the top end of St. Giles feeding the meter for an hour. I started to stroll down Little Clarendon Street towards the Gallery. I had walked no more than a few paces before I could see that there was a knot of people grouped around the entrance and window. As I drew near, I identified that several of them had cameras and that a tall woman with straggly blonde hair standing at the threshold was denying entry to everyone. At the forefront of the throng I recognised the arts critic from the Oxford Guardian who had attended the Fullmere concert. I surmised that the blonde holding the fort was Valerie Wyngarde. Sensibly, Gaby was keeping her head down inside. I pushed my way forward and made myself known to her.

"Come on in. Reinforcements are welcome; you'll find her downstairs," Valerie said.

The Oxford Guardian man seemed to recognize me too. "You were at the concert last weekend, weren't you?" he asked.

"Yes, you'd better come in with me," I said. "But no photographs."

I pushed him in before me and told Valerie to shut the door and lock it. We moved to the back of the ground floor showroom and introduced ourselves.

"This is Valerie Wyngarde, a Gallery director, and I'm Julian Radclive, a friend of Mrs. Deakin's husband. My wife Gaby is downstairs helping Ms Wyngarde out for the time-being," I explained.

"And I'm Charlie Dibbs, Arts Editor for the Guardian. I expect you're wondering why it's me here," he replied. We shook hands formally.

"Yes, I would have expected a crime reporter from the Oxford Evening News."

"That's our sister newspaper and we try to cover for each other's stories. Since I was at the concert our editors thought that I might be better able to research Mrs. Deakin's background. My crime colleague was at the police Press briefing at Kidlington this morning."

Gaby had heard my voice from the basement and came upstairs to join us. "Did the police issue a formal statement?" I asked.

Charlie Dibbs withdrew a single sheet from his pocket and handed it to me. The typed statement on headed paper over the signature of Commander Trevor Wiggins and dated 28 June, 1996 was quite short:

In the course of the investigations into the murder of Mrs. Theodora Deakin of St. Winifred's College Oxford and Miss Molly Bennett of Fullmere at Fullmere Mill on the evening of 21 June, Aubrey Pinkerton of Garden Cottage, Fullmere Mill was taken into custody on 27 June and has been assisting the police in their enquiries overnight. Mr. Pinkerton was released this morning without charge at 0915. The police continue to pursue other lines of enquiry.

"Does that mean that Aubrey Pinkerton is in the clear?" Valerie asked.

"Not at all. It simply labels him as a leading suspect. They can bring him in again for further questioning at any time without charging him," I said.

"Perhaps the police hope to flush out any collaborators. It's unlikely that the same person murdered both Mrs. Deakin and the girl," Charlie suggested.

I looked at Charlie Dibbs carefully for the first time. He seemed a little younger than me but time had not treated him kindly. His face was deeply-lined with shaggy eyebrows and grey hair scraped back into a man-bun at the back of his neck; his suit was well worn, his tie stringy and shirt cuffs ragged. However, his eyes twinkled and his mouth was set in a humorous expression which seemed familiar.

"Haven't we met before?" I asked him.

"I doubt it. You may remember me from my acting days with the Playhouse repertory company under Frank Hauser or later at Chichester with Peter Dews. But after long periods of 'resting' I decided to try my hand as a journalist and I've been back in Oxford for some years."

"That must be it. Now tell me what you want from Ms Wyngarde."

"Background really about the Clarendon Gallery and Theodora Deakin's role in it."

"Theodora was our managing director and the inspiration for nearly all our exhibitions," Valerie answered. "She was well-known in the art gallery world; she was very successful in persuading artists to exhibit their works here and in retaining their loyalty once they started to sell well. I don't know how we can possibly replace her."

Charlie Dibbs turned his attention to Gaby. "I saw that you were sitting at the same table as Mr. and Mrs. Deakin during the supper interval at the concert, Mrs. Radclive. How did you find her?"

Gaby's response was relaxed and delivered with candour – so far as it went. "I didn't know Theodora very well. We'd met once or twice before socially but nothing more. At the concert, she was vivacious and good company; she was excited about the coming tourist season and how it might generate more visitors to the Gallery."

"Nothing to suggest that she felt threatened or in danger?"

"Absolutely not," said Gaby.

"And you, Mr. Radclive. We all saw the incident with Aubrey Pinkerton and the waitress. Did you see him again after he was carried off?" Charlie asked changing direction.

"Actually, I did. When Mrs. Deakin disappeared after the concert I was part of the search party and we called on him in his cottage, He was upstairs in his bedroom and bad-tempered at being knocked up."

"Well, that helps to explain why the police had to release him. There's no news story here; so I won't take up any more of your time. Would you feel able to contact me if anything more develops involving the Gallery?" Dibbs handed me a dog-eared business card.

"I'll make a deal with you, Charlie," I answered. "If you can get rid of the other reporters outside now and let me know of any developments in police enquiries which you hear of, I'll give you an exclusive on any news from our end."

"You have a deal, Mr. Radclive," Charlie Dibbs replied.

Valerie let him out, and within two minutes he had dispersed the crowd. "Why on earth did you make a deal with him on exchanging information?" she demanded.

"That's simple. He'll take ownership of anything we tell him and that will make it less likely that you will be hounded by other members of the Press. They don't usually go for secondhand stories."

"You have a point. He seems relatively civilised," Valerie conceded.

On that note she decided to close the gallery for the rest of the day and I invited her to join us for a late lunch. We repaired to Brown's at the top of the street in the Woodstock Road, the all-day oasis for Oxford's hungry, open from breakfast to late evening. We settled ourselves at a table in the back of the almost empty restaurant and ordered from the modestly priced menu: a steak sandwich for Valerie and spaghetti Bolognese for Gaby and me. It was still short of 2:00p.m.; so I added a carafe of the House Red to our order to wash it down.

"Have you decided what to do with the Gallery?" I asked.

"It's not just my decision. Catherine thinks we should bring in a manager, but we couldn't really afford to. In any case, she and I together hold only twenty per cent of the shares. Theodora owned the rest and I suppose those will pass to Alexander. I haven't yet talked to him. What do you think he will want to do?"

"I've no idea. I know that he's not normally a risk taker but, if the Gallery is now paying its way, he might be happy to let it run on under your direction." I wound spaghetti round my fork and took a mouthful.

"I'm not sure I'd want to do that, although we seem to have turned the corner in the last few months."

"Has the income from the cleaning service for old paintings made a difference?" Gaby asked, knowing the answer but seeking to introduce the subject.

"Mm, that's certainly made a difference," Valerie agreed, biting into her steak sandwich. "Of course, that's entirely down to Theodora. She had the connections to the colleges, and she found a restorer in Amsterdam to do the expert cleaning. Without Theodora I don't know how to attract more colleges." I plied her with a second glass of House Red – a thin wine with rather more tannins than I would normally drink.

"Yes, I was in Latimer earlier – my old college – and they told me that their De Hooch was returned to them last Monday. The Master has invited us to view on Sunday."

"Aubrey Pinkerton dropped it down for me. He was in the Gallery to ask if he could help"."

"He's a friend of yours then?" I enquired casually.

"Oh no," Valerie replied rather too quickly. "I think he knew Theodora for a long time and occasionally she called for his advice, but I seldom saw him – only when he visited the Gallery."

Gazing into her vacant expression, I found it impossible to decide whether or not she was telling the truth. The fact that Latimer's painting had been delivered with a typed invoice dated 24 June suggested that Valerie Wyngarde had more than the passing acquaintance with the picture cleanng activity that she professed.

---ooo0ooo---

CHAPTER 12

June 29, Fullmere

THERE HAD BEEN no messages when we returned home; just a bounding Fred who had missed any company since breakfast. I had expected to hear from the Digger in Amsterdam to tell us when we could expect him back. We were also eager to share the information we had gleaned between us in Oxford but he didn't call until breakfast time on Saturday. He telephoned from the luxury of his room at the Amstel Hotel to tell us that the raid on Van den Groot BV's studio had been successful – although "not entirely without incident" he added. A total of twenty-three paintings had been recovered and had been taken to the Rijksmuseum for its experts to distinguish between the originals and copies. Duncan had booked a flight back that evening and hoped to bring their findings and photographs of them all with him. There was just time to tell him of our day in Oxford and the arrangements I had made for Sunday to view the painting that had been returned to Latimer College before he called off. Commissar Visser had arrived to take him to the Rijksmusuem for the verdict on the paintings left with them overnight.

Soon after this, there were two further calls: the first from Percy Mansfield to tell me that Robert Schindler had invited him to lunch the following Tuesday to discuss his book project and the second from Bill Fentiman. Not one word of thanks from Percy for the introduction – he assumed that Robert had been overwhelmed by the quality of his literary offering. I didn't tell him that the decision whether or not to publish would be taken largely on

Robert's impression of him, nor that Robert had a low tolerance of arrogance. To be truthful, I was not smitten by the prospect of editing his text.

The conversation with Bill was of more consequence. He had heard back from Bernie Klein, his attorney friend in New York. There were holes in Georgina Delahaye's story. There was evidence of past dealings with the Mob through a mouthpiece attorney called Tony Panata and it was uncertain whether she still had connections. She had made monthly payments to the office of their lawyers for the period up to her sale of the property on Long Island.

"I can keep the National Press from publishing stories on her business activities over the weekend, if they show interest, but I need more to head them off from any Mafia connection. Can you question her again today or tomorrow?" he asked. I assured him that I would speak to her again before the day was out and call him back. I tried telephoning Georgina but there was no ringing tone. Either the line was out of order or she had taken the receiver off the hook.

We had woken to a dull and rainy day with leaden skies. The steady drizzle was depressing but it was the first wet day for more than a fortnight and the garden needed the rain; we couldn't complain. We were debating where to do our shopping when a large black BMW swept into the yard and turned a circle pointing back towards the exit before coming to a halt. Two men emerged: from the driver's seat: a foxy-faced fellow with pointy ears and ginger hair; his passenger a more reassuring thickset figure in attendance with a briefcase and the aura of a policeman. From the Digger's description there was no doubt in identifying the driver as Commander Trevor Wiggins. I met them at the kitchen door and took them to the drawing room while Gaby put on coffee. Fred gave them an un-Labrador like growl and preferred to stay in the kitchen.

"I'm sure I don't need to tell you why I'm here, Mr. Radclive," he began, seating himself in the centre of one of our twin sofas while his sergeant took a wing chair at the back of the room and withdrew a notebook from his briefcase. "You and your wife were in conversation with Mr.and Mrs.Deakin on the evening of 21 June, more than anyone else and among the last to see the deceased alive. Sergeant Meadows here will be taking notes and we may be asking you for a signed statement."

I sat on the other sofa facing him with the coffee table between us.

"I've already made a statement to Chief Inspector Cartwright and I doubt that there is anything useful I could add," I said.

"Perhaps, but I prefer to ask my own questions. If your answers differ materially from whatever you said previously, I may have to ask you to come back to the station with us."

"Is this what one would call 'giving a statement under caution'?" I asked.

Commander Wiggins smiled mirthlessly. "Hardly. You'll know if we reach that point. "Now, I want you to tell me about the argument between the deceased and her husband. Would you say that there was bitter disagreement between them?"

"It was plainly a carry-over from an ongoing disagreement. Mr. Deakin was upset that his wife would not join him on a trip to Hong Kong on behalf of St. Winifred's and at the College's expense to drum up student recruitment. She preferred to stay in Oxford to manage her Gallery during the vacation and he thought she was being unreasonable. Aside from that they were both enjoying themselves and good company for the rest of us at our table."

"So, would you say that he was holding her refusal to travel with him against her?"

"I've known Aleaxander Deakin for some years and he's not a man to bear grudges against people who disagree with him. In this case, I would say that he was more hurt than annoyed."

"In other words, they were a perfectly normal happy married couple having a tiff?" said Wiggins pressing the point.

"Whatever a perfectly happy normal married couple may be." Enough of his leading question style of interrogation. The response was met with the same mirthless smile. The Commander changed his line of attack.

"After Mrs. Deakin's absence gave cause for concern, I understand that you took part in the search, Mr. Radclive?"

"Yes. Mr. Fentiman and I were assigned the task of looking for her the other side of the house – the front side - the car parks and grounds."

"And that included the cottage where Mr. Pinkerton lives." Delivered as a statement rather than a question. I realised now that Commander Wiggins carried no notes to prompt him and that each interview was carefully pre-planned. There were no pauses between his questions which made him a very formidable interrogator.

"That's right. We attracted Mr. Pinkerton's attention from outside – he was upstairs and may have been asleep"

"How did he appear to you? We're told that he caused a disturbance earlier in the evening when under the influence of drink."

"He took his time coming to the window. Then he was very abusive shooing us off. I suppose he could have been suffering the after-effects."

"Or he could have been stone cold sober throughout the evening," Wiggins commented, offering the alternative. I wondered if he had talked to Emma Fullerton yet.

Gaby entered the room with four steaming mugs of coffee, milk and sugar on a tray. She placed the tray on the table and sat down next to me. Sergeant Meadows put away his notebook and stood politely when she arrived; Trevor Wiggins remained seated. My dislike of the man mounted, but perhaps it was his intention to annoy. When Gaby had dispensed the coffee, he resumed his inquisition.

"Now, Mrs. Radclive, I have some questions for you," and to me "Perhaps, you would leave us for a few minutes, Mr. Radclive, while I talk to you wife." Gaby and I glanced at each other. Being told to leave the room in my own house was a new experience, but I kept my cool, picked up my coffee and headed for the door.

"I'll be in my study, Gaby, if you need me," I said over my shoulder. As I reached the door, the Commander spoke again.

"One final question, Mr. Radclive. How long do you think Mr Deakin has known his friend Aubrey Pinkerton?"

"So, far as I know, Mr Wiggins, Alexander Deakin had never seen Pinkerton before the evening of the concert." I was getting the measure of the man now; so, I managed to answer him casually without turning back.

After about a quarter of an hour Sergeant Meadows appeared at the study door. "Commander Wiggins has finished his interview of your wife, sir. We're about to leave."

"Thank you, sergeant," I said and remained seated at my desk. If I was hoping to have disengaged from Trevor Wiggins, I was disappointed. He appeared in the doorway.

"That will be all for now, Mr. Radclive, but I may need to see you again. I take it that you will not be going anywhere," he said.

"As a matter of fact, I may be visiting Hong Kong in ten days time for the inside of a week," I told him. The Commander was disgruntled and I could see that the antipathy between us was now mutual.

"For what reason?"

"Publishing business," I replied and stood up to face him across my desk.

He held his annoyance in check and paused before saying more. A vulpine grin spread over his face, before he beat a tactical retreat.

"In that case, Mr. Radclive, you will please inform my sergeant before you leave of your flight arrangements and the name of the hotel where you will be staying."

I showed them to the back door while Gaby brought through the coffee tray and Fred growled his opinion of the visitors again from under the kitchen table.

"Thank you for the coffee, Mrs. Radclive," said Sergeant Meadows. Commander Trevor Wiggins said nothing. The BMW drove off at speed with a spurt of gravel.

---oooOooo---

Gaby and I turned to each other. "Did he give you a bad time?" I asked.

"No, just aggressive but what a very unpleasant man. Do you think that you should have wound him up quite so much?"

"You know that I have a lifelong aversion to control freaks – especially when they're bullies. But Trevor Wiggins is something more. He's an intelligent man seeking to promote himself without regard to anyone else. I think he's after a quick arrest and hoped to pin at least Theodora's murder on Aubrey Pinkerton without caring too much whether or not he's guilty. But bringing him in and grilling him didn't work. Pinkerton held his ground and Wiggins needs to identify a motive before he has another go at him."

"How do you arrive at that conclusion?" Gaby asked.

"I think he realises that it is likely that someone different murdered the girl Molly and that Pinkerton did not have the motive himself but was acting under instruction with the someone who does have a motive. Therefore, he needs to find out who was the instigator of the first murder. The second murder of the waitress was clearly unplanned to conceal the identity of whoever came down the steps from the lake."

"That's logical but entirely your conjecture."

"Not entirely. You heard Wiggins' final question to me. He was seeking to establish a relationship between Aubrey Pinkerton and Alexander Deakin with a motive for Alexander to want his wife dead."

"That means he's trying to place Alexander in the firing line. It's all a bit thin though."

"Yes. But maybe enough for an arrest if he can establish a connection."

The skies had cleared a little and the rain abated to a light drizzle as we drove into Bicester for our supermarket shopping. We continued to debate the subject on our way there and back.

---oooOooo---

After lunch the steady drizzle was replaced by heavy rain and a wind that gusted across the yard hurling sheets of water against the kitchen windows. I tried telephoning Georgina again; as before the line was dead. I concluded that she was still blocking calls and that, in order to question her as Bill asked, I would have to drive over to the Mill in the filthy weather. Leaving Gaby to prepare a cottage pie which she could serve up for supper whenever the Digger appeared, I shrugged into and zipped up a Barbour, added a waterproof shooting hat and made for the back door. "Don't forget the Worcestershire sauce," I called back to Gaby and made a dash for the Range Rover.

The windscreen wipers were working overtime as I turned into the entrance to Fullmere Mill. Coming towards me on dipped headlights was Giles Delahaye's Alfa Romeo, on his way over to see Emma I guessed. We flashed our lights at each other as we passed. I brought the Range Rover to rest in front of the house where Georgina's Bentley was parked. Before I could ring the bell or knock, the front door opened and she appeared. She had been on her way out and was dressed for the weather in a shiny black trench coat and knee-high patent leather boots with a sou'wester in her hand.

"Why Julian. I was going to call you later. Come on in," Georgina greeted me. "I've had the 'phone off the hook all day to avoid reporters."

"You were on your way out. I don't want to hold you up but Bill Fentiman has a couple of questions he wants me to put to you," I said.

"Sure. Why don't we make ourselves comfortable inside?" Georgina tossed her hat on to the hall table and with a swish of her trench coat led the way into a large reception room. I discarded my Barbour and followed her.

Barbara and Gaby's description of the red walls and soft furnishings had prepared me for a gin palace but I found it more refined. With subdued wall lighting and warmer light cast from the table lamps at either end of the three long sofas arranged as an open square in the centre of the room, it was not a family drawing room by any standard; but it worked as a comfortable and relaxed living space for Georgina's house party guests. We sat on adjacent sofas and she helped herself to a long cigarette from a silver box at her side which she lit with a silver Dunhill table lighter. Tossing back her copper-coloured mane, she crossed one leg over the other exposing an expanse of bare thigh and waited for me to start.

"Bill says he has enough to keep the Press at bay on any story about you since you arrived in the UK but that there is a hole in the back story of your escort agency club on Long Island," I began.

"Okay, I did say that I was giving you the concise version last time. So, tell me what's missing and I'll fill you in."

"You didn't say that you'd paid money to the Mob, specifically to one Tony Panata," I said evenly, keeping any accusatory tone out of my voice.

"How the hell did Fentiman come up with that?" Georgina demanded

"Bill has associates in New York; they keep themselves informed about what the Mob's attorneys are up to. They say that you made monthly payments to them for the six months before you left."

"I suppose that means that the cops and the FBI have it on record too."

"Yes. That also means that Scotland Yard can probably run a sheet on you over there," I added.

"What about the Press?"

"Who knows. Anyhow, Georgina, you haven't answered Bill's query."

Georgina took a deep drag on her cigarette, stubbed it out in an onyx ashtray and exhaled.

"That's easy," she drawled. "When the Mob first put the bite on me and I decided to leave the US of A, I needed to keep them off my back while I sold up. Paying my dues through Panata gave me a clear run."

"Makes sense to me and should be enough for Bill to block the Press on libel but they can still publish the facts," I said. "Have you had many reporters around today?"

"There was a pack of them outside Aubrey's cottage this morning trying to interview him but he wouldn't open the door and closed all the curtains. Then, when the downpour started they melted away. I turned the 'phone off here after the first call before breakfast. So far, so good, I guess," Georgina said uncertainly.

"They may start door-stepping you tomorrow, but I have an idea how you might get them to lay off. You remember that the Arts Editor of The Oxford Guardian was here on the evening of the festival and at the police inquiry on Sunday?" I asked.

"Sure, grey-faced little guy in an old timer's tuxedo."

"Well, his name's Charlie Dibbs. I met him yesterday at the Gallery and he seemed a fair-minded sort of journalist. If you gave him an exclusive interview and told him most of what you told me on Thursday about your UK business, he could syndicate it to the national press, which would dampen speculation."

"Sounds good. Would you call him for me, Julian, and suggest he comes here tomorrow at midday or before. By the time we drive back to London he might have filed his copy."

Sounding genuinely grateful, Georgina gathered the folds of her trench coat about her and made to stand up. She seemed rather more relieved than I felt she should. A nagging doubt prompted me to go on.

"While we're still here, is there anything else that could fall out of the woodwork as the murder investigation proceeds? Commander Wiggins is a very impatient and abrasive kind of policeman and he's looking for someone other than your tenant that he can put in the firing line fast. I'm sorry to pressure you, Georgina, but this is the time to own up if there is anything that could put you in his sights."

She sat back again and recrossed her legs, right over left this time, exposing another expanse of bare thigh. There was a pause while she made up her mind and cast me an old-fashioned look.

"I guess that it's better you should know now rather than later. When you arrived I was about to set out for tea with the Master of St. Winifred's in his rooms at College," she answered finally.

"You mean Alexander Deakin? I didn't realise that you knew him before the other night," I said.

"Oh, Alex and I go back a long way to when I was still in New York after Bart died. We met at a book launch party at Barnes & Noble when he was in town on OUP business and I was drumming up clients for my new agency. He was kind and attentive and we got on well. Then, when I opened the club in the Hamptons someone brought him out one weekend before the New York Book Fair. Alex was planning to host a party for the trade and wanted a few escorts for his guests. He wasn't too impressed by the girls he met but he did latch on to me; he asked me to be his hostess at the party and to accompany him to other big parties during the week of the Fair – particularly the Random House shindig, a major social event in publishers' diaries. Strictly against the rules that I had set for myself and the agency, but what the hell; he was such a lost lamb in the Big Apple scene and he needed someone to give him a leg up. Besides, I liked the guy and knew he'd behave like an English gentleman."

"And what then?" I interrupted.

"Well, we had a great week and after that, whenever he was over every month or so, he came out to spend time with me at the Club. And, of course – before you ask – one thing led to another. Then Alex left OUP just before I moved over here and we lost touch. At least, I didn't get in touch when I bought this place. I knew he had become Principal of St. Winifred and that he was married; so it seemed better to keep it cool. Last Saturday, was the first time I saw him again."

"Why on earth did you not open up about your connection with Alexander before? If the police get hold of it they're sure to say that gave him a motive for murdering Theodora."

"You've just answered your own question," Georgina replied and we both stood up.

There was nothing more to say after her bombshell. I had wondered before why she had remained in her trench coat during our conversation; now I noticed that she was bare at the throat as well as her thighs. She cinched the belt tighter as she sashayed to the door. The material clung to her hips and rustled about her legs as she moved. What else was she wearing underneath? Very little, I thought.

I called out after her. "You mustn't keep Alex any longer from his tea and sympathy."

---ooo0ooo---

CHAPTER 13

June 29, Fullmere

GABY WAS PUTTING finishing touches to her cottage pie when I reached home: grated cheese over a mashed potato topping to the mince in a large oven-proof dish; ready to pop in the oven when the Digger returned and we were ready to eat. It was too early for a drink; so we were seated at the kitchen table with mugs of tea. I left a message for Charlie Dibbs on his home answer 'phone that he could visit Georgina Delahaye for an exclusive interview at midday the next morning; then, I gave Gaby as near a verbatim account of my meeting with Georgina as I could recall. She is a good listener and heard me out before commenting.

"I never dreamed that Alexander had it in him. So, she gave him a leg up in New York and he gave her a leg over on Long Island."

"Don't be too judgmental," I cautioned. "Georgina can be very alluring and I should think she set out to vamp him."

"But there's more to it than that, isn't there? It gives them both a motive for bumping off Theodora."

"On the face of it, yes – and you can imagine Wiggins dragging them in for questioning, if he finds out. However, there's the question of opportunity. In the period after we came down from the lake they were both around. Georgina was everywhere, chatting up the audience and departing guests, and I noticed Alexander several times talking to people he knew in small groups near the bar. Neither of them could have climbed back up to the lake unseen to commit the murder. And in Alexander's case, there's no possible reason why Theodora would have gone with him when they could talk together anytime they wished."

"That means that if they planned to do away with Theodora, there must have been a 'hit man' whom they engaged to carry out the job," Gaby mused. "And the obvious accomplice is Aubrey Pinkerton whom she knew well and could have lured her up to the lake."

"Very risky employing someone else and probably very expensive. I really don't see Alexander involving himself in some complicated conspiracy to murder. Actually, Georgina acting on her own is a more plausible scenario. She's tough and ruthless enough and Pinkerton is her tenant, but it's all very far-fetched," I said.

"Of course, Georgina could have slit Molly's throat herself if the girl saw the murderer up at the lake or Aubrey coming back. She was moving mong the waitresses as well as the guests," Gaby persisted continuing her theme. Then another thought struck her. "Are you going to tell Duncan about your visit this afternoon?"

"If I relate the conversation to Duncan, he may feel obliged to pass it on to Trevor Wiggins when he next visits the Kidlington police station. So far as we know, it doesn't relate to the art fraud investigation; I think we can keep it to ourselves for a couple of days. But I must tell Bill and I should do that before he arrives."

While we had been talking the rain had eased off; so we took advantage of the improvement, put on our boots, weather coats and hats and took Fred for his constitutional. Our field is a water meadow and so, after torrential rain overnight and throughout the day, the lower slopes down to the stream were flooded to a depth of a foot or more. Two families of mallard had taken possession of the stream – much to Fred's delight. He charged down the hill at full tilt and to no avail, like a French knight at Agincourt. By the time he reached the stream the ducks had taken off in disciplined flight order with the green heads of the drakes gleaming in the evening sunshine. Fred was left floundering midstream but honour was satisfied; he had seen off the intruders. After more splashing up and down to make sure that there were no other trespassers we resumed our walk around the hedgerows which formed the perimeter of the field before returning to the house.

As we turned into the stable yard a familiar Jaguar XJS swept in off the street. There were two people in the car and Duncan was in the passenger seat. The reason why he was not driving became apparent when he stepped out. His head was heavily bandaged with a black patch over his right eye. The driver, also in plain clothes with a short cut of ginger hair was unmistakably a policeman. Recognising his car from afar, Fred bounded forward and, despite the bandages, gave Duncan a hero's welcome.

"Duncan, you've been in the wars" Gaby exclaimed.

"You should see the other feller." The Digger spread out his hands and gave us a crooked grin.

"Come on in and tell your tale over a drink. You're staying here with us tonight us until you're sorted out," I insisted.

Mallory thanked us and told his driver to take the car home with him to Neasden and to stay there until he was called. The three of us and a very wet Labrador entered the house. Gaby installed Duncan upstairs in a spare bedroom and drew him a bath while I dried Fred and retired to the study to call Bill Fentiman. Since the sun was just about over the yardarm, I took a tumbler of Ballantine's and soda with me.

Bill was satisfied with my report on Georgina's explanation of her payments to the Mob attorney and my arrangements for the exclusive interview with Charlie Dibbs. "That will help to keep the Press dogs at bay for the time-being," he pronounced. However, the revelation of the liaison between Georgina and Alexander Deakin left him almost speechless.

"What on earth does the silly cow thinks she's doing? Doesn't she realise that by consoling Deakin like a toasted crumpet she's putting herself forward as a murder suspect?" he spluttered over the telephone.

"I don't think she understands the risk of reviving the romance; and, if she does, maybe she doesn't care. If it's going to come out anyway, it could be more suspicious to hide it away."

"Do you think she could be a murderess?"

"Well, she couldn't have killed Theodora herself, but she could have had an accomplice who was up there waiting at the lake after enticing her there. And, as Gaby points out, Aubrey Pinkerton is still the prime suspect; he knew Theodora and is Georgina's tenant."

"But where's the motive?" Bill asked. "From what she's told us, we know that Georgina's a tough cookie and tough cookies don't normally murder for love or lust."

We left it at that and I promised to keep him informed of any developments on the local front in the coming week.

---ooo0ooo---

CHAPTER 14

June 28 and 29, Amsterdam

AN HOUR LATER we had re-assembled. Gaby and I had showered and changed clothes; Duncan Mallory joined us looking more relaxed after his bath and dressed casually in polo shirt and jeans. With eyepatch and bandages he was still a wounded soldier but one in convalescence. He had brought down with him a large manilla envelope which he placed on the kitchen table. I had opened a bottle of Muscadet for starters and poured us each a glass before sitting down to hear the full story of the Digger's adventures in Amsterdam. "I'll tell it to you as it happened," he said reaching for his glass and proceeded to do so.

On his arrival at Schipol airport on Friday morning Duncan Mallory had been met by Commissaris Cornelius Visser and whisked away to the handsome canal-side house in Herengracht where Van den Groot BV was located. An unmarked minibus with a fully armed team of policeman was already in place outside awaiting their arrival. The young, uniformed officer in charge stepped out of the minibus and saluted Visser smartly, informing them that van den Groot occupied the top floor of the five-storey building with access by entry phone. Someone would have to press the button against 'Van den Groot' on a panel at the side of the front door in order to gain entry. After a short debate it was agree at Mallory's suggestion that, to avoid suspicion, Mallory would press the button and say in English "Package from Oxford." The ruse worked perfectly: an answering buzz and click from the door and they were in.

The black and white tiled floor of the entrance hall echoed the paintings of 17th century Dutch interiors, the same period as that of the building itself. On one side there was a notice board giving names of the occupants on each floor and, at the rear, was the staircase and a metal-framed lift of Victorian design in which passengers were visible through the wire mesh of the sides and door. Commissaris Visser, Mallory and two of the squad crammed themselves into the lift which had room for four only, and the elevator began its dignified ascent with a muffled creaking while the young officer and four remaining members of his squad took to the stairs. The advance party reached the fifth floor first while the rest of the team were still two floors below. And this, Duncan told us, was where the operation started to go wrong. Demonstrating his authority and leadership, Visser pulled back the door to the lift, strode to the door of Van den Groot BV's premises and pressed the buzzer. He should, of course, have waited for the back-up team to arrive. "Politie" he shouted as the door was opened and he burst in followed by Mallory and the two policemen with them.

"It wasn't at all what we expected. More like a bloody factory than an office," Duncan said. "We found ourselves in a large open space occupying the whole fifth floor with a small glass-fronted office at the far end. On each side a row of easels was set-up with a dozen or so men and women working on canvases – either painting or cleaning. As we found out later, each painter had a finished painting at his or her side which they were copying on the canvas in front of them. When we entered there was a commotion. We were clearly outnumbered; a group of them rushed us, trying to get out, and we found ourselves in a fight. I noticed that there was one man in the office, perhaps Van den Groot himself, and I tried to barge my way through to get to him before he could destroy any evidence. I was nearly there when a beefy youth – more of a yob than a painter –

charged me with a palette knife and caught me in the face. One of Visser's men clobbered him from behind but too late to prevent the damage." He touched his eyepatch and bandages ruefully.

"Go on," I prompted and refilled his glass.

"By that time, the rest of the squad had arrived. At the sight of their guns and body armour the fight went out of them. They were all arrested, including the man in the back office, and taken off to the local station in police vans that Visser called up. All the finished paintings that were found there, either those in the office and those being cleaned or alongside the easels where they were being copied, were packaged up carefully and carried off to the Rijksmuseum in another wagon for examination. There were twenty-three as I told you on the 'phone this morning."

"But what about you, Digger?" Gaby asked. "You couldn't have played an active part."

"I wasn't out of action for long. Cornelius Visser held himself responsible; he took me to the accident emergency department of the nearest general hospital himself and waited while they stitched me up and gave me eye tests to make sure there was no permanent damage. Then we went on to the police station. At his direction they'd booked all those arrested but let everyone go home except for my attacker, who was charged with assault, and the manager who was held awaiting interview. I sat in on the interrogation which Visser conducted partly in English for my benefit. The preliminaries were in Dutch but I gathered that we were questioning Van den Groot himself, as I had hoped. Their body language told me that he and Visser were already acquainted; and that there was a kind of wary mutual respect between them."

"So, what did you make of Van den Groot?" I asked him,

"There was an interesting contrast between the two men: Cornelius Visser stocky and broad-shouldered, almost bald with a round, cheerful face and Johannes Van den Groot, tall, thin and ascetic with a fine head of hair and a trim goatee beard. What I didn't realise before the interview is that copying old masters or any other painting and selling the copies is not against the law in the Netherlands, provided that the copies are unsigned and are not passed off as the original. If you wander around the lanes off the Dam there are a number of art shops and galleries openly selling copies of famous paintings or paintings in the style of famous artists. Of course, the quality of these 'reproductions' is variable. Van den Groot's are among the best and he is considered by many to be the finest copyist in the country. When he and Visser had last met his studio was in Dordrecht; he had moved to Amsterdam some five years before when the opportunity arose to rent the top floor at a prestigious canal side address with attic windows giving good natural light for his team of copyists. He claimed immediately that all twenty-three of the paintings we had recovered were copies. When the Commissaris told him that they were now being examined by the Rijksmuseum he expressed bland amusement."

"Why the amusement?" I asked.

"Because the art experts would be doing the opposite of their normal examination; instead of authenticating they were searching for signatures which had been painted over. Cornelius Visser thought it was a good joke too."

"So, a good time was had by one and all. Getting back to the object of your visit, what did he have to say about his dealings with the Clarendon Art Gallery?"

"It all started towards the end of last year when he was approached by Theodora Deakin asking if he was willing to offer a cleaning service for the treasured paintings of Oxford Colleges. She visited him in Amsterdam and they agreed a deal. The Gallery would be responsible for shipping each painting to Van den Groot and back to Oxford. Van den Groot's team would clean each canvas, send it back using the packaging and labels provided and then invoice the Clarendon Gallery. On receipt of payment in full commission of ten per cent would be paid into a numbered account in a Swiss bank. There would be no direct contact between the colleges and Van den Groot so that the ownership of the paintings remained unknown to him. There was a second part to the deal. Van den Groot could make up to twenty unsigned copies of each canvas and sell them on the open market such as Amsterdam art shops. As with the cleaning service, he would pay royalties of ten per cent into the same numbered Swiss bank account."

"And, from what you say, under Dutch law that would be perfectly legal?"

"Legal but dodgy. Strictly speaking, you should have the owner's consent to copy any original painting but Van den Groot has written consent in his agreement with the gallery. That protects him sufficiently, although there is cause for civil action against Clarendon in the UK by the colleges if they chose to pursue it. Of course, there's no copyright issue because the artists are long dead."

"Have the police kept him in custody?"

"Visser kept him in overnight until the Rijksmuseum confirms that all the canvases we took to them are copies. They did this morning. We still need to confirm that the first two paintings returned to Oxford are originals and that the third is a copy; we know that its original was sent to Hong Kong. Then he will be in the clear. Meantime, there wasn't enough to hold him but we did retrieve some useful information from him. The first two originals were collected by DHL and shipped back to Oxford to the Clarendon Art Gallery; the De Hooch was also collected by DHL but the destination specified on the packaging was an address in Hong Kong and it was given a special courier service. The fourth and last painting was treated quite differently. It was collected in person ten days ago at the front door by an envoy with a letter of authority on Gallery letterhead and driven away in a private car. Van den Groot saw it off himself; he says that it had UK plates and he thinks that the driver was a woman. Of course, DHL gave him receipts for each of the first three and he has a sort of receipt with an illegible signature for the fourth collection by hand."

While I was digesting this information the Digger continued his report, answering the questions which sprang to mind.

"As you would expect, we asked him for a description of the man who collected the fourth original. He wasn't very clear. The man wore dark clothes and was wearing a wide-brimmed hat pulled over his eyes. Van den Groot said that he only had a glimpse of his face; once the man had taken possession of the painting he held it between them; he did remember that the man was tall and heavy. From his voice he was certainly British. Inspecteur Visser sent one of his men back to Herengracht to recover the video tape from the CCTV at the front door but that didn't provide a better image. They've given me a copy in case it means anything to you or anyone at the Gallery. We also asked him for details of the Swiss bank account and his deposits into it which he gave us."

Duncan Mallory withdrew a sheaf of colour photographs from his manila envelope and spread them out on the kitchen table in four separate piles with several black and white frames from the Herengracht CCTV. He was having difficulty with his spectacles because of the eyepatch; so I fetched a magnifying glass from my study. Gaby poured the last of the Muscadet into our glasses.

"Reading from left to right are the copies of the four paintings sent to Van den Groot BV in the date order that the originals were returned," Duncan explained. "They painted twelve copies of each and, as you can see, the numbers remaining in each pile are those which have not yet been sold."

The first painting in line was of a dark, sombre scene with a scantily clad woman plunging a dagger into the heart of a swarthy, bearded man lying in disarray on a canopied bed. As with the other three there was no signature. The second was a full-length study of an elegant lady in eighteenth century dress with an arrogant expression set in a rural landscape; it looked familiarly English. The third in line was of the De Hooch interior now on offer in Hong Kong and the fourth a colourful Impressionist landscape of a sweeping coastline.

"Did Van den Groot tell you who the artists were?" Gaby asked.

"Yes. The first is a Caravaggio, the second is by Joshua Reynolds and the fourth by Claude Monet. You can see that we recovered ten of the Caravaggio, six of the Reynolds, three of the De Hooch and four of the Monet. And, of course, we know that another De Hooch was returned to Oxford."

"What did he have to say about the De Hooch copy sent back to the Gallery?" I said.

"He claims that he was acting under instruction from Theodora. Apparently, he was called and told to add a signature and it was collected and despatched by DHL as before. Her story was that the College who owned it were selling the original and wanted to keep it to themselves."

"That's superficially plausible, but didn't he smell a rat?"

"Throughout the interview he took the line that he is a simple, honest copyist and cleaner of fine paintings acting for clients and following their instructions. In this case, there's no way of confirming what he was told to do verbally since Theodora is dead. Visser had his telephone records checked and there was an incoming call from Oxford two days before DHL collected the original. We traced the number back to the Clarendon Gallery."

"And so Van den Groot sails off blithely into the sunset."

"Quite so. He made his exit with bland charm. He's in the clear unless we trip him up on the originals which he returned to the Gallery or the De Hooch which he despatched to Hong Kong. Now, have a look at the CCTV frames and see if you can recognize the man who collected the Monet."

Gaby and I pored over the film and agreed that we couldn't say with any certainty who it was. It was definitely a man taking pains to conceal his identity. Judging by his height and bulk, it might be Aubrey Pinkerton in the frames. Both Alexander Deakin and Percy Mansfield, who were also at the concert, were tall men if not similarly well built, but neither seemed a likely courier.

It was time for us to eat. While Gaby dished up generous helpings of her cottage pie with baby carrots and French beans, Duncan Mallory set the table and I uncorked a bottle of rioja. The cottage pie was excellent – plenty of Worcestershire sauce. We ate contentedly in silence for several minutes before Duncan reopened the discussion.

"Let's summarise where we are. We believe that the original De Hooch is in Hong Kong waiting to be auctioned as something less valuable. We expect to confirm that the painting at Latimer College is a copy. We've been told by Van den Groot that the original Caravaggio and the original Reynolds were returned to the Clarendon Gallery. During the coming week I shall hope to confirm that they were returned to the colleges that own them. He also tells us that he was instructed by the Clarendon Gallery to hand over the original Monet to a courier for delivery back to Oxford and the CCTV tape at the front door of his Herengracht premises confirms that it was collected. The identity of the courier is obscure because he took care to conceal who he was. We don't know whether or not the Monet reached the

Gallery or if it was delivered to its owner because there's no Clarendon Gallery invoice to corroborate."

"As to the second and third paintings, from the timing of the invoices recorded at the Clarendon Gallery, we know that the original or copy of the Caravaggio was returned to Curzon and of the Reynolds to Hereford Colleges," Gaby added.

"Assuming then that they check out," Mallory resumed "we're left with two sets of questions to answer before we can identify who is behind it all. First, what do he, she or they plan for the De Hooch at and after the auction in Hong Kong; second, to which college does the Monet belong and where is it?,

"We should be able to find out who owns the Monet by asking a few questions in Oxford, telephoning round the colleges if we have to. And plainly you'll have to follow up on who authorised its collection and no doubt question Aubrey Pinkerton," I said.

"That's straightforward routine if I can keep Trevor Wiggins and his sergeant from interfering. The Hong Kong investigation is more difficult. I have to get permission to attend the auction and authority for my travel expenses. I'll need to make the case to my gaffer and possibly in person to the Commissioner. They're particularly tough on budgets this year and, with handover to the Chinese next year, Hong Kong is not exactly flavour of the month."

It wasn't the right moment to tell him that I could be there to give him support if he wished. The first step was for him to get approval for his visit; I held my peace. Gaby had been examining the four piles of photographs more carefully through the magnifying glass added a further comment.

"I know that these are all copies meant for sale through tourist shops, Duncan, but some of them are better painted than others and look more authentic."

"That's what you'd expect. The skills and talent of the copyists vary; some of them will improve over time, others won't stay the course."

"You can take bets that the one we view tomorrow at Latimer will be one of the best; probably painted by Van den Groot himself, the master copyist," I added.

---oooOooo---

CHAPTER 15

June 30, Oxford and Fullmere

WE WERE ON THE ROAD in good time the next morning. No lie-in this Sunday for us. Gaby and I were up and about promptly, in the kitchen having watered Fred by 9.00 a.m. We left the Digger undisturbed until we had breakfasted. Having eaten my croissants and drunk a first cup of coffee, I took Fred out again for a scamper in the fields while Gaby served Duncan Mallory with his breakfast on a tray in bed. He looked in better shape today. The swelling had gone down and the bruising was less livid, but the eyepatch remained.

We collected Basil Gore-Smith from his flat in Summertown on the way into Oxford. He was sporting another floppy bow tie, this time with a straw-coloured linen suit. Duncan looked at him doubtfully but thawed after engaging him in a discussion about recent art frauds. By the time we drew up in front of Latimer College just before twelve-thirty Basil was chatting with him like an old friend. As I parked at the entrance, Jessop popped out through the postern gate like a figure signalling bad weather from a cuckoo clock. He recognised and admonished me firmly.

"You know you can't park there, Mr. Radclive," he said. Then, as Duncan Mallory alighted with eyepatch and bruised face, and remembering his previous visit, Jessop retired with an air of malignant dissatisfaction into the porter's lodge.

The four of us entered the Front Quad where the strains of organ music came to us from the college chapel through the passage to our left. As we stood there, the college clock struck the hour and there was a brief silence; then the organ swelled with J. S. Bach's cantata 79, "Now thank we all our God", as the chapel doors opened and the congregation emerged. They came through the passage from the back quad with Geoffrey Randle as Master of Latimer in the lead. He was wearing his academic gown and hood with scarlet silk lining. With his actor's profile and the gown billowing slightly behind him he cut a dashing figure – and knew it.

"There you are, Julian, and Gaby. How lovely to see you; an unexpected pleasure. Now introduce me to your entourage," he declaimed.

More members of the congregation strolled through into the Front Quad, postgraduates and members of the Senior Common Room with a few undergraduates who had delayed going down at the end of term among the stragglers. Hamish McAllister clad in MA gown over grey Harris tweed joined us. He still managed to look more like a Scots estate manager than an academic. I performed the introductions and the six of us proceeded to the Senior Common Room where the De Hooch was hung. McAllister turned on its picture light and we stood back from the painting behind Basil Gore-Smith to await his opinion.

"It's very good," he said after a pause for reflection. "Surprisingly bright and clear, but that could be the result of cleaning. Let's take a closer look." Basil took a lens from an inside pocket of his jacket and moved close to the painting. Duncan moved forward with him but the rest of us held back to give him space.

"The varnish is recent but, of course, that would also be down to cleaning," Basil murmured.

"There's no signature," Mallory commented.

"De Hooch didn't always sign in the usual place at the bottom of the canvas. We need to look within the picture." Gore-Smith peered closely through his lens at the detail of the painting. "Ah, there it is. Look at the underside of the chimneypiece to the right of the foreground." He handed the lens to Mallory who confirmed that a signature was there in small manuscript.

"The brushstrokes look genuine. In fact, if it is a copy, it's very well done," Basil said turning to face us after further examination.

"Does that mean you think it may be genuine?" the Geoffrey Randle enquired.

"I need to look at the back of the painting before I can give a clear opinion. May I take it down?"

The Master nodded; McAllister and I stepped forward, unhitched the picture carefully and laid it face down on a refectory table. The ornate gilt frame kept the canvas itself from the tabletop surface. Basil took his lens and inspected the canvas minutely, the battens to which it was attached and the dowels which secured the painting to the frame. He paused to marshal his thoughts, straightened and addressed us again.

"The wooden pegs and inner frame are old but I can't date them. The canvas is the giveaway. It's certainly a hundred years old but definitely not nearly as old as the seventeenth century. I can confirm that it's not right – a brilliantly executed painting but definitely a fake."

Our reactions were mixed. The Master and Bursar, having been warned, were disappointed but not shocked. Mallory was smugly pleased. Gaby and I looked at each and tried not to show any excitement. It was time for the Digger to say his piece while Basil and I returned the painting to its place on the wall.

"Gentlemen," he said directing his remarks to Geoffrey Randle and Hamish McAllister. "The next step is clear. Mr. Gore-Smith's appraisal confirms that the painting on offer at auction in Hong Kong next week is our original. We want to let the auction go ahead to help us identify who are the villains at the back of this crime, but the police will be there and I can assure you that they will confiscate the painting immediately afterwards before it can leave the auction room. After the formalities it will be returned to you within two or three weeks."

I could see that Basil would have added something to the statement but had decided to hold back.

"In that case, Inspector, we're in your hands. Hamish, you should inform our insurers in the morning in case they want to have someone at the auction to verify that we are getting our De Hooch back. Thank you, Mr. Gore-Smith for your professional opinion," said the Master, like a chairman closing his meeting. Geoffrey Randle had become more formal as a reaction, I thought, to confirmation that the substitution of a fake for a valuable painting had happened on his watch as college head.

There was nothing more to be said and no reason for us to prolong our visit to Latimer. Not even the offer of a Senior Common Room lunch.

---ooo0ooo---

I drove back into The High to return the way we had come. Unexpectedly, Digger Mallory invited us to lunch. "I've been living for free in Fullmere with nothing to bill to my expense sheet. You choose where we go." Basil suggested the Lamb and Flag and I parked outside in St. Giles. The pub was still serving its Sunday roast: pork with roast potatoes, green beans, carrots and apple sauce. We ordered and settled ourselves at a far corner table with a glass of the house Australian Chardonnay for Gaby and pints of draught bitter for the rest of us.

"I think you had something to add to Duncan's assurances at Latimer just now, Basil?" I asked.

Basil looked uneasy. "There is another uncomfortable possibility, but they but they wouldn't have been pleased to hear it and you won't be either," he said looking apologetic. He brushed away the lock of hair which had flopped over his forehead.

"You should level with us now," Duncan reacted sharply. "You weren't asked to give an incomplete assessment." The waitress delivered our meal giving Basil time to frame his answer.

"Well, the painting to be auctioned in Hong Kong might be an original but not a De Hooch."

"Explain yourself. How could that be?" The normally phlegmatic Digger was now visibly on edge. Ignoring the plates of food in front of us we craned forward to hear Basil better.

"What I mean is that it could be on old canvas of a later period, originally without a signature. And, in that case, it is probably a contemporary copy painted by someone else in the school or that of another Dutch Master – quite common practice at the time."

"In other words, the catalogue description as 'school of Vermeer' could be accurate," Gaby spoke for the first time and Basil nodded unhappily.

Digesting this information, we started to eat our food. The pork proved tough, the crackling was limp and soggy and the roast potatoes like cottonwool under their crisp exterior. Overall, the meal was a disappointment but matched the gloom which Basil's pronouncement had caused.

"How does the auction price of a genuine De Hooch original compare with that of a later unsigned copy?" Duncan Mallory asked at length. He seemed to have recovered his customary composure.

"I would expect the copy to fetch one to two thousand pounds," Basil replied putting on an Antiques Roadshow expression and voice "but a genuine signed De Hooch in good condition could make fifty thousand US dollars at auction in New York."

"So, if we return an unsigned copy from Hong Kong, however genuine, the College won't be best pleased, because it shows that they never had a genuine De Hooch original in the first placc" I said sharing a glimpse of the obvious.

"Which means that we would have to prove conclusively that the painting came from Latimer," Duncan finished for me.

"All the more reason why you should go to Hong Kong yourself."

"Would it help," Basil asked diffidently "if I asked a former colleague of mine at Christie's, now in Hong Kong, to attend the auction with you?"

---oooOooo---

We finished our lunch on a more positive note. Duncan had recovered his good humour with a helping of apple pie and custard. He accepted Basil's offer of help and invited him to view the Caravaggio at Curzon and the Reynolds at Hereford College with him the next day for a modest personal fee. The two of them agreed that Basil would join the Digger at the Randolph Hotel across the street from the Ashmolean in the early evening after Duncan had set up arrangements for them to view. We dropped him off on our way home.

The rest of the day passed pleasantly but uneventfully. We took Fred for a late afternoon ramble over the still waterlogged fields. Later I drove Duncan Mallory over to Finmere Mill to show him the lie of the land and where Aubrey Pinkerton lived. Of course, Georgina had already left for London but we had hoped that we might encounter Pinkerton while Duncan was free from Trevor Wiggins' supervision. However, the cottage was locked up and there was no green Volvo parked outside. I took Duncan over the back route that Pinkerton could have taken to reach the lake without being seen on the night of the Festival. We stood at the near end where the musicians had played while Mallory shared his thoughts.

"I need to question Pinkerton; he's my odds-on favourite for the mystery courier who collected the Monet painting in Amsterdam although I can't prove it. I need to have hard evidence and until then I'm inclined to let him run," Mallory said.

"We do know that he delivered the De Hooch copy from the Clarendon Gallery to Latimer and that he was a friend of Theodora Deakin," I countered.

"That's not enough. Look what happened when Wiggins brought him in for questioning under caution. He couldn't hold him. I must have more on him than that. If you see Pinkerton's car around in the next day or so, take the registration number. I will run a check with all the car ferries to see whether he made a cross-Channel journey in the past fortnight and when he returned. Meantime, I'll have the Yard investigate his past activities in the art world."

"Do you think he could have killed Theodora Deakins?"

Duncan thought carefully before replying. "He certainly had the means and opportunity but we don't have a motive."

"Maybe he fell out with Theodora over the theft of the original paintings" I hazarded.

"Maybe he was no more than the collection and delivery man and not a prime mover in the art scam. And we won't know the extent of the scam until we can explore how it's planned to operate in Hong Kong."

---ooo0ooo---

CHAPTER 16

July 1 and 2, Oxfordshire

THE FOLLOWING MORNING Gaby drove Duncan into Oxford on her way to the Clarendon Art Gallery and deposited him at the Radcliffe Infirmary where he had made an appointment to have his dressings changed. He would then walk down to the Gallery to interview Valerie Wyngarde before proceeding to the Randolph Hotel which would be his base for the rest of the day. I remained at Home Farm with several days' work ahead of me editing manuscripts and assembling contents for *Managing Business Abroad*.

We still had no idea where the original Monet had been delivered, nor to which college it belonged, unless there was Gallery paperwork about the painting which Gaby had overlooked or Valerie could enlighten us. If they drew a blank, Gaby had volunteered to telephone each college in turn in the Gallery's name to make enquiries, a tedious but necessary task. By the time Mallory arrived she had scoured the correspondence and accounting files again but could find no reference to the missing Monet.

Valerie recognized Duncan from the previous week and greeted him on entrance as 'Mr. Mumford'. Something in his expression and his formal manner alerted her that this was a different kind of visit. He showed his warrant card and suggested that they sit down in the basement office. Gaby related to me later how Mallory conducted the interview. Valerie had clearly enjoyed a heavy weekend and was still suffering from a hangover; he was at pains not to scare her but she remained on edge. His opening remarks were to the point:

"I'm investigating an art fraud on Oxford colleges, Ms Wyngarde. I apologize for the deception last week but I was unsure then that the Clarendon Art Gallery was involved. Following further investigations over the weekend in Amsterdam and in Oxford, I now believe that your Gallery is a link in the chain and could be playing a major role. I need to ask you some questions." He was careful not to give any indication of his previous association with Gaby.

Duncan's first questions centred around Valerie's acquaintance with Aubrey Pinkerton. She stuck to the story she had given Gaby and me the week before: he was a friend of Theodora and she had only ever seen him at the Gallery: more frequently, it was true, in recent weeks. Had he been authorized to collect a painting from Amsterdam recently? "Perhaps," she revealed. She had heard him quite recently, about two weeks ago, telephoning someone on behalf of the Gallery in Theodora's absence one morning to instruct them to hand over a painting to an authorised courier when he called. "No," she didn't know whom he was calling. It could have been someone abroad. He was talking very slowly and loudly as British people do when speaking to foreigners who have little or no English. At the time she had thought that he was talking to someone hard of hearing.

Mallory changed the direction of questioning to her knowledge of the paintings that had passed through the Gallery on their way to Van Den Groot BV for cleaning. Again, as before, she claimed to have had minimum knowledge. The only picture she could identify was the De Hooch which she had unwrapped on the Monday after Theodora's murder and which Aubrey Pinkerton had volunteered to deliver to Latimer College. Duncan persisted. Had she any recollection of the French Impressionist painting which was the last to be sent to

Amsterdam, he asked. Again, Valerie professed ignorance. On balance, he thought she was probably telling the truth but was less certain that there was nothing further that she could have told him. He closed the interview with the customary warning that if he found evidence contrary to that which she had told him, she might be required to make a written statement under caution. He left her shaken but not stirred.

---oooOooo---

I laboured on with my editing throughout the day. There were still two texts outstanding; I harried the authors on the telephone and was promised delivery not later than first post Wednesday. With some burning of midnight oil I would be able to fulfil my promise to Robert to submit the complete book by the end of the week. Gaby returned home from the Gallery shortly before 6:00 p.m. in ebullient mood. Shortly after lunch she had taken a telephone call from St.Winifred's College. Alexander Deakin came on the line; he asked her how she was getting on but seemed little interested in the account she gave him of how the Gallery was managing. His reason for calling was to enquire whether there was any news of the College painting which Theodora had sent away for cleaning several weeks before her death. Gaby promised to investigate. "What was the painting?" she asked. It was "a coastal sea and landscape by Monet," he said – rather valuable, he thought. One mystery was solved with every reason for Gaby to feel pleased with herself. Mallory's interview of Valerie Wyngarde paled by comparison.

Time for a drink. Looking forward to a relaxed domestic evening, I selected a congratulatory bottle of Sancerre for Gaby and poured a generous Ballantine's for myself. With Fred fed and watered we were deciding whether to bath or shower together when the telephone rang. It was the Digger on his cell phone as he was being driven back to London.

"Wotcha. How's tricks, you two?" he hailed us cheerfully. "I've had a busy day and I'm on my way back to Town to see the Deputy Commissioner in the morning."

"Before you tell us how you got on this afternoon," I replied "Gaby's got news for you. I'll let her tell you herself." I passed the receiver to Gaby and fetched a second handset from the study. I picked up the last sentence of the exchange as I returned t the kitchen.

".......so we know that the call to Amsterdam from the Gallery was not made by Theodora and that the Monet was collected but we don't have a clue where it is now."

"I'll have the 'phone records checked in the morning to confirm date and time of the call, but you're right. I think we've nearly got enough on Pinkerton. I just need his registration number to check that his Volvo crossed the Channel and I can arrest him on suspicion," Duncan replied with satisfaction.

I rejoined the conversation. "Leave that to me. I'll locate the Volvo tomorrow and let you know. Now tell us your tale."

"Our friend Basil did his stuff at Hereford and Curzon Colleges. He was confident that both the Reynolds and the Caravaggio are genuine. He seemed to convince both Bursars but they'll probably take second opinions from their insurers. So that leaves us with two avenues of enquiry – the De Hooch in Hong Kong and location of the Monet. I would place bets that the two are connected."

"Do you think you'll persuade your bosses tomorrow to approve your attendance at the Hong Kong auction?"

"I may have a clincher. During the day I had Basil Gore-Smith call a chum at Christie's. He gave the description of the Monet from the photo of a copy. His pal said that it sounds like a companion piece to his *Sur La Falaise pres de Dieppe, Soleil Couchant.*" Mallory read the French from his notes haltingly. "And if it is, it would probably raise up to £10 million at auction."

"Wow," said Gaby with a squawk – one of my least favourite expressions in the English language. "*Sacre bleu,*" I added seeking to raise the tone.

Duncan concluded his argument. "So, case for going to Hong Kong is that it's the best way of finding out at first-hand how the scam works and who is behind it there and in the UK."

"And nipping the scam in the bud if this is their trial run," Gaby added.

"Can you brief me on Hong Kong, Julian, if I get permission?" Duncan asked. "I know an Inspector in the police there because we were at Hendon together on a course several years ago, but I've never been there and I have no other contacts."

"I can do better than that. If I won't be in the way, I can be in Hong Kong with you next week. I have to negotiate sponsorship for the next edition of my China book, and it might just as well be sooner rather than later."

My suggestion was greeted gratefully and clearly with some relief. He promised to call me the next day as soon as he had a decision and rang off. Gaby gave me her old-fashioned look and delivered a caution.

"Are you sure you know what you're getting yourself into? With handover coming up next year and a Governor at odds with Chinese government, Hong Kong won't be the stable place it was when we were last there."

"I'll only be there with the Digger as an observer and his unofficial advisor," I protested.

"Cast your mind back eighteen years when you agreed to help old Max Salinger with his crusade in Germany. You nearly lost your life then."

"This is quite different. Duncan Mallory is a competent and experience detective - not an old man in a hurry past his sell-by date."

"But this time," Gaby argued "you won't have me on the spot to back you up."

As most sensible husbands know, there are some arguments you can't win; It's better to throw in the towel. "Time for a bath," I reminded her.

---ooo0ooo---

On Tuesday morning, while Gaby set out for the Clarendon Gallery again, I began making arrangements to visit Hong Kong. The first of the missing chapters for *Managing Business Abroad* had arrived overnight as an email attachment. I saved it online and printed a hard copy for editing later. I decided to test the water for sponsoring a new edition of my China book with the international bank which had supported previous editions. The head of international marketing was based at London's Docklands in a Canary Wharf tower block but was a frequent globetrotter. I was lucky to reach her on her mobile in the first-class lounge at Heathrow waiting for a flight to Abu Dhabi. We exchanged greetings and I asked her direct whether the bank was ready to sponsor again.

"In principle yes, but how are you going to handle Hong Kong with handover coming up next year?" Laura Bendix asked.

"Sensitively," I said.

"What does that mean? Don't forget our Asian business is centred on Shanghai."

"It means that I'll write the Hong King chapter myself, Laura."

"Uh huh. And how much are you asking for" she replied without enthusiasm.

"Same as before with the bank's logo on the cover and a preface if you wish."

"I'll have to talk to the guys out there." A non-committal answer was not what I wanted. I felt that I was losing her.

"I can offer you exclusivity over any other bank sponsorship and an editorial veto on the Hong Kong chapter, if that makes a difference," I said as casually as I could.

There was a short pause. "You're twisting my arm, Julian," Laura said "but you can send me the order confirmation. I'll be back in London in ten days."

A few more friendly words between us; then I could hear her flight being called. "Have a good trip, Laura," I said and let her hang up first.

On the strength of Laura Bendix's verbal acceptance, I called Robert Schindler next to tell him that the bank was on board and that I planned to visit Hong Kong at the beginning of the coming week. I was able to assure him that the complete text of *Managing Business Abroad* would be with him on Friday. With his agreement I asked Velma to book me a Club seat on Sunday evening's British Airways flight and a return flight on the Thursday following. That would give me two days to pursue sponsors in Hong Kong before the auction and a day after to follow up.

---oooOooo---

Feeling quite pleased with myself, I decided to give Fred his long walk earlier than usual; we strode down through the village, then up the hill and over the cattle grid and into the grounds of Eastwick Hall. As we approached the house, I heard repeated gunshots. I put Fred on his lead and we pressed forward with caution to investigate. The shooting was coming from the front of the house; so we crossed the stable yard and edged round the corner of the main building to be met by an unusual sight. With her back to us, Lucinda Mansfield stood foursquare with a shotgun in her hands. She was dressed for action in moleskin breeches and an olive green gilet with padded shoulders over a check shirt. To her right-hand was a table with several boxes of cartridges and a second gun with its breech open. Ahead of her, on either side of the far end of the lawn some forty yards away, were Silas Grimshaw and Agnes Black, each crouched behind a spring-loaded trap with open boxes of clay pigeons by their sides. Lucy was addressing her retainers.

"Next time I want you, Black, to count two seconds only before you pull and you, Silas, to pull yours immediately," she commanded, leading her gun with cartridges. Then, holding her gun at waist level she shouted:

"PULL"

Immediately, Grimshaw released the lever on his trap, catapaulting a clay disk in a trajectory of sixty degrees across the lawn from the right-hand side. Lucy mounted the shotgun to her right shoulder in an instant and pulled the front trigger. The first clay shattered before reaching its full height but, already while it was still on the rise, Agnes had released her trap on her left and the second clay pigeon was in the air. Lucy swung her gun and pulled the back trigger, despatching the clay with the same aplomb and ejecting the used cartridges. The traps were reloaded while Lucy changed to her second gun and inserted cartridges. I noticed that there were a score or more of spent cartridge cases on the grass behind her.

"And now," she ordered "this time both of you release your clays together as soon as I call."

Fred was sitting to my left watching intently with professional gundog interest. We waited for the next part of the display.

"PULL"

This time the traps were released almost simultaneously and two clay pigeons were projected into the air while Lucinda mounted her shotgun. Their paths crossed just as they reached the peak of their trajectories. She fired and both disks disintegrated. Lucy turned and noticed us.

"Good shooting," I called. "I'm impressed."

"I'm preparing for the grouse next month. I'll be shooting in Yorkshire on the 12th with the Ropers and I want to keep my end up," she said.

"I've never managed to master low flying birds on a grouse moor," I admitted. "Tell me, why did your change your gun just now?"

"They're a matched pair of Holland & Holland 16 bore, but this one has both barrels choked. They have a tighter pattern of shot which is what I wanted for that shot."

She handed the beautifully crafted weapon to me. It was amazingly light and well balanced and shrieked quality with its fine mahogany stock, etched steel sidelocks and gleaming tapered barrels – as close to a precision instrument as any shotgun could be. I handed it back to her.

"What a wonderful gun. You could carry it in the field all day without being conscious of any weight," I said. Lucy looked pleased at the compliment.

"Are you a shooting man yourself?" she asked.

"I enjoy a day out for pheasant or partridge but I cannot claim to be any kind of a good shot. I inherited a Churchill 12 bore from my father and had the stock lengthened to suit me but living in London seldom had the chance to shoot."

"You must shoot with us here this season. I'll tell Percy to put you on the guest list when we start up in October. Is your dog trained to the gun?" she asked looking at Fred doubtfully.

"He was sold to us as fully trained when we moved here, but I haven't had a chance to try him out yet." With attention focussed upon him, Fred put on his most knowing expression and came forward wagging his tail.

"Well, we can try him out but if he runs wild he'll have to be sent home. I can't stand an undisciplined dog." Or husband too, I thought to myself.

"Now, do you want to see Percy while you're here? He's closeted in his study writing his wretched memoirs for you to edit," she added.

"No. I prefer to wait until he can show me a draft list of contents and a couple of chapters. Until then I can't make any useful comment. If he can deliver that to me by the end of next week when I'm back from Hong Kong, that would be good," I said firmly.

"Hong Kong. Why on earth are you going there?" Lucy asked sharply.

"I'm meeting contributors to the next edition of my book on China. Just for a few days, but my publisher wants me to get started."

I disengaged politely and started walking back with Fred still on his lead. Over my shoulder I could hear Lucinda Mansfield continuing to instruct her troops. "When you've tidied all this up and taken the clays back to the stable, Silas, Black will have prepared the vegetables for lunch; then you can drive her back to the village." I was already closing the gates to Home Farm, when Silas drove by.

---ooo0ooo---

CHAPTER 17

Oxfordshire, July 2

I DIDN'T FEEL LIKE making lunch for myself; so, I gave Fred his and decided to drive up to the Eastwick Arms for a pie and a pint. Barry Fullerton and Emma were both there behind the saloon bar and a handful of locals, seated at tables, were finishing their lunches. Those whom I knew nodded politely and Barry greeted me in his usual friendly fashion. Mounting a bar stool I glanced at the clock and noted that it was almost 2:00 p.m.

"I'm a bit late for lunch but what can you do?" I asked Barry as he pulled me a pint of bitter. I settled for an individual steak pie with a packet of cheese and onion crisps while Barry brought me up to date on the progress of Piroska's concert tour. She had called him from Baltimore where she had received particular acclaim and was now heading for California. I had finished eating and was pushing my plate away when I felt a heavy hand on my shoulder. I looked up and found the threatening figure of Aubrey Pinkerton looming over me.

"I've a bone to pick with you," he growled.

"Sit down and have a drink, won't you," I answered equably. Seemingly disconcerted by my mild reply, he perched on the bar stool next to me while Barry pulled a pint of Hook Norton ale for him.

"Now, Pinkerton, what's your problem?" I asked in the same even tone.

"Your wife and your fancy detective friend have been asking questions about me at the Clarendon Art Gallery. I've already been grilled by the police and I don't need any more from busybodies." I realised that he had been talking with Valerie Wyngarde and that their relationship was probably more than the nodding acquaintance that she had claimed. I decided to take the initiative.

"My wife is helping out at Professor Deakin's request with administration of the Gallery until the shareholders decide what to do. Valerie was telling her how helpful you've been and that you introduced Theodora to the picture restorer in Amsterdam which she used for College paintings. Do you get to Amsterdam much yourself?"

Pinkerton lent forward invading my space; he grabbed me by the lapels and glared at me intently. "The 17th century Dutch Masters are not my period. I have no reason to go there. Now, keep your nose out of my affairs," he growled, shaking me none too gently and raising me to my feet as he stood up himself.

He was several inches taller than me, a heavier man with bad breath and some twenty years younger. If my inclination was to hit him, I let discretion be the better part of valour and relied on Barry to intervene.

"That's enough, Aubrey," Barry's parade ground voice rang out. "I've told you before not to bring your personal quarrels into my pub. Unhand Mr. Radclive and sit down or I'll throw you out."

Pinkerton let go my coat and subsided back on to his stool. By now everyone else left in the saloon bar was paying attention and enjoying the drama. Time for a graceful exit. I drained my glass and turned to him speaking clearly for all to hear. "If you have anything further to say, you know where we live." A nod to Barry and I walked away without looking back.

In the car park Pinkerton's mud-spattered green Volvo stood alongside the Range Rover. I managed to read and commit to memory the registration number and was unlocking my car door when he strode out purposefully from the hotel and headed towards me.

"Hey you. I haven't finished talking to you," he shouted.

I had half expected him to follow me and realised that this time I had no option but to face up to him. His fists were clenched confirming that further assault was intended. My mind flashed back to the unarmed combat instructor on my military training course nearly forty years ago. "Don't wait for him to hit you. Go for the bugger and take him out first." I pivoted, stepped forward and stamped on Pinkerton's right instep as hard as I could, stopping him in his tracks as he reached out for me. I was still wearing heavy field shoes from my walk and he grunted with pain. Then, I kicked him savagely on the shin of his left leg and, while he was off balance, pushed him hard in the chest causing him to stagger back into a rank of wheelie bins at the side of the car park and slither to the ground. Not waiting for him to recover, I slid into the driver's seat of my car, pressed the doorlock and reversed smartly. As I drove off, Pinkerton was clambering to his feet and I could see that Emma Fullerton was watching from the pub door with amusement.

---ooo0ooo---

Back at Home Farm, I was careful to lock outside doors in case Aubrey Pinkerton was in pursuit and to write down the Volvo's registration number on my desk pad while it was still in my mind. Steadying my nerves and blood pressure with a cup of tea, I took advantage of the time gap to email my contacts at the Hong Kong offices where I hoped to visit them the following week. Given that they were five hours ahead of the UK, they would receive the emails when they returned to their offices the next morning and I could expect some replies when I logged in after breakfast.

"We're on," the Digger said when he called shortly before Gaby was due back. He was in ebullient mood. "They're allowing me forty-eight hours in Hong Kong; so

I'm booking a day flight out on Tuesday and my flight back overnight Thursday. But I've no idea where to stay. What shall you do?"

"That depends. Where are they holding the auction?"

Duncan Mallory consulted his catalogue. "Wednesday 10th July at 7:00 p.m. in the Regent Hotel ballroom, it says here."

"That's Kowloon side, We might as well stay there then. For meetings on the island, we can take the Star Ferry across to Central; it's only a short walk from the Regent. I'll reserve us both rooms in the morning," I suggested. We agreed that I would also ask Basil Gore-Smith to line up and brief his friend at the local Christie's offices for me to call on arrival. Duncan would brief his colleague in the Hong Kong police.

"All settled then," he said. "Now back to our friend Aubrey Pinkerton. We've done our homework. He has form here in London although he's never been charged. Five years ago he was a working partner in a fashionable West End art gallery until he got himself into trouble. It seems that he advised a client that her painting was a copy of a Degas rather than the real thing. He helped her to sell it at a price above his valuation; result, one satisfied client. Then six months later the same picture was sold at auction to a collector at ten times the price paid to the client. Pinkerton's partner, who was the one with money in the gallery dismissed him to salvage the gallery's reputation. The attempt failed and the gallery folded within the year."

"It could have been a genuine misjudgement; nothing criminal in that, surely?"

"That's what many people thought, and there was quite a lot of sympathy for him at the time. He left the London scene and worked as a self-employed consultant. But opinions changed when it was revealed that the same collector had appointed Pinkerton as adviser a few weeks after the auction. All very fishy, but we couldn't touch him."

"It helps to explain why he's so sensitive now about people asking questions about him." I related to Mallory the details of my encounter with Pinkerton at the Eastwick Arms and gave him the registration number of the Volvo.

"That's good," he said. "I'll have them call the ferry operators in the morning. If we establish that he made the crossing on the day or the day before the collection of the Monet in Amsterdam, we can be sure that he is involved in the Oxford art scam," Duncan said.

"Not just involved but perhaps the originator?" I suggested. "Based on the back story that you have uncovered and his friendship with Theodora Deakin, he could have come up with the whole scheme to rip off Oxford colleges."

"The evidence so far is all circumstantial and I shall need more than that to pin it on him. But, if you're right – and it's still a big if - the auction in Hong Kong may be a dress rehearsal for the disposal of the more valuable Monet ……"

"…. which is the object of the whole exercise." I added triumphantly.

"All the more reason to lay off Pinkerton until after we come back next week, hopefully with more insight and supporting evidence. I want you to avoid him from now until you depart on Sunday. If we leave him undisturbed for ten days that may lull him into a false sense that he is in the clear."

"What about your friend Trevor Wiggins and his murder enquiry, Will he leave Pinkerton alone in the meantime?"

"You have a point," admitted Mallory. "I'm meeting with him on Thursday for a catch-up and I'll have to give him some kind of a report on our investigation. I'll call you again Friday."

---ooo0ooo---

Wednesday was less remarkable. There were three positive replies overnight to my Hong King emails which I set aside to answer later in the day. The final chapter for *Managing Business Abroad* had also arrived overnight and by lunchtime I had finished the edit, added it to the contents and given the complete text a final review before sending it off to Robert Schindler. With rooms reserved at *The Regent* for the following week I made myself a toasted cheese and salami sandwich and was taking the first bite when the telephone rang. I could barely recognise the cheerful friendly tones of my caller.

"Julian, it's Percy – Percy Mansfield – here. I understand from Lucy that you want to see a contents list with the opening chapters of my book," the voice said.

"That's right, - er – Percy. I can't really comment usefully on the text of the early chapters until I have the context of the complete book. I need a list of contents, the skeleton, if you like, for the body of the work."

"I see. I've never attempted to write a book before and need guidance. Look, if it's not too inconvenient could I pop down this afternoon for half an hour for bit of tutoring," he said and managed to sound genuinely apologetic. The marked difference between the peremptory tones of our previous encounter and his present manner stimulated my curiosity.

"Alright, why don't you come down here for a drink at about 6:00 p.m. and we can talk it through without any interference from the telephone," I suggested. I wasn't expecting any incoming calls but I thought it would be good to have Gaby on hand for her impressions of the 'new' Sir Percy.

That left the afternoon clear to set up meetings with the Hong Kong offices of the London law firm which had written for me several times before; China Light and Power, the monopoly supplier of electricity; and Swayne Mackenzie, the trading and industrial conglomerate founded in the early nineteenth century and one of the original Hongs.

There was just time to brief Gaby on my 'phone call when she returned before Percy Mansfield's middle-aged Rover pulled into our yard. I met him at the door as he alighted and took him through my study on to the terrace. Dressed in a linen jacket over navy blue trousers with a polka dot scarf at his throat, he was the very model of a senior British civil servant enjoying a summer in retirement. He accepted a gin and tonic with ice and a slice of lemon from the drinks trolley; I poured my usual Ballantine's and we settled ourselves in garden chairs. The French windows behind us had been opened before he arrived so that Gaby could hear us while she flitted about the drawing room.

"Damn civil of you to let me disturb your evening. What a delightful place you have here," he said continuing his charm offensive.

"What can I tell you to help you get started?" I replied to open the conversation, and took a first taste of whisky.

"Not sure what you mean by a skeleton for my book and list of contents. You and Robert have already read my synopsis and said that you liked it." He sounded less laid back and more querulous now.

I explained that he would find it easier to write if he laid down the structure of the book first with a short abstract of what he intended to say in each chapter, with or without chapter headings. In response to further questioning I advised him on the optimum length of the book and of the text in each chapter.

"For your kind of book fifty thousand to sixty thousand words would be a good length. You need to keep it reader friendly which means that chapter length should be no more than three thousand and no less than two thousand words. So, it's a matter of arithmetic. For example, twenty chapters of two thousand five hundred words average would get you there, but it's flexible."

"H'm, see what you mean. But how do you set your chapter length parameters?"

"We're guided by reader attention span; from experience, about 20 minutes. Depending on the density of the text that works out at from two to three thousand words. You'll get the feel of it as you write."

There was a pause while Percy digested my words of wisdom and swigged another dose of gin and tonic. "Never realised that writing a book is such a disciplined process," he said at length. "Always thought that the author just wrote his manuscript, y'know, and delivered it to the publisher to monkey about with."

"That works sometimes for creative writing, such as romantic novelists or established authors of crime fiction, but not for academic or business book publishers such as Schindler Lyne," I said stifling any lingering thought he might have of privileged treatment.

"Well, Julian, you've given me my marching orders. I'll concentrate now on planning it all out during the coming week." He assumed an air of gruff jocularity but I suspected that he was already familiar with the advice I had given him. Having apparently answered his questions, I called Gaby out to join us and poured her a glass of chilled Chardonnay while she sat herself on the two-seat sofa alongside. Percy had tossed back most of his gin and tonic; so, I refreshed his glass and topped up my own with more ice and soda water.

"Your husband has sorted me out," he declared. "I'm very fortunate to have my own local friendly editor." He sounded proprietorial, as if conveying his patronage on a favoured butcher or grocer and Gaby bridled.

"You may find Julian more difficult to satisfy when you start to submit text," she cautioned.

"I understand from Lucy that you're going to Hong Kong next week, Julian?" Mansfield asked changing the subject; then, as if casually. "Shall you be gone long?"

"Just for the inside of the week. I'm meeting with potential contributors to the next edition of my China business book. Hong Kong will account for only a minor part of the book but, hopefully, much of the sponsorship from companies with mainland connections."

"I can give you introductions to people in Government House, if you like," offered Mansfield. "Might help you with some inside political connections."

"Thank you, but no," I said. The book has to be non-political; my co-editor in Beijing works for an offshoot of MOFTEC, the Chinese Ministry of Foreign Trade. In Hong Kong I'm meeting only with people who will remain in position after next year's handover."

I thought that Percy might be offended, but – was I imagining it – he seemed relieved. "That's splendid, then," he said with the fake bonhomie of a TV quiz show host. "I'll have the outline for my book ready for you by the time you return at the end of next week."

---ooo0ooo---

"What was that all about?" Gaby asked after Percy Mansfield left. He hsd knocked back the rest of his drink with minimal small talk and showed himself out after muttering something about "leaving you good people alone to enjoy your evening."

"I could have given him that briefing in ten minutes over the telephone," I replied.

"The sudden friendliness seemed out of character. He seemed more interested in your visit to Hong Kong than your editorial advice and somehow *relieved* after you refused his offer of an introduction to Government House. Why would that be?"

"Your guess is as good as mine. I agree that there was an element of play-acting about the visit. Perhaps he was concerned that I might be talking to his old cronies. In view of his opinions about our Government's bargaining on the handover treaty, he's probably no longer flavour of the month over there," I suggested.

"Or with the Chinese," Gaby added.

---ooo0ooo---

CHAPTER 18

July 4 to 7, Oxfordshire or London

THE REST OF THE WEEK PASSED PLEASANTLY ENOUGH. The fine weather held and I had time to mow the lawns as well as a lengthy ramble with Fred while Gaby was in Oxford on Thursday. My airline tickets arrived by the midday post and I started to put my notes together for meetings in Hong Kong. A call to Basil Gore-Smith at the Ashmolean confirmed that he had contacted his chum at Christie's office there; his name was Felix Blandford. Basil had briefed him fully on attendance at the auction and what was expected of him. Felix would expect me to telephone him on Monday when I had checked in at my hotel. I wrote his number in my pocket diary and promised Basil to keep him informed.

When Gaby returned she brought with her copies of the *Oxford Guardian*. Charlie Dibbs had gone to town in a full-page feature article on page five. Under the eye-catching headline - **OXFORDSHIRE'S HOSTESS WITH THE MOSTEST** - there was a photograph of Fullmere Mill taken from the lawn with a head and shoulders inset of Georgina Delahaye. The opening text of the article under Charlie's byline was no less attention grabbing:

Fullmere Mill, the country home of Mrs. Georgina Delahaye was the elegant location for a Music Festival on 21 June featuring the Piroska Szabó quartet. The audience enjoyed a stimulating programme of East European music, but the evening ended

tragically with two violent deaths shortly after the concert.

Guests were treated to a champagne reception on the lawn on arrival, supper in the interval and hot punch after the concert. The final item was an aria from Smetana's *The Bartered Bride* sung by the group's soprano from a boat on the lake.

Georgina Delahaye herself presided over the evening with charm and elegance ensuring that everyone felt personally welcome and involved. "I just love entertaining," she told me "particularly in my own home. We were so fortunate that Piroska and her musicians could fit us into her busy summer schedule."

A talent to amuse

An accomplished hostess, Mrs. Delahaye is no stranger to the world of hospitality. She is Chairman of the prestigious *Wigmore Escort Agency* in London which she founded three years ago after moving to England from America. The agency numbers foreign embassies, government departments and well-known multinational companies and banks among its clients providing staff for their social events to entertain guests. In the United States she was the owner of an exclusive country club on Long Island whose members were drawn from similar business and government circles.

> Looking ahead, further concerts at Fullmere Mill are planned for next year. "I want to develop the Fullmere Festival into an annual cultural event for Oxfordshire residents and their friends introducing them to lesser known classical music with international musicians in relaxed surroundings over two or three days each year." Georgina says. "In time, we hope to achieve similar standing to the leading literary festivals in which Great Britain abounds and to attract music lovers from abroad as well as throughout the UK."

The article continued with a description of the music programme and a profile of Szabó Piroska and her glittering international career. Finally, as a footnote, Charlie Dibbs had added a paragraph summarizing the murders and the state of police inquiries.

> As reported in the *Oxford Evening News* last week, Mrs. Theodora Deakin, managing director of the Clarendon Art Gallery, was found bludgeoned to death on 22nd June, the following morning, at a lake in the grounds where the final item of the programme was played to the concert audience. The body of local teenager Molly Bennett was also found in a nearby location. It is believed that the two incidents may be connected. After almost two weeks there have been no arrests. Commander Trevor Wiggins of Scotland Yard's murder squad, who is leading the investigation, told the *Oxford*

Guardian "We are pursuing several lines of enquiry and have interviewed many of those present that evening. An early arrest is now expected."

I cut out the article with kitchen scissors and faxed it to Bill Fentiman at his home and office and awaited his call. No covering note was necessary. Within the hour Bill telephoned back.

"Not bad," he commented. "There's enough there as a reference for the national newspapers seeking to recap on the story. Only those who decide to write a feature article on Georgina will need to delve deeper."

"What about the final paragraph summarising the details of the two murders?" I asked.

"Commander Wiggins won't be pleased; it puts the pressure on him to make another arrest and to charge someone. If he finds out about Georgina's friendship with Alexander Deakin, he may have a pop at them both. I'm lining up Kenworthy-Green to represent her if she's arrested for questioning. He's the best defence lawyer I know for people who can afford him."

I told Bill that I would be on my Hong Kong trip from Sunday until the Friday following; we left it that Gaby would be in touch with him while I was away. if anything happened locally which might affect Georgina Delahaye.

---ooo0ooo---

"We've got a match," Duncan Mallory reported with satisfaction when he called the following morning. "Pinkerton and his Volvo with one other passenger took the night ferry from Harwich on 18th June arriving at The Hook at 0745 the next day in good time to collect the Monet from van den Groot in Amsterdam that afternoon."

"Did you find out who was the other passenger?" I asked.

"The name given was Monica Lester and they shared a sleeper cabin on the ferry but it must have been an assumed name. If we've got it right, it was really Theodora Deakin."

"What about the return journey?"

"The Volvo returned from The Hook on the day ferry 20th June but this time the only passenger registered was Aubrey Pinkerton," Mallory replied. "That means that his companion came back some other way."

"Maybe she flew back from Schipol on the evening of the 19th," I said.

"We've checked all the flights to Heathrow and Birmingham – there were none to Gatwick – under the names of Monica Lester or Theodora Deakin. We drew blanks."

"How was your meeting with Trevor Wiggins?" I asked changing the subject.

"No more friendly than last time. He still has little interest in our investigation and won't consider that the art fraud might have a bearing on the murder. He was keen to impress me with his diligence. He's interviewed individually each of the house guests at Fullmere Mill on the night of the Festival with particular attention to Hugo and Trixie, the two who sloped off to bed together in the interval. Also, he has it in for somebody called Gerald Marl who wasn't there but seems to have interfered with his interviewing process. Have you come across him?" Mallory asked.

"Yes, he's Georgina Delahaye's right hand man at the Wigmore Escort Agency. He lives over the shop and acts as general manager. Rather a downy bird; Wiggins would loathe him. But how did he become involved?"

"Wiggins called at the agency and asked Marl to arrange for each of the girls to come in there for interview. Saved him the trouble of trying to track them down at their flats, digs or places of work if they had day jobs. The only trouble was that Marl had lined up a solicitor to sit in at each interview."

"Must have cramped Wiggins usual confrontational style of questioning," I commented. "Did he do the same with the men?"

"No. He called them all by telephone at their offices and arranged to interview them at home or at the Metropolitan Police station in the Barbican. That is, except for Hugo Bassinger whom he had down as a suspect. Two plainclothes detectives turned up at his office without warning, announced who they were and took him off to the station. Maximum embarrassment for Basinger but it didn't do much good. Wiggins couldn't pin anything on him and had to let him go after an hour or so. He didn't call for a solicitor because he didn't want to have to confess to the bank how he had spent his weekend."

I wouldn't have wished Wiggins on anyone but it was hard to feel sympathy for the arrogant Hugo with his sense of self-entitlement.

"So where does that leave Trevor Wiggins now?" I asked. "He must be under pressure from above, let alone the Press, to arrest and charge someone."

"He's back on Aubrey Pinkerton as the perpetrator – this time acting under instruction for Alexander Deakin. And he's found a motive – not just a husband at odds with his wife. He checked out Mrs. Delahaye with the FBI and found her connection with Deakin when he was in New York as CEO for Oxford University Press. He thinks they could have planned it together," Mallory elaborated.

The twinge of guilt I had felt at not telling Duncan before about Georgina's liaison with Alexander evaporated. "You mean Wiggins is now viewing Theodora's murder as a *crime passionel* on Georgina's part?"

"Well, Pinkerton is her tenant," Mallory argued "and she could have slit the throat of the waitress while she was moving around between the guests."

"That's far-fetched and, as for motive, she's a feisty lady but the idea of her having someone bumped off out of sexual jealousy is sheer fantasy – a business competitor, just conceivable, but for a lover – no way." I was aware that perhaps I was being too vehement in Georgina's defence.

"OK, Julian, don't shoot the messenger. I don't believe it either. But I do think he means to arrest and charge Deakin as soon as he can make a plausible case. Wiggins is interviewing and taking statements from his friends and colleagues in Oxford from tomorrow. He told me that he has already sent someone over to New York to interview OUP staff there."

---ooo0ooo---

CHAPTER 19

July 8 and 9, Hong Kong

THE BOEING 747 SIDE-SLIPPED past hillside apartments, hotels and the downtown shopping centre of Kowloon to complete its descent and land at Kai Tak International airport. Among the world's most dangerous for long haul aircraft, runway 13 taxed the professional skills of pilots unable to rely on their instruments to land safely. Passengers flying into Kai Tak for the first time found the experience surreal. Viewing TV screens through apartment windows as their jumbo slid by was unnerving. They disembarked with relief, many still in a daze. Old hands like myself were the first to reach passport control and reclaim our baggage. A red and white Mazda taxi delivered me to the Regent Hotel within fifteen minutes.

The Regent was my favourite Hong Kong hotel. From the modern décor of the spacious lobby with its circular reception counter to the fashionable harbour bistro and gourmet restaurant below, from the immaculate service provided to the luxurious en suite accommodation for residents, a stay at The Regent was a comfortable and stylish experience for the world weary traveller. If that were all, I might have preferred the opulent splendour of the Peninsula Hotel nearby with its air of stylish 1930s high life and a fleet of Rolls Royce limousines parked permanently outside to convey guests wherever bidden. But one feature of the Regent trumped everything else: its open-air swimming pool. Located six floors up, the kidney-shaped roof top pool overlooked Victoria Harbour; floating in the pool or lolling on a lounger guests had a panoramic view of

Hong Kong island from the high rise building dominated by the Bank of China tower to Central from which the Star Ferry plied its trade to and from the Tsimshatsui terminal Kowloon side.

By the time I had checked into my tenth floor room with its balcony giving on to a sea view it was approaching sunset. I hastened down to the pool for a quick dip having telephoned Gaby at the gallery to confirm my safe arrival. With the seven hour time difference we left it that I would check in again the following night before going to bed and the same again on Wednesday to report on the outcome of the auction.

I was the only person in the pool. I swam half a dozen lengths; then dried off and sat on one of the loungers in the towelling bathrobe which I had worn down from my room. As I gazed across the harbour in the gathering twilight, the lights in the apartment blocks and offices opposite came on in quick succession and, as if by the flick of a single switch, the neon advertising signs and corporate logos atop office buildings were illuminated simultaneously against the backdrop of the darkened Peak. If there had been a pool attendant still on duty I would have ordered a drink. Sitting there by myself I reflected on the future of the prosperous business centre before me and its hardworking entrepreneurial people. Until now the glittering jewel in Britain's Far Eastern crown, how would Hong Kong fare under the ultimate authority of Beijing after the handover in a year's time? After more than a decade of visiting the mainland on business I was apprehensive. For the first five years of visiting it had seemed that the commercial development of China as a free enterprise economy "with Chinese characteristics" might even evolve into a kind of para-democracy but that had been wishful thinking. After the Tianamen Square uprising of 1989 the Chinese Communist Party had clamped down firmly on the levers of government and it seemed less likely now that the "one country, two systems" approach to Hong Kong rule would endure. Tomorrow I would begin to get a feel for how Hong Kongers viewed their future.

---ooo0ooo---

After a good night's sleep I took breakfast in my room and started telephoning to confirm meetings for the day and the following morning. I also called Felix Blandford at Christie's local office and invited him to join us for an early dinner at The Regent before the auction the following evening. He had been fully briefed by Basil Gore-Smith and would come prepared; he seemed to relish involvement in an international art theft investigation. By 10:00 a.m. I was on the Star Ferry in good time for my first meeting at Swayne Mackenzie, one of the oldest trading houses, in their tower block in Central close by the Hilton Hotel. My appointment was with Alasdair Swayne, a junior member of the founding family entrusted with business development in mainland China; his uncle was the present Chairman. I had dressed accordingly in my best lightweight blue suit with a rather dashing pink tie, appropriate to a publisher. The imposing outer office was staffed by a pair of elegant Hong Kong ladies who checked me in and seated me in a well-furnished meeting room with a cup of green tea. I was ten minutes early but it was more than twenty-five minutes before I was joined by Alasdair Swayne, accompanied by an older, very polite but expressionless Hong Kongese, or more likely Chinese, introduced as 'Mr. Tao'. Unusually, no business card was proffered and I did not identify his function or management position until later.

Swayne, an overweight young man in a chalk stripe bankers' suit with an oversize signet ring and a supercilious smile, examined cursorily the copy of the current edition of my book that I had brought with me before passing it to his companion. "How will the new edition differ from this book?" he asked. "What shall you say about the future of Hong Kong after handover?"

"I am hoping that Swayne Mackenzie with its extensive mainland interests in trade, commerce and shipping will contribute a chapter on the subject as a sponsor," I said doing my best to look smoothly confident.

"I see. I can tell you, in strict confidence, that we are in negotiation with a powerful Chinese corporation to take a financial interest in our group. So, I shall have to consult with them before taking a decision," he replied pompously.

I didn't care for his patronising tone and decided to knock him off his perch. "Does that mean that you are discussing a joint venture or that your Chinese friends will be purchasing a shareholding in Swayne Mackenzie?" I questioned.

Swayne flushed to the roots of his ginger hair and glanced nervously at Mr. Tao. "I've already said more than I should, Mr. Radclive. You'll have to be patient; no comment."

The inscrutable Mr. Tao intervened. "Please to answer one question if I may ask, Mr. Radclive?" His English was almost perfect with only the slightest accent.

"Of course, Mr. Tao. Ask away," I replied.

"Will your new edition have the support of MOFTEC and the same Chinese joint editor?"

"Certainly," I assured him. "Mr. Xing Yu Zhu is my trusted colleague and now an old friend. I rely on him for all the chapters contributed by Chinese authors."

Mr. Tao nodded. "You are wise, Mr. Radclive. Old friends are best." He held the book in both hands, tapped it on the table before him. Turning to Swayne he nodded again. His approval was clear, but Alasdair Swayne was not going to lose face.

"I shall have to discuss your proposal with the Chairman before I can give you an answer," he said self-importantly.

"I'm staying at the Regent," I told him. "I fly back to the UK on Thursday evening; you can fax me at my office at the end of the week if you prefer."

We stood up and moved towards the door. Mr. Tao shook my hand formally and remained impassive. Swayne steered me towards the elevator in Reception and offered a limp handshake. "Remember me to your uncle," I said as the lift arrived. "We met in London last autumn at an Institute of Directors conference where we were both speaking."

Having delivered my parting shot, I stepped into the lift and the doors closed behind me. Of course, the point scoring had been childish. I had been introduced to Gerald Swayne at the IoD but he had spoken before me and hadn't stayed for my address. I thought it unlikely that he would remember me.

---ooo0ooo---

My next meeting was more congenial. Wingate's were a leading law firm in Hong Kong, an offshoot of the parent partnership in Sydney. I had known Greg Barlow, the local partner, for more than ten years since we met in Tianjin on both our first visits to China. He cut a lanky figure with one of those mournful, pinched Australian faces but was good company; he had a mordant wit and we had got on well from the start. Wingate's had contributed to the previous editions of my China book and I expected him to write again this time. He greeted me with a knowing smile.

"How's tricks, mate. What are you going to talk me into this time?" he asked in the Australian twang which he took pleasure in exaggerating among friends.

"Good to see you, Greg, as always. I'm hoping you'll write for me this time on the outlook for business in Hong King after the handover."

He waved me towards the comfortable chair and sofa in his spacious office, drew two bottles of chilled Tsingtao beer from the refrigerator concealed in a cupboard and set them down before us.

"Do you want me to repeat what the Governor says and the Happy Valley crowd of Poms are peddling, or do you want the opinion of an old Ozzie cynic?" He necked a draught of beer from his bottle,

"I'd like to read the same opinion that you give your regular clients and businessmen coming to Hong Kong for the first time," I replied taking a first swig to keep him company.

"That's easy," Greg replied. "To those who are here I say get yourself a mainland partner and, if they have a trading or joint venture partner already, encourage him to buy into your company so that he can float his Chinese business through yours on the Honkie Stock Exchange."

"And to those who aren't already here?"

"Stay away, sport, until you have the protection of Chinese investment in your business."

"Surely not a great way to gain new clients," I reflected.

"On the contrary, Julian, we've followed our own advice," Greg retorted. "Those that are serious engage us to find Mainland partners. And that's why we're opening an office in Beijing with Chinese associates."

"Good on you, Greg," I congratulated him in my own imitation Ozzie accent. "I've just come from a meeting at Swayne Mackenzie; it's what they seem to be doing too, although pretty coy about it."

"Who did you see there?"

"Alasdair Swayne and a mysterious Mr. Tao," I said.

"Alasdair's a plonker but his uncle Gerard is a wily bird. Your Mr. Tao – I wonder. Not an uncommon Chinese family name Can you describe him?"

"Not very well. Usual black hair; impossible to say how old but I would say well over fifty; horn-rimmed spectacles;

didn't speak much but excellent English with very little accent. No distinguishing features but an air of authority," I told him.

"Sounds like Tao Qi Wei; the manager of QITIC's Hong Kong office. And, if it is, Gerard Swayne has picked a powerful pal," Greg replied, sounding uncharacteristically impressed.

"What's QITIC?" I asked. "I'm no good at these Chinese acronyms."

"Qingdao International Trust and Investment Company. It's the sovereign wealth fund of Shandong Province and its major port."

"In that case shouldn't it be called SHITIC?"

"Shanghai already has the rights to that name. In any case, Qingdao is where this beer comes from; so it already has a high international profile" And so saying Greg took another long draught from his bottle and motioned me to do the same. "Drink up," he added "and I'll buy you lunch."

---ooo0ooo---

We wandered companionably down on foot to The Hong Club on Victoria Harbour where Greg was a member. Founded in 1846 by the eight taipans of the time for themselves, heads of trading houses and senior government officials and known more simply as 'The Club' it remains exclusive with membership by invitation only. Greg selected one of the four restaurants overlooking the harbour where we were seated by the head witer at a table with a good view of the whole bay. We decided to eat Chinese food and Greg ordered for us both. Like most food in Southern China, the cuisine is Cantonese which I normally find rather dull and insipid but I had to concede that the Chow Mein with bean shoots and dim sun which Greg chose were delicious.

"Avoid the Western food here," he cautioned. "Aside from the steaks flown in from Brisbane or the lamb from Wellington, it's even worse than your Pommie clubs in London."

While thinking of a suitable reply to the insult I surveyed other members and their guests who were lunching at neighbouring tables. My attention was drawn to a pair who were just entering the room: an elderly Chinese with horn-rimmed spectacles and another taller man who could have been Hong Kong Chinese or from further away, perhaps Thailand or Singapore. Unlike his companion of conservative appearance, the somewhat younger man was flamboyantly dressed in a white suit with what, at a distance, could be mistaken for an Old Etonian tie.

"That's Mr. Tao," I whispered to Greg Barlow "do you know who that is with him?"

"Well, your Mr. Tao is Tao Qi Wei alright and the other character who calls himself Canning Kwok is a swagman originally from Vietnam who owns a chain of restaurants and nightclubs in Kowloon up the Nathan Road."

"That sounds like a strange relationship," I commented.

"Not so strange, but probably not respectable either. Kwok is into all sorts of fringe illegal activities and Tao is said to enjoy making something on the side for himself from the sale of antique artefacts from the mainland."

The waiter led them past our table to be seated. Mr. Tao recognised me and we exchanged nods. Canning Kwok seemed curious, looked coldly at Greg and addressed him, "Good morning, Mr. Barlow."

"Good afternoon, Mr, Kwok," Greg acknowledged him.

"So, you're acquainted with the dodgy Canning Kwok," I said after they had passed by.

"We've never spoken before, but I acted for someone who was suing Kwok for his sale of stolen goods to him. We won our case," Greg replied with satisfaction. Hardly the basis for a beautiful friendship, I thought.

---oooOooo---

From The Club I took a taxi to Telford Plaza for my scheduled meeting at the headquarters of the Mass Transit Railway. As a public utility the MTR provides the vital communications system for commuters and rapid movement between the island, Kowloon and the New Territories. Offering exemplary service it was a source of pride to the Hong Kong government and was currently extending its network to the new airport opening in two years time on Lantau Island. I was warmly received and spent the next hour or so being briefed by an enthusiastic deputy General Manager. He was happy to provide the material for a chapter in my book, but it was soon clear that the MTR was wholly occupied in its own business with no interest in reaching a wider audience. Indeed, in all my times in Hong Kong I never saw an advertisement for the MTR. It was an interesting afternoon but there was no scope for sponsorship. By 5:00 p.m. I was back at The Regent in a towelling robe and swimming shorts at the side of the pool. Of all the businesses in Hong Kong, I mused, the MTR was the least likely to suffer interference after the handover, The Chinese knew a good thing when they saw it.

Back in my room I decided to wait dinner for Duncan Mallory who was arriving by the same flight that I had taken the previous day and called down to reception to leave a message for him. Then, with nearly two hours to spare, I helped myself to a drink from the duty-free half bottle purchased at Heathrow and settled down with a lined pad and ballpoint to summarize on paper the thoughts that had been circulating in my mind over the past ten days on the murders after the concert and the art fraud which had brought us to Hong Kong. I was convinced that the two events were connected but tried to list potential suspects with columns for motive and opportunity against each name. Starting with the concert murders I took it as read that the brutal killings of Theodora Deakin and of Molly Bennett had been perpetrated by the same person or different persons working together. My written notes were speculative and hardly grounded in fact :

Murder of TD at after concert   *Motive*   *Opportunity*

Alexander Deakin   Removal of obstacle to affair with Georgina D/ discovery that his wife was about to steal from college
    No

Georgina Delahaye   Removal of obstacle to affair with Alexander D   No

Aubrey Pinkerton   Removal of partner in art scam or under contract to X   Yes

Hugo Bassinger   None known   Yes

Sir Percy Mansfield   " " "   Perhaps

Lucinda Mansfield   " " "   Perhaps

Murder of MB by Marquee

Any of above suspects   Prevent identification of TD killer
    All

I looked at the page in front of me with disfavour. The odds on favourite for Theodora's murder was Aubrey Pinkerton and, if you denied any link to the art fraud on Oxford colleges, I had to admit that Commander Wiggins' theory of his doing it on behalf of Georgina was plausible; and that it was also possible that Georgina was responsible for Molly Bennett's death if the girl had observed Aubrey returning from the lake.

On the other hand, if you believed in a link between the murder and the art scam, Aubrey was still the odds-on favourite as Theodora's killer although the motivation was unclear. If he wanted to dispose of a partner who had served her usefulness, how likely was it that he could handle the sale of genuine paintings or relationships with the colleges by himself? True that his connection with the Clarendon Gallery through Valerie Wyngarde was stronger than she made out and that he was in her confidence to some degree, but I couldn't see her as more than an accomplice and certainly not as 'X' if he had been acting under instruction. And that, of course, made the point that if there was an 'X' it could very well be someone who had not attended the concert.

My analysis was getting me nowhere. I had to hope that tomorrow's auction would take us closer to identifying the identity of Aubrey Pinkerton's collaborators. I took another look at my notes and consigned them to the wastepaper basket.

---oooOooo---

CHAPTER 20

July 10, Hong Kong

WE WENT OUR SEPARATE WAYS on Wednesday morning. Duncan Mallory had checked in late the evening before; his flight had been delayed by a freak electric storm over the Indian ocean. Having enjoyed little sleep, his priority was to get his head down and we didn't meet up before breakfasting together. I tod him about the arrangements for Felix Blandford to join us in the evening and Duncan informed me that he was meeting with his contact in the Hong Kong Police Force that morning. His former Hendon police college colleague, Inspector Harry Foung, was ready to help in any way he could.

Meantime, I was attending a meeting at the head office of China Light and Power in Kowloon; so, while Mallory headed for the Star Ferry, I took the MTR to the nearest station. Unlike MTR under public ownership, China Light and Power had been controlled by the Kadoorie family since the 1930s through its parent company CLP Holdings listed on the Hong Kong stock exchange. Therefore, I reasoned, its international standing in the face of the pending handover was of concern to its directors and it was more likely that they would want CLP to be showcased in my book. That was the logic behind my discussion with its management and my approach was well received. However, the price of sponsorship was that I should write their chapter to which I agreed reluctantly. This involved several sessions with individual managers and the collection of company literature covering past and current activity which kept me with CLP until mid-afternoon. I undertook to send them a draft for approval within two or three weeks.

Back at The Regent I found Digger Mallory wallowing in the pool. He was lying on his back paddling idly and wearing designer sunglasses. I took a quick dip myself; then we both clambered out and settled down on the loungers which Duncan had reserved with towels and a pair of auction catalogues - I was reminded of German tourists booking places on the private beach of an exclusive hotel in Crete where Gaby and I had stayed some years before. Duncan's choice of flowered swimming trunks added to the Mediterranean analogy. Mindful of the evening ahead, we ordered coca colas rather than anything stronger.

"How was your day? What have you arranged with Inspector Foung for a police presence this evening?" I enquired.

Duncan picked up one of the catalogues and leafed through the pages; sucking cola through a straw he answered me obliquely. "There are 175 lots in the auction and our painting is set for number 95. Most of the lots before ours are Chinese porcelain or jade. Harry thinks we should allow an average of no more than two minutes per lot. The auction starts at 6:30 p.m; so we should be in our seats before 9:00 p.m. Harry Foung will be there in good time and I've invited him to join us if he's early."

I had studied the other catalogue and noted that the name of the auction house, Challoner Chen, was displayed prominently on the front cover with their contact details. Underneath in smaller print was the phrase *"Correspondents in San Francisco, Manchester and Geneva"*. The first two locations made sense as they were both cities with large Chinese populations; Geneva could only be there for its banking and tax haven status.

"Did Inspector Foung have anything to tell you about Challoner Chen?" I asked.

"Harry says that they are just about respectable and on the right side of the law, but there have been stories about unauthorised exports of artefacts from the mainland. The firm was founded by Raymond Challoner in the 1960s and specialises in jade, jewellery, pottery and furniture imported from China whose owners are seeking buyers in the international market. Some of the sellers are Chinese Government agencies; others are Chinese individuals, often in positions of influence. Whether or not they are the actual owners is sometimes uncertain."

"And is there a Mr. Chen as well?"

"Alive and kicking. Challoner brought Chen Yu Bo in as his partner more than ten years ago. Chen was born in Shanghai and came to Hong Kong about then; he handles the China connections. They'll probably both be there tonight," Duncan explained.

With Felix Blandford due at 7:00 p.m. it was time to shower and change; so we downed the last of our drinks, took another quick dip in the pool and retired reluctantly to our rooms.

---oooOooo---

We took our early dinner in the Harbour restaurant and were seated there with our guest by 7:15 p.m. He was not what I had expected. Where Basil Gore-Smith, his friend from the Ashmolean, was gangly, bow-tied and diffident of manner, Felix Blandford was compact, sober-suited and precise. Only the twinkle in his brown eyes and an infectious grin betrayed a cynical wit and sense of humour. Duncan Mallory completed the rather sketchy briefing that Basil and I had given him in separate telephone calls and outlined our plan of action. We would attend the bidding on Lot 95 and then follow the purchaser when he retired to the area reserved for payment and collection. There, we would challenge the authenticity of the painting; Felix and I would examine the canvas while Mallory would interview the purchaser and the representatives of Challoner Chen tasked with completing the transaction. Inspector Foung would stand by to support Duncan and, if necessary, arrest for further questioning.

"Is there anyone in particular we should expect to see at the auction among the bidders or as a seller?" I asked Felix.

"The usual suspects and a sprinkling of tourists just there looking for bargains to display at home as evidence of their encounters with the *real* Orient," he replied.

"What about local collectors with a taste for European art?"

"Mostly businessmen with houses on the Peak seeking to demonstrate their culture or looking to add prestige to their offices to impress clients. No-one in particular springs to mind," Felix responded wryly.

Mindful of Greg Barlow's advice I ordered lamb chops for my main course and selected carefully from the salad bar for my starter. The other two followed my example although I suspected that Felix would have been more adventurous in other company. We washed our meal down with Tsingtao beer, decided against taking dessert and made our way towards The Regent's grand ballroom on the mezzanine floor where the auction was being held. The ballroom was approached by a wide sweeping staircase from the hotel's rear lobby; it was used normally for private functions, mainly wedding receptions for the well-heeled or shareholder meetings of Hong Kong companies listed on the stock exchange. There were side rooms off the main area for private meetings and cloakrooms at the head of the stairs for guests arriving. The whole suite was carpeted in thick blue Wilton including sections of carpet in the ballroom itself which could be rolled back when used for dances.

We registered at a desk outside the ballroom and were equipped with numbered paddles to be raised when bidding which provided a degree of anonymity. On entry we could see that tonight's auction was well attended with many of the ten rows of gilt painted chairs occupied; they faced a dais on which the auctioneer was positioned at a rostrum. We found ourselves three chairs together in a row towards the back of the room from which we could survey the proceedings. The auctioneer, a tall figure with craggy features, a mane of white hair and a booming voice was in full flow.

"Lot 82," he intoned "a jade Buddha believed to be of the Tang dynasty."

A porter in green overalls and white gloves carried the quarter metre high light green figurine to the centre of the dais and placed it reverently on a plinth.

"That's Raymond Challoner himself running the auction," Felix whispered in my ear. "He'll be taking bids in US dollars - hard currency only at this time."

"I'm opening at $200, ladies and gentlemen. Am I bid $300?" Challoner called. A paddle was raised at the front of the room.

"$300. I am taking advances now of $100 or more."

There was a flurry of bids around the room and the price rose rapidly to $900.

" Am I bid $1,000. Thank you, sir," to a raised paddle from the left-hand side of the room. "Any advance on $1,000 for this outstanding piece of Tang dynasty jade?"

There were a few seconds pause and Raymonf Challoner picked up his gavel. Then, from the original bidder at the front "$1,500" in a clear male voice. There was no answering counterbid.

"Final offers, then ….. Going to the gentleman in the front row……..Going, going…" Challoner brought his hammer down on its pad and the porter in white gloves removed the jade Buddha from the dais.

The next few lots were ceramic tableware objects attributed to the Yongzheng period of the Qing dynasty, some offered singly and some in sets of bowls or plates. I had time to scan the room and examine the assembly while Raymond Challoner auctioned off each lot with professional enthusiasm and practised efficiency. I noted that all items sold were removed to another room at the side where they were presumably held for collection by their new owners following payment. Turning my attention to the audience I was surprised to see both Canning Kwok and the enigmatic Mr. Tao seated apart on opposite sides of the room. I nudged Felix and pointed to each of them in turn.

"Do you know either of those two?" I asked him.

"I can identify them both. The Chinese cove with spectacles is Tao Qi Wei. He's a seller rather than buyer, either acting for QITIC whom he represents or for himself – he sells quite a lot on his own account, sometimes through us. Respectable but said to be an enemy to avoid. The other character is Canning Kwok, a very slippery customer and into all kinds of borderline business. He wouldn't be here unless there are one or more lots in which he has an interest. The big man on his left is his minder and comes from Outer Mongolia. You don't want to be on his shopping list."

The auction proceeded to Lot 95 in short order and we watched Raymond Challoner expectantly as he gave his introduction. "This next Lot is an unusual item in tonight's auction – an unsigned painting of 17th century origin probably from the school of one of the most famous Dutch Masters," he paused for effect "Johannes Vermeer. I shall start the bidding at $500." He looked around the audience until a first paddle was raised from the back of the room.

While I looked in the direction of the bid, Mallory lent across Felix to tell me that Inspector Foung had arrived in plainclothes and was seated in a row behind us with two uniformed policeman stationed at the entrance. A second bid of $750 came from the centre of the room which the first bidder raised to $1,000. After a short pause, that was raised in turn to $1,250 when the bidding stalled.

"Surely there are other bidders for this genuine 17th century painting from the golden age of Dutch art fit to grace the boardroom any Hong Kong enterprise of standing. I have $1,250 in the room. What am I bid now, ladies and gentlemen?"

A massive arm with paddle was raised from the right-hand side; "$2,000" a deep voice called. There were no further bids and the painting was knocked down to him. It was removed carefully by two porters towards the exit. The bidder was revealed as Canning Kwok's minder when the two of them moved towards the anteroom passing the policemen on the door. Duncan Mallory, Felix Blandford and I followed with Inspector Foung in our wake.

We gathered in the auction office at the side of the lobby, accessible by a door at the head of the stairs. If Canning Kwok was surprised by the arrival of our group of four, he gave no indication. Advancing to the counter where payment was taken, he produced a large cheque book from the breast pocket of his beautifully tailored silk evening suit. Only Kwok had changed into formal evening attire; the rest of us were clad in our day clothes.

"That will be $2,400 with 20 per cent buyer's commission, Mr. Kwok, for Lot 95," a sharp-faced Chinese told him from behind the counter.

"Just a moment." Mallory interrupted producing his warrant card. "We need to verify that the painting you are about to pay for is not stolen property."

"You have no jurisdiction here," Canning Kwok retorted. "Mr. Chen will accept my cheque and the painting will become my property."

"But I do have authority, Mr. Kwok," Inspector Foung said stepping forward, and addressing the Chinese across the counter "You are Chen Yu Bo, I assume, a partner in this auction house?" Mr. Chen nodded weakly. "In that case, you will have the painting brought in here for my colleagues' inspection."

Canning Kwok held his peace and Chen summoned two white gloved porters to bring forth the painting which they laid carefully on a table at Felix's direction. He examined first the back of the canvas, pegs and stretchers before studying the face of the painting through a lens. To laymen such as the Digger and myself the picture had a mellower, albeit darker appearance than the cleaned canvas that Basil Gore-Smith had examined at Latimer College in our presence barely ten days before. But Felix gave greater scrutiny to the search for an artist's signature. From the breast of his jacket he produced a small bottle of clear liquid and from a side pocket a packet of cottonwool buds; then, with extreme care, he applied a drop or two of the liquid to the cottonwool and dabbed gently to the areas at the bottom of the picture where artists usually signed their names and the chimneypiece where Basil had found a signature on the copy.

"Only turpentine," he explained. "It will do no damage to the original varnish or paint, but will remove anything more recent." There was no result from the bottom of the painting and the cottonwool remained clean. Chen Yu Bo relaxed and Canning Kwok looked bland.

"As expected," Felix commented and sprinkled turpentine on another cottonwool bud before applying it carefully to the underside of the chimneypiece on the right of the painting. This time, there was a positive result. Gradually, as he continued to dab, writing was revealed. We craned forward to read an unmistakable signature: *Pieter De Hooch*. Felix straightened up and faced us.

"This is a genuine De Hooch painting," he announced solemnly. "You may want corroboration from the Rijksmuseum experts when you take it back or one of the London auction houses, but I have no doubt myself."

This was the cue for Duncan Mallory to step forward and assert his authority. "Inspector Foung, will you please take this painting and hold it in custody until I can make arrangements for shipment back to the UK and return to its rightful owner."

Then, turning to Chen Yu Bo, he added "And, unless you can offer a satisfactory explanation of how you accepted this valuable work of art for auction, Challoner Chen and its partners will face charges for accepting stolen goods."

Inspector Foung accepted his commission and called in his two uniformed officers to take away the De Hooch covered in a dustsheet. Mr. Chen, looking shocked, received his caution and agreed to attend the police station the following morning at 10:00 a.m. for questioning. Canning Kwok, while remaining calm, seemed amused but mildly irritated. "How tiresome," he said and tore his oversize cheque dramatically into pieces which he placed into an ashtray. "A wasted evening but quite instructive. Thank you, gentlemen, for saving me from embarrassment. I take it that I am free to go home?"

The two inspectors looked at each other and Mallory nodded. "Thank you, Mr Kwok," Foung answered him. "We know where to reach you if we have any questions."

After Canning Kwok had swept out with his Mongolian minder Mallory turned again to Harry Foung. "I've only one question for that downy bird, but you can probably give me a more reliable answer," he said. "Has he had any telephone conversations with the UK or Netherlands in the past few weeks?"

"I can find out from the telephone company by submitting an official request in the morning. I'll put one in for his flat and one for his office," Foung promised. There was nothing more that could be done that night; so, the inspector and Felix Blandford left with our thanks for a successful mission completed.

---ooo0ooo---

We decided to take a nightcap together in my room and I poured us both stiff measures from my duty-free bottle of Ballantine's. "Do you think that Canning Kwok knew what he was buying?" I asked.

"Almost certainly. He was in on the scam and his role was to find buyers for the stolen paintings, probably for private collections not exhibited to the public. That sort of buyer would pay close to the market price, particularly of he was in competition with other wealthy collectors. I expect to find that Kwok is in direct contact with the Clarendon Art Gallery or more secretly with whoever is running the operation," Duncan Mallory replied.

I remembered that I had promised to telephone Gaby after the auction and put in my call through the operator while Duncan lounged on the one comfortable chair. "Give her my love," he said raising his glass contentedly as she came on the line.

"Gaby, darling," I said. "I'm here with Duncan who sends his love and we are flushed with success. The painting is the original De Hooch and it will be back in Latimer in a week or so. You can ring Geoffrey Randle and give him the good tidings when you have a moment."

"Before you ask," Gaby broke in "there's big news here too. Alexander Deakin was taken in for questioning yesterday evening. I've just heard what happened from Georgina."

"As Duncan expected. Where is he now?" I asked.

"Back home at St. Winifred's. It was all very dramatic. When he was arrested, they allowed him to telephone his solicitor before taking him to Kidlington police station; he sprang into action and called the Vice Chancellor. The Vice Chancellor couldn't do much about it himself – he'd called in Scotland Yard in the first place – but he could pass it on to the Chancellor whom he caught in the bath at his London home. As luck would have it, the Chancellor was getting ready to attend a dinner at the Carlton Club where the Home

Secretary was guest speaker. The two of them had served together in the last Government; so it was easy to take him on one side at the pre-dinner reception. Within the hour the Commissioner had instructed Kidlington to release Alexander and he was returned by police car to his lodgings at the college."

"And who says that the Old Boy network doesn't operate anymore?" I commented and related the story to Mallory.

"Ask Gaby how Trevor Wiggins reacted," Duncan requested.

I relayed the question to her. "What did our chum Commander Wiggins do next aside from spitting feathers?"

"Georgina says that he was recalled to Scotland Yard and – this is the best bit – because he has got nowhere with his investigation the case has been handed back to Chief Inspector Cartwright."

"That certainly makes it easier for us to connect the murders to the attempted art fraud. Tomorrow, we hope to pin down who was involved in the chain of communications between the Gallery and the auction house here in Hong Kong. And that will give Duncan something useful to tell the Chief Inspector."

"We're looking forward to having you back. Fred misses you terribly. See you at the airport on Friday morning. Hugs and kisses," she said and rang off.

---oooOooo---

Canning Kwok strode through The Regent to the entrance lobby followed closely by his minder. He could barely conceal his anger. The auction of the De Hooch had been the pilot for a series of disposals of other paintings disguised as copies. If it had gone according to plan the next in line would have been the far more valuable Monet for which he already had a buyer in China pre-arranged through Tao Qi Wei. He was deprived now of a highly promising source of income and potentially at risk personally if the connection with his partners in the UK was unearthed.

His first reaction was to telephone his primary contact in Oxfordshire as soon as he reached his apartment but that would be foolish. An examination of his telephone records would reveal the call. A moment's reflection and he realised there was a risk anyway that the zealous British police inspector would call for copies of his records over recent months. It was unlikely that the Hong Kong police would do so on their own initiative, he reflected, since the case was hardly of much interest to them. His chauffeur-driven black Mercedes 500 was waiting for him on the forecourt; as he neared the car he reached a decision. Turning to the Mongolian behind him he gave his instructions.

"Zhang," he said "See to it that neither of the two Englishmen ever leaves this hotel."

---ooo0ooo---

CHAPTER 21

Hong Kong and Home, July 11 and 12

I HAD STARTED TO SHAVE the following morning when the maid delivered my full English breakfast on a trolley. She left the scrambled eggs and bacon in their covered dish and decanted fresh orange juice from a jug. "May I pour you a cup of coffee, sir?" she asked as I applied a razor to my well lathered face at the bathroom hand basin. "Please do, thank you," I replied and started to scrape. Looking in the mirror, I could see the white-overalled maid over my shoulder as she busied herself with the coffee pot. Then, unexpectedly. she took a small phial from a pocket and sprinkled the contents into the poured cup of coffee. I turned swiftly wiping the last of the shaving soap from my face and stepped back into the room.

"What's in that bottle?" I demanded. "Hand it over."

Instead, the maid dropped the glass tube on the trolley and, extracting a long-bladed dagger from the inside of her overall, advanced upon me. With only a towel around my waist the scope for action was limited. I grasped the edge of the trolley nearest to me and steered it hard at her driving her back towards the open door to the balcony. She tried to stab me across the trolley but couldn't touch me. I continued to propel her backwards and, as we reached the threshold, she stumbled on the lintel and lost her footing. I crashed the trolley into the maid's ankles and, as she fell back, the edge of the table surface cat her squarely in the chest knocking her across the balcony and off her feet. Unable to recover her balance, the back of her head connected with the balcony rail with stunning force and she sank unconscious to the ground. I picked up the dagger, flung it into space and took the phial off the trolley.

Reality hit me. I was safe but had Duncan Mallory suffered a similar attempt on his life? Shrugging on a towelling robe, I dashed from the room down the corridor to his door. Fortunately, there was a housemaid with a cleaning cart several doors before his; I enlisted her help to open up, It must have been my distraught cries of "Emergency" rather than my wild, barefoot appearance that persuaded her to apply her passkey promptly. We burst in and were confronted by the sight of Duncan slumped over the remains of his breakfast. There was a half-empty cup before him and a teapot with empty plates, a glass and a basket of fruit on the table. I tried to rouse him but to no avail. His mouth was slack and his head lolled forward uncontrollably when I pulled him up in his chair. With the housemaid's help I managed to lever him up and manoeuvre him on to the bed. There was no muscular reaction from his arms or legs and his breathing was faint; it was like handling a very heavy stuffed toy. I called for the hotel doctor and hotel security on the house 'phone and then telephoned Inspector Foung on an outside line. He promised to send a sergeant immediately and to come over himself as soon as he had interviewed Chen Yu Bo.

The hotel doctor was an elderly, precise man whom I judged to be past normal retirement age, but he seemed to know what he was doing. While he examined Mallory I explained the circumstances including my narrow escape and produced the contaminated phial. The doctor didn't attempt a diagnosis.

"This man's in a critical condition. His nervous system seems to have been disabled by some kind of toxin, He needs to be in intensive care as soon as possible. I will call for an ambulance and telephone the emergency team at the hospital to prepare." He made his calls and took the phial from me. "This I will deliver to the pathology lab myself to save time."

I stayed with Duncan Mallory until the ambulance paramedics arrived after less than twenty minutes and stretchered him away. His breath was now no more than whisper and they put a mask on him with a portable oxygen supply before moving him. I was joined by the hotel security manager and related details of the incident to him while I packed up Duncan's belongings. We moved back to my room. It was in much the same condition as I had left it with one difference: the only trace of my attacker was a bloodstain on the balcony rail where the back of her head had struck. The security manager left me to question room service staff and identify the intruder from those on duty at the time and I completed my own packing for checkout until Sergeant Li Peng arrived – the same sergeant who had attended the auction. He insisted that everything be left as it was on the balcony until a forensics team inspected the trolley for fingerprints and scrapings of dried blood from the rail.

Harry Foung arrived shortly after midday and went through my story again. His sergeant had already called in forensics who were diligently at work taking whatever evidence they could find including my fingerprints - "for the purposes of elimination, sir" I was assured. By now the security manager had established that the housemaid was not a regular employee of The Regent; she had been taken on the previous evening to replace another girl who had called in sick and had given an address on Nathan Road where she normally worked as a waitress. Foung recognized the address as one of Canning Kwok's nightclubs and sent Li Peng to find her home address and interview her there.

It was my turn to quiz the Inspector on his meeting with Chen Yu Bo, an encounter that I knew Duncan Mallory would regret missing. "He was well prepared, but nervous," Foung commented.

"Perhaps he'd not been interviewed by the police before." I ventured.

"No, quite the opposite. We had him and his partner in last year for auctioning as Ming a vase which turned out to be a fake. They were sued for damages but not prosecuted. This time they are probably in the clear," he said.

"He explained how they had acquired last night's painting as a lot in the auction. The first contact came from someone called Aubrey Pinkerton who telephoned from the UK. Apparently, Raymond Challoner had done business with him before; at first, he was reluctant to have anything to do with him again."

"What persuaded Challoner to change his mind?" I asked.

Foung consulted his notes. "A letter came requesting Challoner Chen to accept an unsigned 17th century Dutch interior painting for auction. It was on the letterhead of a Swiss company with an address in Geneva and signed in the name of Monica Lester, a director. It seemed genuine; so, he accepted the commission and passed it over to Chen to complete the arrangements. The painting was delivered by DHL in good time. Chen did wonder why it had been shipped from Amsterdam but didn't raise any question. By that time they had received instructions to pay the sale proceeds, after deducting commissions, into a numbered Swiss bank account. I have the account number here."

"That seems to add up," I said. "We already knew that the painting was collected by DHL from Van den Groot in Amsterdam. We also know that Monica Lister is the name on the passenger list of the woman who travelled there with Aubrey Pinkerton and drove the car in which he collected the Monet more recently. Duncan will be able to confirm when he recovers whether the bank account number is the same number given to Van den Groot to remit profits from his sale of copies over there."

"What we need to know now are the dates and telephone numbers of Canning Kwok's calls to and from the UK. I have put in the request, but it has to be sanctioned by our police commissioner before the telephone company will provide information from its records. It may take me up to a week before I can pass on the information," Foung replied apologetically.

"Do you think you can add to your request information on calls any there might have been between Challoner Cheng and the UK over the same period?" I asked. "We might be able to find out if Aubrey Pinkerton called from the Clarendon Gallery or some other number."

---oooOooo---

We called through to the Prince of Wales hospital where Duncan Mallory had been taken to inquire about his condition and were told that there was no news yet; no bulletin was likely before mid-afternoon. Sergeant Li returned and reported that he had tracked down the maid. She had been found with her throat cut in an alleyway outside the tenement building where she had lived. The Inspector asked me to identify the corpse before it was transferred to the morgue and we set out through the maze of narrow lanes at the back of the Nathan Road, an area of Kowloon seldom visited by tourists. She was lying on her back, a pathetic limp figure; her face held an expression of surprise. She was certainly the intruder who had assaulted me at the hotel, although she seemed older now than I remembered. The contusion on the back of her head was proof of identity. Sergeant Li had already summoned the morgue and waited with the body until the ambulance arrived while Foung and I retraced our steps to the main thoroughfare.

"Shall you interview Canning Kwok?" I asked.

"I tried to reach him before leaving the police station but he had taken the early flight to Shanghai and his office says that he would not be returning for at least a week," the Inspector replied.

"By then the telephone records may reveal a connection with the people involved in the fraud in Oxford which will give us a firmer base for questioning him," Harry Foung agreed.

We decided to visit the hospital in person to find out how Duncan Mallory was faring. Arriving by police car which remained at the front entrance in a clearly marked No Parking space, we entered and were directed to the intensive care unit on the second floor. The nurse in reception tried to fob us off with a sister who adamantly denied us any update on the last bulletin or detail on Mallory's condition. Harry Foung was having nothing of it and insisted on speaking to the doctor in charge. In the face of his Inspector's uniform the sister's resolution wilted and a senior physician, a grizzled Briton with a dour manner, was summoned. His report was bleak and comfortless.

"Your colleague was poisoned with botulism toxin. If it had been injected intravenously he would have died before admission to the hospital. We are pumping him with as much anti-toxin as he can take and he is in an oxygen tent, but he may not survive."

"When shall you know, Doctor," I asked him.

"If he is still with us in 24 hours' time, there is a fair chance of recovery. Fortunately, his heart is strong and he is a relatively fit man, but the full recovery of his nervous system will take time. You may call me tomorrow evening when I shall be on duty again," he replied offering a glimmer of hope.

Dr. Gavin Fairchild, FRCP I read on the card which he gave us. At least, Duncan is in well-qualified hands. With nothing further to be done in Hong Kong, I let Harry Foung drop me back at The Regent where we said our goodbyes agreeing to keep in touch.

"You may rely on me to look after our friend when he comes out of hospital. I won't let him fly back until he is quite fit," Harry reassured me. I shook his hand warmly.

---oooOooo---

It was good to be home. Gaby had met me at Terminal 4 with a warm embrace when I came out of baggage claim. I had taken time to call her briefly from the Club lounge at Kai Tak where I had indulged in several free whiskies before boarding. The line had been bad and she plainly had not understood what I had tried to say. Her first words now were: "What news of Duncan?"

On the journey back to Fullmere with Gaby driving I brought her up to date. Her conclusions echoed mine.

"So, we've established now that the Clarendon Gallery and Aubrey Pinkerton were both involved in the attempt to auction off the Latimer College De Hooch as an unsigned canvas. It seems likely, doesn't it, that the mysterious Monica Lister who made the arrangements and accompanied Aubrey to Amsterdam to collect the Monet was Theodora Deakin?" she asked.

"Yes, but we don't know why she fell out with Pinkerton resulting in her death," I commented.

"Nor whether there is someone else involved, a sleeping partner who participated in the murder," Gaby countered.

I had slept some of the flight back but needed a few hours' sleep before grappling with the problem further. Gaby had been up early herself. After an ecstatic welcome from Fred, we retired to bed with Fred at the foot and stayed there for the rest of the morning. We were woken by the insistent ring of the telephone which Gaby answered.

"Yes, he's back. I'll hand you over to him, Chief Inspector," she said passing the receiver to me.

"Mr. Radclive, Cartwright here. I've just heard from the Fraud Squad; I understand that Duncan Mallory is in hospital in Hong Kong and that you were with him much of the time. We need all the help we can get on the Deakin murder case and I think you may be able to help me. What happened in Hong Kong?"

"Certainly, Chief Inspector. First, the good news. The mission was a success. The painting auctioned was revealed as the original belonging to Latimer College and we established the connection with Aubrey Pinkerton and the Clarendon Art Gallery. The bad news, which you already know, is that Duncan Mallory was poisoned at the hotel in an attempt on both our lives. I was lucky to escape myself, but Duncan is going to be in hospital for several days with the effects of botulism toxin - if they succeed in saving him. We think that the attempted fraud was a dry run for the much more valuable Monet painting from St. Winifred's also sent to the Gallery for cleaning."

"Does that mean there is a definite link between the art frauds and the murder of Theodora Deakin?"

"It's difficult to conclude otherwise or that Mrs. Deakin was not involved in the scam, but I can't offer you firm proof."

"That's good enough to be going on with. I shall have to question Mr. Deakin myself at St. Winifred's this time. It's highly irregular but I wonder of you would accompany me. Someone has to tell him about the College's painting and it would be better to give him a first-hand account coming from you. Can I arrange a meeting with him for tomorrow morning?" the Chief Inspector suggested.

I had some reservations about getting further involved in the murder investigation but agreed to take part as a friend of Alexander Deakin. My immediate concern was Duncan Mallory's condition and I decided that Harry Foung would have gleaned more information than I could from the hospital. He was still at his desk and had spoken to Dr.

Fairchild within the last two hours. His news was that Mallory was still hanging on but that they had reached the limit of anti-toxin that his body could tolerate. If he could hang on for another twenty-four hours, the doctor thought he might make it.

---ooo0ooo---

CHAPTER 22

July 13, Oxfordshire

ONE OF OXFORD'S NEWER COLLEGES, St. Winifred's was built in the 1920's as an exclusively female college and did not open its doors to male students until the 1980's. Unlike the traditional pre-nineteenth century colleges, it is constructed in the shape of a double 'E' rather than to the traditional two quad design. It is also built mainly of brick with only the chapel at the back at the rear end of one leg and the Master's lodgings forming the shorter central leg faced in mellow Cotswold stone. St.Winifred's is located between the Banbury Road and the Parks. Visitors can park their cars at the rear of the College approached from Norham Gardens.

I had left the Range Rover at Kidlington and travelled into Oxford with Chief Inspector Bernard Cartwright. He had decided to keep the forthcoming meeting as informal as possible. To that end he had left his sergeant back at the police station and was driving himself. My attendance is intended to reassure. The College porter checked with his appointment book, telephoned the Master to inform him of our arrival and showed us through to his lodgings. Alexander Deakin greeted us at the door of the fine high-ceilinged first floor room which served as his study. Wide open casement windows give on to an immaculately mown lawn. He waved us to comfortable chairs and sofa in front of the marble mantelpiece and empty grate.

"Shall I need to ask my solicitor to join us?" were his opening words.

"No, Professor Deakin. We're here this morning to discuss a possible motive for your wife's murder connected to a planned art fraud involving the Clarendon Gallery. Mr. Radclive has been helping Scotland Yard Fraud Squad with their investigation," the Chief Inspector explained.

Alexander looked more interested than surprised. "I felt sure that it had something to do with the Gallery. But how have you become involved in this, Julian?" he asked.

I look at Alexander carefully before replying. In the three weeks since the night of the concert his face has become gaunt with deep lines etched into his cheeks. He used to project a youthful air; now he is showing his age.

"The Fraud Squad inspector is an old friend. He consulted me about Oxford and the colleges in particular. His investigation was sparked by the catalogue for an auction abroad brought to his attention which included an unsigned 17th century Dutch painting. It appeared to match an original De Hooch which is the property of Latimer College. When he visited Latimer he found out that their painting had been sent away for cleaning through the Clarendon Gallery. It had recently been returned when the Inspector interviewed the Bursar. I helped him to arrange for an appraisal by the resident expert at the Ashmolean. In his opinion the canvas now hanging in the Senior Common Room was a copy," I told him.

"And I suppose you've found out that Theodora took our Monet away for cleaning. We're still waiting for it to be returned although I asked Theodora several times for it to be brought back."

"The Gallery records show that paintings from four Colleges were sent away to be cleaned. The first two returned by the Gallery were originals. The Latimer De Hooch was the third and your Monet the most recent. We know that the De Hooch was sent direct to the auction house in Hong Kong from the copyist in Amsterdam, on Gallery instructions, after painting over the signature. I was at the auction on Wednesday when it was knocked down for a fraction of its real price. It was impounded afterwards by the police and confirmed as the original. The plan was to sell it on as a genuine De Hooch and we believe that this was the pilot exercise for a similar disposal of your Monet as the next in line."

"What part in all this did Theodora play? Could she have been unaware of what was going on?" Alexander questioned.

"That's not very plausible," Cartwright broke in. "The Amsterdam police took a statement from the owner of the studio where the paintings were cleaned and copied who is a well-known copyist himself. The arrangements with the Gallery which allow him to sell unsigned copies of the paintings locally were set up personally with Mrs. Deakin."

Alexander rose from the wingchair where he had been sitting and walked to the open window. Butterflies fluttered in the sunshine on the dark purple flowers of a buddleia which climbed up to the sill. He gazed wistfully over the garden before turning back to us.

"I don't doubt that she made the arrangements originally for cleaning as managing director of the Gallery but that doesn't mean she was involved in the planned fraud. That sounds more like the rogue Pinkerton who was always hanging around the Gallery. I don't know why she insisted on consulting him," he replied.

"I'm afraid that there's more to it than that, Professor," the Chief Inspector continued. "You're correct that Aubrey Pinkerton is a prime mover in this matter. Indeed, the whole concept of the fraud may have been his and we do know that he personally collected your Monet from the Amsterdam studio in his car last month. However, he was accompanied by a woman travelling under an assumed name who took a night ferry to Rotterdam with him and drove the car. We think that this woman may have been your wife."

"That's preposterous, Chief Inspector. Theodora never stays away except when she visits her aunt in Devon occasionally and stays overnight."

"In that case perhaps we can establish whether she was there on the night of the eleventh last month."

Alexander consulted the appointments diary on his desk. "I can see that I was in London that evening for a dinner and stayed overnight at my Club. I can recall now that she did drive to Budleigh Salterton that morning and did not return until after me the following day. While you're both here I'll telephone her aunt to confirm." He picked up the telephone and dialled an eleven digit number. We could hear the bell at the other end ringing repeatedly before the receiver was picked up but only his side of the conversation that followed.

"Nora, it's Alexander, I hope I haven't taken you away from anything important ...... you were in the greenhouse watering ..... yes, I'm managing alright here – everyone's being very kind ..... David and Kate have been in touch and they're both coming to the Memorial Service next week. I hope you'll be coming too ..... that's splendid ..... yes, of course, I can put you up in College. Nora, the reason why I'm calling you is that the police are trying to establish all Theodora's movements on the week or so before she was killed - did she visit you last month? ..... Tuesday 11th June and stayed with you until the following morning, That's fine. Look forward to seeing you next week ..... I'll meet you at the station if you tell me the train you are taking."

Deakin turned to us triumphantly. "That proves conclusively that Theodora played no part in collecting the Monet in Amsterdam and it gives you a motive for her murder. She found out what had happened, wanted to return the original to St. Winifred's and was murdered to shut her up," he declared. That wasn't my conclusion but I didn't want to contest it. I was spared comment by the Chief Inspector.

"That certainly suggests a motive, Professor Deakin, and I shall take it as a working hypothesis" he said with a twitch of his military moustache and rose to his feet.

"That takes us as for as we can go for now, I think. I shall probably have to trouble you again, but thank you for your help this morning," he concluded walking towards the door. "Oh, one more question. If a signed copy of your painting had been returned, how long do you think it would have been before it was detected as a fake?"

"No more than a few weeks. We are having all the College's movable assets revalued for insurance purposes and the fine art valuer will be coming next week," Alexander replied. "I explained to Theodora that was why we needed the Monet back as soon as possible and, of course, I'm worried now that it has still not been returned. Do you know where it is?"

"We know that Aubrey Pinkerton collected it from the studio in Amsterdam on 12th June, but nothing more yet. So far, it hasn't turned up at the auction house in Hong Kong; it may be with him here in the UK. The police are working on it but there is no news yet," I told him.

As I prepared to follow Cartwright, he called after me. "You will come to the Memorial Service on Tuesday, won't you Julian?"

"Of course, Alexander. Gaby and I will both be there," I assured him.

---oooOooo---

"What do you make of that?" the Chief Inspector asked turning a gloomy face towards me as he drove us back to Kidlington.

"I find it difficult to believe that Theodora Deakin was not involved in the scam from the start. It seems more likely that she and Pinkerton planned it together, but I think someone else must have been involved in setting up the disposal plan in Hong Kong through Canning Kwok," I replied.

"I agree with you. There's also the question of the real identity of the woman who travelled to Amsterdam with Pinkerton and drove his car. Whoever it may have been she was a collaborator but not necessarily a partner in the enterprise. In that role, Valerie Wyngarde as an associate is a candidate."

"Will you bring Pinkerton in for questioning again?" I asked.

"I shall have to find out where he has taken the Monet, but next time I arrest him I want to charge him for murder at the same time and I don't have enough evidence for that yet. No, my next step is to interview Miss Wyngarde this afternoon. If she admits to the Amsterdam trip, she may have insight on any agitating by Mrs. Deakin for return of the painting. After that, I shall have to do Inspector Mallory's job for him and find out where Pinkerton has taken the Monet," Cartwright answered.

"She couldn't have participated in the killing herself because she wasn't at the concert," I remarked.

"Quite so. Either way, we have to discover now who else might be Pinkerton's partner in the whole enterprise. I may have to consider Commander Wiggins' suspicion that Georgina Delahaye is behind him."

If it was the Chief Inspector's intention to provoke a reaction from me, I wasn't playing. We travelled the rest of the way to Kidlington in silence.

---oooOooo---

It had started to drizzle as I left Kidlington and the rain had turned into a downpour by the time I reached home. I found Gaby in the kitchen struggling with a cryptic crossword, made myself a toasted cheese sandwich and retired to the study to read the opening chapters of Percy Mansfield's book which he had delivered during the morning. I was pleasantly surprised. He wrote fluently without any of the pomposity I had expected; his accounts of discussions with representatives of the Chinese government were both lucid and detailed with touches of insight. They were highly readable. The difficulty arose with his observations on the Governor's attitudes towards the mainland and conversations with him. Here, his comments were not only critical but personal and descended sometimes into the libellous: attention grabbing for sure but likely to attract the lawyers' red pencil when referred to them. I made my own notes and copied the complete manuscript to be mailed to Robert Schindler on Monday. I did not relish discussion with the author after the weekend.

Saturday afternoon was an unlikely time to reach Harry Foung in his Hong Kong office: so, I telephoned the Prince of Wales hospital direct for news about the Digger. Dr. Fairchild was not there but he had left a bulletin on Ward Reception for those enquiring after his patient from the UK. "Douglas Mallory remains in intensive care. He is, however no longer on the critical list," it said. That was reassuring but it was clear that Duncan would not be back to support Detective Inspector Cartwright soon. I wondered if I would be called upon for more assistance in his place.

By early evening the rain had eased off. Fred, who had been gazing mournfully at the weather from his vantage point on the kitchen window seat decided that he had been patient long enough and started to agitate for a walk. His whingeing and wagging tail became irresistible; Gaby and I clothed ourselves in boots and mackintoshes and set forth up the garden and into the field. For the second time in a month the water meadow was flooded and the stream had overflowed its banks. As before, Fred galloped joyfully down the field and dashed into the water. But this time his behaviour differed. There was something in the middle of the stream, a dark bundle, caught up in the roots of a willow, which seemed to distress him. He barked loudly, splashed around the bundle and ran back towards us, agitating for us to join in his investigation. Leaving Gaby in the shallows, I waded into the stream and, pulling Fred's discovery free, towed it back towards her. The bundle was heavier and bigger than I had first thought and it took both our efforts with Fred tugging at loose corners to land it on dry ground.

It soon became all too clear that we were handling a human corpse in a full suit of sodden clothes. I turned the body on its back. Looking up at us was the blank face of Aubrey Pinkerton.

---ooo0ooo---

CHAPTER 23

July 13 to 20, Fullmere

THE POLICE SURGEON PULLED OFF her latex gloves and stepped back from the body.

"No doubt about cause of death here," she said.

Chief-Inspector Cartwright, Sergeant Fellows and I were grouped behind her with the scene of crime team, also in protective clothing, standing by ready to remove the corpse when instructed. The area of the stream and bank around where Fred had made his discovery were already cordoned off with police tape. In the past hour, since calling the police, the rain had eased off and a watery evening sun had poked through the grey sky. Dr. Celia Armitage, rosy-cheeked and in her mid-fifties, pushed back a lock of unruly grey hair from her forehead and pointed at the gaping wound in Aubrey Pinkerton's chest.

"Typical shotgun death at nearly point blank range. Death almost instantaneous. But he probably wasn't killed here," she pronounced.

"Do you mean he was shot elsewhere and the body was dumped here later?" Cartwright asked. "What is your first estimate for of time of death, Doctor?"

"You know better than to ask me that, Chief Inspector. I don't make guesses. I'll give you a firm estimate when I have him back in the lab. and have completed my post mortem. As to where he was killed, I believe the body may have floated downstream this afternoon. In which case he was probably shot on a neighbouring property upstream and dumped in the water there."

For a non-guesser this sounded more like supposition than deduction, and the Chief Inspector chose not to take Dr. Armitage up on it. Instead, he enquired at what time she would hold the post-mortem the following morning and insisted politely that he would be present at the appointed hour. He walked with me up the hill with Sergeant Fellows in attendance back to the house where he had left his car.

"This would seem to confirm that there is someone else involved as a principal in the fraud," I suggested.

"But Aubrey Pinkerton's killing also removes our No, 1 suspect for the murder of Mrs. Deakin," Cartwright replied mournfully.

"How did you get on with Valerie Wyngarde. Did she admit to being Pinkerton's companion?"

"Far from it. Miss Wyngarde has a firm alibi for the night of 11th June. She was at her weekly Tai Chi class in Walton Street from 7:00 p.m. until 9:00 p.m. and then in the pub on Gloucester Green with her friends until closing time."

"What's the next step?" I asked knowing full well that the Chief-Inspector was under no obligation to involve me further in his investigations.

"I shall focus on this killing while keeping any eye on the two previous murders," he replied; then turning to Sergeant Fellows "I want you to check on the movements in the last 24 hours of all those present at the concert on 21st June from whom we took statements. In particular, we need to identify who owns shotguns and could have been in the fields between here and Fullmere Mill."

"By definition that includes Gaby and myself," I said.

"Yes. You can start here, Nigel, with Mr. and Mrs. Radclive," Cartwright acknowledged without any hint of humour.

---oooOooo---

On Sunday Barry Fullerton gave a lunch to celebrate Piroska Szabó's safe return from her American tour. The party consisted of Georgina and Giles Delahaye, Gaby and me, Barry and Emma Fullerton and Piroska herself as guest of honour. The good weather had returned overnight and we ate alfresco in a private section of the Eastwick Arms garden with a high yew hedge between us and the main area, blocking the view of lunchtime customers. We were welcomed with glasses of chilled Cremant de Jura and smoked salmon canapês. Not surprisingly, even before we sat down, the first topic of conversation was the Aubrey Pinkerton shooting. Gaby and I gave a colourful description of Fred's discovery, which Giles thought was beyond a Labrador retriever's normal call of duty, and a more sober account of the police action and Dr. Armitage's on the spot conclusions. Georgina said that she had noticed Chief Inspector Cartwright's police car outside the cottage and thought that he must have received notice of my call while he was still there. That explained why he and Sergeant Fellows had arrived so promptly upon the scene. All of us had received visits from the Sergeant last night or this morning. None of us had been able to give complete alibis when questioned except for Emma and Giles who had been in each other's company day and night throughout the period. Everyone admitted to having access to a shotgun. No-one expressed much sympathy for Aubrey Pinkerton.

Our first course for lunch was asparagus from the local farm shop served warm with melted butter and a light white wine from the Medoc. Remembering the reason why we had been invited, we congratulated Piroska on the success of her tour and Gaby asked her which of the concerts she had enjoyed most, which had been the best audiences and in which newspapers she had received the best reviews.

"Nincs verseny," she announced. "Philadelphia is my favourite city in America and they were very nice. In Dallas and Los Angeles zey were wun-duhrfuhl. Boston was schrecklich. The people are so hidegrerú - so cold-blooded. As for the newspapers, the *Baltimore Sun* was ihn-creh-du-buhl and the *New York Times* is something for my agent's albumot."

Some of this was almost incomprehensible but the general meaning was clear; the tour had been a triumph. Seated here in Barry's garden she was basking in the experience with no sign of fatigue although she was barely forty-eight hours home. Barry was watching over her with almost proprietorial pleasure while Emma and Giles cleared away our plates and served the next course. Her accompanist Werner had also enjoyed a successful tour, not just reflected glory in her shadow but in his own right. In San Francisco he had been approached by a cellist of international standing to join a chamber music quintet planning to tour Europe the following year and in Chicago a prestigious conservatory invited him to lecture and deliver a course of tuition on the art of piano accompaniment. These assignments were not only career-building but also extremely well-paid by British standards. I asked Petroska to pass on to him our best wishes.

Our main course was cold salmon with baby new potatoes and petit pois. The mayonnaise had been prepared by Barry himself together with garlic French dressing for the tossed green salad to which we helped ourselves. The vintage Meursault which he served with the salmon was another gourmet treat. Barry had certainly pushed the boat out. By the time we reached the summer pudding as dessert and the cheeseboard that followed all his guests were mellow and enjoying each other's company. We were offered a Sauvignon Blanc to drink with the cheese; both Gaby and I preferred to stay with the Meursault. It was especially good with the Reblochon,

The conversation never flagged. Georgina asked me how I had enjoyed my brief trip to Hong Kong. I gave a light-hearted account of my meetings with contributors to the new China book and then explained how I had come to attend the auction. I hadn't intended at first to tell them about the attempt to pass off Latimer College's De Hooch as an unattributed painting but, having started, was encouraged to continue. Gaby kicked me under the table; so I restricted myself to telling them how the original had been passed through the Clarendon Gallery for cleaning in Amsterdam and had been sent to Hong Kong after the artist's signature had been painted over. I was careful not to tell them about the attempt on my and Duncan Mallory's lives. Barry Fullerton was the first to question me.

"Was Aubrey Pinkerton involved in the scam?" he asked "I know that he helped out at the Gallery."

"Definitely. At the least he collected paintings for cleaning from the Colleges and returned the fake to Latimer."

"You say Colleges. How many others entrusted their artworks to the Gallery?" It was Emma's turn to pursue her father's line of questioning.

"Three others so far. Two of them have received their original pictures back in good condition; the third is still waiting," I answered anticipating the next question.

"How long do you think that will be?" Giles Delahaye this time.

"I haven't the faintest idea. The police are working on it." My reply was truthful, so far as it went. I felt that Georgina had more to say but was keeping it to herself. Could she have been the mystery woman in the Volvo with Pinkerton when he collected the Monet, I wondered?

"I suppose Mrs. Deakin must have known what was going on, and that is why she was killed," Piroska observed thoughtfully.

"That seems to be the theory the police are working on. Pinkerton was their leading suspect but I suppose they'll be looking for someone else now."

"To think that all this could happen in North Oxfordshire. When we moved here we thought that we would be entering a world of rural calm, not exchanging London life for mayhem and murder," Gaby sighed with mock regret.

"How did you find Aubrey as a tenant, Georgina?" Barry asked as he poured her coffee.

"No problem. He paid a reduced rent and looked after the property during the week. I only saw him at the weekends. Sometimes, he drank too much and he tried to make advances once until a knee in the nuts showed him I was off limits."

"You knew him better than most, didn't you Barry?" I asked.

"As a customer, yes. He could be good company and quite entertaining, but there was always a hint in the background of dodginess. It doesn't surprise me that he was up to no good with the Gallery."

"Aubrey Pinkerton was a creep," said Emma forcefully. Remembering her experience of him at the concert, no-one disagreed. "Still you knocked him down here in the car park, Julian, the other week," she added.

"That doesn't count." I replied. "When you're my age and don't have your Dad's skills, you forget about Marquess of Queensberry rules and beat a retreat as best you can."

---ooo0ooo---

It was almost 3:30 p.m. when the lunch party broke up and we drove the short distance home. "You almost said too much," Gaby admonished me.

"I know but I wanted to test reactions, particularly from Georgina. Chief Inspector Cartwright as his mind set on her as Aubrey Pinkerton's partner in the planned fraud."

"What do you think, Julian."

"I hate to think so because I like her but we have to admit of the possibility," I said.

It was time for Fred's afternoon walkabout; so we took him into the top of the field again with a tennis racquet and balls where he demonstrated his catching ability. He showed little interest in running downhill into the water meadow or stream where we could see that the police cordon was still in place.

When we returned to the house there was a message on the answerphone. Georgina had telephoned us. I called her back.

"There's something more I should have mentioned about Aubrey at lunch, Julian, but I thought you might prefer to hear it without raising general speculation," she announced.

"I had the feeling you might be holding something back. Time now to spill the beans," I replied.

"The weekend before the concert last month, I got down here from London early evening Friday and found him waiting for me. He said he had come into something really valuable and asked me if I would store a package for him for a few weeks. I guessed that he was probably receiving stolen goods and turned him down."

"How did he react. Did he try to persuade you?"

"He wasn't best pleased and made a fuss at first, but he took it rather better than I had expected. He said that there was somewhere else not too far away where he could place it safely."

"You need to tell Chief Inspector Cartwright when you see him," I told her.

"How did you know that he wants to talk to me? I've only just had a call from Sergeant Fellows asking me to stay here tomorrow until Cartwright visits me mid-morning," she asked sharply.

"I was with him yesterday at St. Winifred's when he interviewed Alexander. He wanted to explore how deeply Theodora had been involved in the planned art scam. You see, three days before Pinkerton asked you to store a package for him he had collected the Monet original from the studio in Amsterdam where it was being cleaned and copied. He was accompanied him a by a mystery woman who travelled with him on the night ferry to Rotterdam and drove the Volvo for him the following morning when he went for the painting. Cartwright established that Pinkerton's travel companion couldn't have been Theodora because she stayed overnight with her aunt in Devon. Therefore, you became a suspect."

"Do I need to have a lawyer with me when the Chief Inspector interviews me tomorrow?"

"Not if you can satisfy him that you slept here or in your London flat on the night of 11th June."

Georgina breathed a sigh of relief. "In that case, I guess I'm in the clear. I was at a reception in the Egyptian embassy all evening until about `10.00 p.m. when it broke up. I was there throughout supervising the girls we supplied as escorts," she declared.

"Sounds like an alibi to me," I said.

We rang off and I related to Gaby what Georgina had said about the approach she had received from Aubrey to store his package and her refusal.

"What's your take on her tale?" I asked.

"Just the sort of cover story she would come up with if she's involved in the theft of the Monet."

"But she couldn't have been Aubrey's companion on the night ferry to Rotterdam, if her alibi holds," I remonstrated.

"Who's the say the woman on the ferry with him and the driver of the Volvo were the same person? Georgina could have taken an early flight to Amsterdam the following morning and met up with him there," she countered.

Gaby had a point – an unlikely one but not impossible.

---ooo0ooo---

CHAPTER 24

July 23, Oxford

MEMORIAL SERVICES BEAT FUNERALS every time as social occasions. On Tuesday afternoon just before 2:00 p.m. we were seated in the chapel at St. Winifred's. It was as well that we had arrived twenty minutes early since the chapel was full. The left-hand side front row was occupied by Alexander Deakin with an elderly lady in a black straw hat on his right, no doubt Aunt Nora, and to his left a family of husband and wife with grown-up son and teenage daughter, also relatives presumably of Theodora. In the two rows behind Alexander were members of his Senior Common Room in academic dress, several of whom I recognized. Amidst them, were Georgina and Giles Delahaye trying not to look incongruous. Gaby and I had found places on the other side of the aisle, also three rows back. Ahead of us in the front row we identified the Vice-Chancellor and, next to him, Geoffrey Randle, unmistakable with his mane of white hair and actor's profile. To his right, showing their respect, were the Masters of Curzon and Hereford Colleges with several of their colleagues. In the second row, within touching distance, were Valerie Wyngarde and Christina Charteris. Valerie seemed unkempt. Her hair was lank and dishevelled; in half profile, it was apparent that she had been crying: her eyes red and swollen and cheeks tear-stained. In contrast, Christina wore her elegant black coat and skirt with confidence; perhaps rather too much makeup and definitely too much of the Gallery's jewellery. Part-time staff from the Clarendon Gallery were ranged alongside them and, in our row, were several senior editors from the Oxford University Press on nodding acquaintance with me. Looking further back before the Service started I could see Charlie Dibbs representing the Oxford Press and, at the rear, Chief Inspector Cartwright and Sergeant Fellows casting an eye over the congregation.

The Service was conducted by the College chaplain with commendable speed and despatch. The first lesson was read by the Vice-Chancellor and the second by the young man in the Deakin family front row. Eulogies were given by one of the better known artists who was a regular exhibitor at the Gallery and by Alexander himself. His address was simple and dignified: fond memories of Theodora as a wife, her love of the Arts and the enthusiasm she had brought in her support of him as Master of St. Winifred's in all aspects of College life. The congregation sang the psalm and hymns lustily. We "lifted our eyes unto the hills", "fought the good fight" and asserted that "no discouragement would make us once relent our first avowed intent." More surprisingly, we also sang our support "for those in peril on the sea," an oblique reference, I supposed, to Theodora's death in the lake at Fullmere Mill.

The congregation stood, allowing the front rows to walk out at the end of the Service, before dispersing. It occurred to me that all those attending, except for Theodora's relatives, were there to support Alexander rather than honour the deceased and I reflected that it was unusual to hold a Memorial Service so soon, barely one month after death compared with the normal three to six months. I shared my thoughts with Gaby as we strolled across to Hall behind Valerie and Christina to join in the reception laid on by the College.

"Don't forget that there was a very private cremation shortly after the body was released by the police. With the story of Theodora's involvement in the Clarendon Gallery scam sure to hit the headlines soon, I expect that Alexander wants to head off the publicity as much as possible for the sake of the College and today offers some kind of closure," Gaby reasoned.

"Quite so," I agreed "and there's another consideration. If Alexander and Georgina have revived their relationship, today will make it easier for them to open up sooner rather than later."

Gaby cast me one of her old-fashioned looks and we mounted the steps into Hall. There was no formal line-up at the entrance. Instead of greeting everyone at the door, Alexander had elected to take up a position at the far end of the chamber by the High Table. Attendees could approach him individually as they wished during the course of the reception. Tea was being served at the Buttery on arrival and a selection of sandwiches, cakes and other edibles was laid out on tables in the centre of the room. We accepted our cups and saucers and decided to wander slowly toward Alexander until the knot of well-wishers around him had thinned. Christina had taken an immediate beeline towards Geoffrey Randle who was already a centre of attention from a cluster of middle-aged female dons drawn as moths to the flame.

Valerie turned towards us; she seemed anxious to speak.

"What a tragedy. He was such a lovely man. Always ready to help deliver and collect exhibits for the Gallery. He was so kind and reliable. Do you think the same person killed them both?"

Her recollections hardly matched mine of the man whom I had encountered in the car park of the Eastwick Arms but I realised she must be referring to Aubrey Pinkerton. I didn't know quite how to respond but Gaby came to my rescue.

"It's too much of a coincidence if it was anyone else, but we didn't know Aubrey as you and Theodora did," she said.

"He was very close to Theodora, you know," Valerie continued. "She relied on him completely in choosing the prints and new paintings which the Gallery exhibits. He was with her there two days before her death but I couldn't really understand what they were saying to each other."

"Tell us what you heard," I urged her.

"I was in the showroom serving a customer and they were downstairs with their voices raised, almost arguing. When the customer left I tried to listen in from the reception desk at the head of the stairs. Theodora was saying '...... so you see, Aubrey, you have to get it back for me by the beginning of next week.' Then he said 'That won't be as easy as you think. They're only interested in the payoff.' And she replied 'If you won't do it I'll have to talk to them myself.' After that, they heard me moving about upstairs and stopped talking. And Aubrey stormed out of the Gallery. What do you think they were talking about?" Valerie questioned.

"Almost certainly the St. Winifred's Monet which is still missing. Did you tell this to the Chief Inspector when he spoke to you last Saturday?"

"No. He only seemed interested in my whereabouts on the evening of June 11th."

"In that case you should tell him as soon as possible," I cautioned her. "He's over there on the other side of Hall."

Looking doubtful she set off across the room, leaving Gaby and me to start working our way in Alexander's direction. We reached the first of the tables bearing food and helped ourselves to precision cut cucumber sandwiches. We were joined by Geoffrey Randle who had escaped from Christina's clutches and the covern of dons who now descended like a swarm of locusts on plates of lobster vols au vent.

"Someone save me from that ghastly woman," he cried. "Why is it that she hounds me at every University social function that I attend?" He wolfed one smoked salmon sandwich and reached for another.

"That's simple. She's looking for a new husband and you're at the top of her list of eligible bachelors. A rather glamorous head of house at one of Oxford's oldest colleges would be quite a catch," Gaby explained.

Geoffrey was mollified and looked complacent. "In that case, the sooner she realises that I'm immune to her charms the better," he declared and changed the subject. "I must thank you, Julian, for your part in recovering our De Hooch. There was a call from Federal Express yesterday to tell us that they would be delivering by the end of the week."

"You should expect no less from any Latimer alumnus," I told him with false modesty.

We continued our advance towards Alexander who was now in conversation with the Master of Curzon. There was no longer a queue waiting to approach him. Georgina appeared at our side carrying cups of tea for the two of them. As always at social occasions with well-dressed women, she and Gaby appraised each other critically before relaxing. Today, Georgina was dressed in a timeless Chanel suit and Gaby in Armani; they both wore pearls but little other jewellery. I judged the contest a draw.

"How did you get on with Chief Inspector Cartwright yesterday?" I asked, foregoing any pleasantries.

"He's a pussycat – full of old-world courtesy. He sent his sergeant off to check my movements with the Egyptian embassy. But I think he's reluctant to take me out of the frame," she said.

"Pussycat's like to catch mice and in this case there aren't too many mice around."

"How's Alexander doing? Today, must be a strain for him," Gaby asked sympathetically.

"You'll see for yourself in a moment. I guess the worst is over for him now," Georgina responded.

And so it seemed. Alexander Deakin had lost weight in the month since we had seen him at the concert but, as I had noted when visiting him three days before, there was no loss of energy and today he was more relaxed and less withdrawn. Gaby kissed him on the cheek.

"This must have been awful for you, Alexander," she empathised. "I know that grieving is a lengthy process but I hope you will feel able to move on again soon. Come out to us soon for Sunday lunch or a dinner if you prefer with one or two of the people you know."

"I'd like that, Gaby. I'm almost ready to start seeing people again. Georgina's been trying to look after me, but that's about the only company I've had except for colleagues here at St. Winifred's." He accepted the cup of tea she had brought him and slurped gratefully.

"I'll feel better when you've managed to find our Monet. Geoffrey's told me what you did in recovering the Latimer De Hooch. I'd like to be able to put the whole of this Gallery business behind me and sell off Theodora's shareholding."

"I think we can be certain that the Monet is back in England," I assured him "and I'm pretty sure that it's being held somewhere locally in Oxfordshire. If I'm right, it should be back at St. Winifred's soon."

"If there's anything you think I can do to help, just ask. Chief Inspector Cartwright seems a decent chap but I'd rather work with you to solve any problems."

One of the OUP editors was waiting to speak to Alexander; so we left them and started to make our way back towards the entrance. The Chief Inspector caught up with us as we neared the Buttery.

"Thank you for directing Miss Wyngarde to me. The conversation which she overheard suggests that the missing painting is around and about and that Pinkerton may have had a local accomplice," Cartwright said.

"I'd place bets on it, but one thing puzzles me," I replied. "From the tone of the eavesdropped conversation, it sounds like more than one person involved and someone giving him instructions."

"Any ideas how we might identify the 'him' or 'them' involved?"

"It's about time that the Hong Kong police come up with some telephone numbers that Canning Kwok was calling in the UK long before the De Hooch auction. That could point us in the right direction," I answered.

I added that Duncan Mallory had been discharged by the hospital as scheduled and that I hoped to speak to him the next day.

We were out of Hall and walking back to the car when a voice hailed us from behind. Charlie Dibbs was struggling to catch up.

"Mr. Radclive, hold on. I want to ask you about the forged painting that was returned to Latimer College by the Clarendon Gallery," he called out. I turned to face him.

"Where on earth did you get that story from, Charlie?" I asked.

"From the horse's mouth – or rather a little bird in the Bursar's office."

"Why don't you ask the Master. Geoffrey Randles's back there inside."

"I already have. He says that you recovered the original for them and know more about it than he does. It's connected to the killing of Mrs. Deakin too, isn't it?" he queried.

How typical of Geoffrey, I thought. Always delegate the difficult ones if you can. I was going to have to say something to Dibbs now to shut him up.

"I'll do another deal with you, Charlie," I said. "Yes, there's a much bigger story, but I don't know all of it yet and I can't talk until the police investigation reaches a conclusion. If you'll hold off now, I'll give you an exclusive on the full inside story as soon as they make an arrest."

"And nothing to the nationals?"

"Not for twenty-four hours," I agreed. He thought carefully for a moment.

"You delivered last time. We have a deal," Charlie Dibbs decided.

---ooo0ooo---

CHAPTER 25

July 25 to 26, Fullmere

THE DIGGER WAS COMING BACK. When I had called Hong Kong on the day before the Memorial Service, Inspector Harry Foung had told me that the hospital were preparing to release Duncan Mallory the next day. He would be staying harbour-side where Harry could keep an eye on him until he was strong enough to fly back. I waited until Wednesday and then telephoned the Holiday Inn to speak to Mallory direct.

"Welcome back to the land of the living, Digger. You've had us all worried."

"Had me worried too, old chum," Duncan said. "I couldn't think clearly until yesterday and I'm still a bit hazy at times, but I'll be back to normal by the time you see me. I'm taking the daytime flight tomorrow and, all being well, I'll be with you on Friday. Is anything happening back at the ranch?"

I brought him up to date on Aubrey Pinkerton's killing, Chief Inspector Cartwright's investigations and the elimination of local suspects as the unknow traveller on the night ferry to Rotterdam.

"He's not making much progress at present. It might help if we can get the records of Canning Kwok's telephone calls to and from the UK. Harry Foung said that he had applied for them nearly a week ago," I said.

"They're promised today and I'll bring a copy with me. Is there anything else I can do from here?"

"One thing crossed my mind. You might ask your pal Visser in Amsterdam to find out from Van den Groot if

Pinkerton and his lady friend collected any other paintings with the Monet original on 12th June. May not be relevant but it would be interesting to know," I suggested.

"You're right, I should have asked when I was there. I'll give him a call now. See you Friday," Mallory repeated.

Gaby had been listening to the exchange and questioned me when I put the receiver down.

"What do you have in mind when you asked him to find out if Pinkerton had brought back more than one painting?"

"It occurred to me yesterday that if they were planning to steal the Monet they would have to return a signed fake to St. Winifred's and that hasn't happened. I wonder why," I explained.

"In which case, we're looking for two paintings somewhere locally," she reasoned.

"Not necessarily together in the same place," I said, complicating the logic.

---ooo0ooo---

Gaby headed off to the Gallery and I started to catch up on my work. There was nothing more to be done for the time-being on Percy Mansfield's Hong Kong book. Surprisingly, he had accepted my criticism of his opening chapters. He had taken the point about libel risk and was now going to substitute verbatim comments made by his Chinese contacts in place of his own personal account of the Governor's private remarks. Robert Schindler thought that would satisfy the lawyers without detracting from the controversial stance of the book. I hoped he was right.

There was progress on my own China book. Both the bank and Swayne Mackenzie had confirmed their sponsorship; so I was ready to start work on commissioning content. I faxed my Chinese co-editor to suggest that for this edition he might prefer to visit us in London, air fares and hotel paid, rather than have me make a more expensive visit to Beijing. After the Hong Kong excursion, my taste for travel to the Orient had dimmed, at least for the time-being. That left me with the rest of the day to ponder further on the criminal goings-on in Oxford and locally in which Aubrey Pinkerton had been a prime mover. I thought that it would be interesting to find out just how long it would take to walk from the bottom field along the stream to Fullmere Mill and this would serve the dual purpose of exercising Fred. When we set out he was still a bit wary of the water meadow but once we were on Eastwick land he perked up and bounded ahead. I found that the Mill was further distant than I had expected. When Bill and I had walked part of the way on the weekend of the Festival it had taken us some twenty minutes. I realised now that our casual amble had covered less than half the distance and it was another half hour's walk at a faster pace before Fred and I reached the boundary fence of the Mill estate. The going was harder over the second leg of the walk but there was something of a track from the fence for the final hundred metres where the grass had been trodden down indicating that Aubrey Pinkerton might have set out on foot along that route the previous Saturday. Where had he encountered his nemesis, I wondered? Unless he had been dragged into our water meadow by his killer, it had to be somewhere from which the swollen stream could have carried him through. On the way back, I kept closer to the stream and looked out for any signs of human activity. Encouraged by my repeated cry of "High-low", the phrase which Fred's trainer had assured me would spur him to adopt retriever mode, he joined in the search. In the penultimate Eastwick field before home he seemed to have detected something, displaying a keen interest in the base of a sturdy willow overhanging the stream. The ground in front of the tree seemed muddier and there were the marks of heavy boots over a flattened area of turf. There were no stray clues in sight which the police might have picked up, but the bark of the tree trunk and branches at head height were scarred by recent gashes consistent with the discharge of a shotgun at short range. Aubrey Pinkerton had received the blast that killed him full in the chest; so it appeared that there hsd been a second shot. Why, I asked myself? Not even the poorest of shots could have missed at that distance. However, if Pinkerton had been flung backwards into the stream at this point, it was at least possible that the body could have been carried during the downpour through into our water meadow.

I became more convinced than ever that the key to exposing the killer was the identify of Pinkerton's collaborators. This took me back to discovering where and with whom he had lodged the painting when he brought it back from Amsterdam. Having eliminated Valerie Wyngarde and Georgina Delahaye from the list, who else was there locally with whom he might have had any kind of relationship? Really, there were only two: Barry Fullerton or the Mansfields. I decided to try Barry first and, instead of returning home, we cut up the hill and through the village football field to the back of the Eastwick Arms. He was presiding behind the bar serving his lunchtime customers. I slid on to a stool and ordered a pie and a pint for myself and "the usual" for my companion. Fred was always a welcome visitor and Barry kept a supply of dogfood behind the bar from which he was now served.

"Barry," I began when we were settled "we were talking about Aubrey on Sunday and I want to ask you another question. Did he ask you to look after a package for him about the size of a painting several weeks ago?"

Barry studied me quizzically. "As a matter of fact he did and I can remember exactly when. It was the weekend before Piroska's concert at the Mill. He wanted to hand it over then and there. I sensed that he was up to something shady and I turned him down pretty sharpish," he recalled. "Why do you ask?"

"We know that he was involved in substituting copies for original paintings from Oxford colleges via the Clarendon Gallery and one of them has gone missing. Is there anyone else locally whom he might have asked?"

"Only the Mansfields up the road. I have to deliver bottles and glasses there this afternoon for the Conservative Party summer drinks party tomorrow evening. Would you like me to ask them for you?" Barry offered.

"Better still, why don't I ride up with you and give you a hand," I suggested.

---ooo0ooo---

Barry picked me up in his flatbed Toyota early evening and we rolled up to the stable yard of the Hall just as Silas Grimshaw was preparing to drive Agnes Black home.

"Oh good," Lady Lucinda Mansfield greeted us. "You've brought someone with you to help with the humping. Let's have the bottles and glasses here in the kitchen overnight and, while you're here, you could set up the trestle tables in front of the house now. It's not expected to rain."

Having received our marching orders we set about our tasks, unloading cases of bottles and glasses from the back of the Toyota. The hardwood tables were stored in a stable and had to be carried one by one between us with separate journeys for the iron trestles; we left them leaning against a wall for assembly the next day.

"Silas and Black can do that in the morning," Lucinda ruled.

Sir Percy Mansfield emerged from the front door having heard the sounds of our table activity.

"Good gracious, Julian. I didn't know you had a second occupation as a furniture removal man," he joked with heavy humour.

"Actually, I came up here with Mr. Fullerton for a quite different reason," I told him.

"In that case, you must enlighten us," Lucinda insisted.

"As you know Aubrey Pinkerton was shot and killed at the weekend in the fields between here and the village. The police have established that he was engaged in a scheme to take original paintings from Oxford colleges and substitute copies through Theodora Deakin's gallery. I'm helping them look for one of the most valuable paintings which has disappeared. We think Aubrey may have parked it with somebody who knew him, and I wondered if he had asked you to keep it for him," I said, repeating roughly the same explanation I had given to Barry.

"I told you we should never have let him store that package in the stables. We were receiving stolen goods," Percy declared.

"Do you still have it?" I asked.

"No longer," Lucinda replied without hesitation. "He brought it to us on the Sunday before the concert at the Mill and he collected it last Thursday. Of course, we had no idea what it was."

The sequence of Pinkerton's actions seemed clear. Having failed to persuade Georgina to take the painting on his return from Amsterdam, and then Barry immediately after, he had lodged it with the Mansfields and then recovered it after he received news of the debacle at the Hong Kong auction. All very well, but it didn't help to determine where the painting was now. I assured Lucinda and Percy that they would not be in trouble if they told Chief Inspector Cartwright what they had just told me. Percy went off to telephone Cartwright at once and we took our leave.

Back at the farm, I found Gaby watering the roses. I gave her the full account of Fred's and my day. Nothing of much of interest had occurred at the Gallery; however, Valerie had been less weepy although still deeply depressed and there had been only two customers whom Gaby had served. I went inside to pour drinks and found a fax waiting for me from Hong Kong which Mallory must have arranged to be sent for him after he left. He had contacted Commissaris Visser in Amsterdam who had interviewed Van den Groot again at the police station. This time, he was able to charge him with sending a signed copy of the De Hooch to the auction house with intent to pass it off as the original and pressed him to make a complete statement. Van Den Groot confirmed that Pinkerton had collected not one but two paintings from his studio on 12th June, the original and a signed copy. He pleaded that both copies had been exported which helped to mitigate the charges, but the Commissaris had enough to shut down the studio and to provide Mallory with the ammunition he sought.

With a large Ballantine's at my elbow and a glass of wine poured for Gaby I sat on the terrace and reviewed my previous conclusions about Pinkerton's disposal of his package. I pondered on whether there was any difference in the significance of his actions if the "package" contained the two paintings rather than one. Probably not. But if he was trying to stash only one, presumably that would be the original. One way to settle the matter was to ask Barry; so I called him.

"You said earlier that Aubrey tried to pass on his package 'then and there'. Did you get a look at it?" I asked.

"It was in the back of his car tied up in a dust cover- Definitely the shape of a picture frame and pretty bulky," Barry replied.

"Could it have been more than one picture?"

There was a pause while he considered. "Certainly, two pictures of the same size; that would explain the bulk. But more than two - I think not.

---ooo0ooo---

Lucinda Mansfield's weather forecast had been optimistic. The sky was overcast with rain clouds from the time we arose on Thursday and there were showers throughout the morning. Chief Inspector Cartwright was interested to hear the results of my findings the previous day although I had the impression that he would have preferred his own team to have come up with the information first on Pinkerton's offloading of the paintings. We agreed to talk again later in the day after Duncan Mallory had arrived.

Georgina and Gaby had been press-ganged by Lucinda to help with the distribution of drinks and nibbles at the constituency party and Gaby had arranged that Georgina would collect her just before 6:00 p.m. giving them half an hour to set up. The invitations stated that the Member would be addressing the assembled gathering at 7:30 p.m. so there was plenty of time for me to join them, provided that the Digger had put in an appearance. The heavens opened just before Georgina's Bentley turned in to the stable yard and Gaby ran out to join her in mackintosh and rain hat. It seemed doubtful how many people would turn up to the event which would now have to be held indoors at Eastwick Hall. I changed into shirt and tie with a lightweight jacket and trousers, fed and watered Fred and continued to wait.

Finally, he arrived close to 7:30 p.m. driven in a police car which decanted him at the door with overnight bag before speeding away. The Digger looked in poor shape: his face was drawn and white and he had lost at least half a stone in the eight days since I had last seen him. His movements were those of an elderly man as he sat down but the old grin and familiar sense of purpose were still there as he faced me across the kitchen table.

"Wotcha, mate," he said, dumping a sheaf of papers in a plastic file in front of me. "Canning Kwok's telephone records for the past three months. The telephone company finally coughed just before I left Hong Kong."

"You look as if you should be tucked up in bed, Duncan. Do you want to go straight up and have a lie down? We can talk later when Gaby and I get back from the drinks party up the road in an hour or so," I suggested.

"I want to get this over. I know we're nearly there. Just scan the records and identify who Kwok was calling. Then we can make an arrest this evening and I'll sleep round the clock. Now give me a Scotch and start reading."

I poured us both a Ballantine's and got to work on the sheets in front of me. Trawling swiftly through the office records produced nothing but local calls and calls to and from mainland China. There had been less traffic through his home telephone but a number were overseas calls. Sorting by country codes I soon found the handful to and from the UK, prefixed by 0044 . They started with a twenty minute inward call in April followed by two shorter outward calls in May and three inward calls in June. All the calls were to and from the same UK telephone number. The last call by Kwok was from the day before the auction. There was no mistaking the identity of his correspondent; I had been there earlier.

---ooo0ooo---

CHAPTER 26

July 26, Fullmere

IT WAS AFTER 8.00 P.M. when we left. I had suggested that Mallory wait until Cartwright passed by but he insisted on coming with me. The Chief Inspector said that he and Sergeant Fellows would be with us in under the hour when I telephoned; he had been hanging on for my call at Kidlington. There were cars coming in the opposite direction on the way there; it seemed that the reception was already over and disgorging its attendees. A few stragglers were still leaving as we swept into the courtyard and parked behind the Bentley. I don't know quite what I expected but I was concerned that my questioning about Aubrey Pinkerton's package could have provoked some precipitate reaction.

An elderly couple, the man on sticks with a hearing aid, were saying their farewells to Lucinda. I was pleased to see that Gaby and Georgina were in their coats and preparing to leave. Any fears that I had about their safety were dissipated.

"I'm so sorry to have missed the party, Lucinda," I said advancing towards her "but I've brought someone with me just back from Hong Kong who has a message for Percy. Let me introduce you. Inspector Duncan Mallory – Lady Lucinda Mansfield." I saw here expression tighten and she withdrew the hand she had started to offer.

We had rehearsed our dialogue on the short drive over from the village and now it was Duncan's turn.

"Yes, I was particularly asked to deliver it in person," he said.

"You'd better come in then," she answered and turned on her heel to lead him inside.,

"You might like to hear this," I added signalling to the others "Do join us, if you have finished clearing up."

"I'll catch you up. I just want to put something in the car," Georgina responded. Gaby and I followed Mallory in Lucinda's wake around to the front of the house and into the drawing room.

"Percy, there's someone here to give you a message from Hong Kong," she called out. He's an Inspector Mallory from the police," she continued.

Sir Percy Mansfield appeared from the study in the same dapper attire he had worn when visiting us at the farm.

"It's always good to hear from old friends in Hong Kong. Do sit down and tell me," he said affably.

We settled ourselves on the sofa and in armchairs with Duncan facing Percy across the fireplace where he remained standing with his arm resting on the mantelpiece.

"Canning Kwok sends you his best regards. He's sorry that things didn't work out at The Regent but he hopes there'll be another opportunity to do business soon," Mallory stated baldly, making no attempt at subtlety.

"Canning Kwok?" Mansfield echoed. "I barely know the man. Met him at one or two of the Governor's receptions for local businessmen but that's all."

Mallory had taken Kwok's home telephone records from his breast pocket. "Well enough to call him at his flat on 22nd April. How do you account for that?" he asked. The colour drained from Percy Mansfield's face and he sat down heavily in a wing chair.

Let me help you to refresh your memory, Sir Percy," Mallory went on. "On July 10th Mr. Radclive here and I attended an auction at The Regent Hotel, Hong Kong, where Mr. Kwok bid for an original painting by Pieter De Hooch, the Dutch Master, disguised as a copy, which was knocked down to him at a fraction of its market price. The painting was taken from Latimer College for cleaning by the Clarendon Art Gallery. We think you were a party to this elaborate fraud. What do you have to say about that?"

"Don't say anything until we have our solicitor present," Lucinda Mansfield intervened.

"That's your right, sir. I can book you in at Kidlington police station for the night and we'll interview you in the morning," Mallory offered.

"I'm sure that we can sort all this out now, Inspector," Percy temporised, trying to sound confident. "I don't deny making that call in April and I'm sure the telephone records will show that there was a continuing flow of call both ways up to the time you were in Hong Kong. It all started with trying to do that fellow Pinkerton a favour. He came to us in April, you see, with this plan to sell off paintings by well-known artists there, passed off as copies, and then for them to be sold on at market value to wealthy Asian collectors. He offered us a share of the profits which would have been very welcome. All we had to do was to find and recruit the collaborator in Hong Kong and then pass him instructions. I realised that we were engaging in something outside the law and I chose Canning Kwok. That's really all there is to it." He smiled hopefully.

"That's very helpful but it's not quite all is it? Some of those calls between you and Mr. Kwok were about the next painting after the De Hooch, weren't they?" Duncan persisted.

"That's enough, Percy. You've told the Inspector what he came here this evening to confirm. You can answer any more questions he has at the police station tomorrow," Lucinda tried again.

"It's no good, Lucinda. Might as well make a clean breast of our involvement with Pinkerton now," Mansfield assured her.

"That would be very sensible, sir." Mallory took out a notebook and pen from the same pocket.

"You're quite right, Inspector. The De Hooch sale was meant as a test case. If it went well, the next one down the line would be a more modern seascape painted by Claude Monet. Kwok was quite confident that he could sell it on for several million pounds. So, we talked about that as well and the financial arrangements between us."

"What were those financial arrangements and how did you organize the share-out?"

"The share-out was simple; each of us, Kwok, Pinkerton, ourselves and Theodora Deakin who procured the paintings through her Gallery would receive 25 per cent of the profit. To protect ourselves we set up a numbered bank account at a Swiss Bank into which all the money collected from the auction house, the end purchaser and even the copyist in Amsterdam would be credited."

"And who organised and administered these arrangements?" Mallory pressed him.

"We did, of course," Lucinda re-entered the conversation. "I made it a condition of our participation. We wanted to avoid the risk of being ripped off by any of the others."

Mallory was making a good job of extracting an admission but so far he hadn't really implicated Lady Mansfield as a key player. A brief nod from him signalled that it was time for me to have a go.

"Let's see if we can understand the timeline a bit better," I suggested. "We know that the De Hooch original with signature obscured was sent by DHL from Amsterdam to the auction house in Hong Kong and the fake to the Clarendon Gallery from which Pinkerton delivered it himself to Latimer where we saw it. But what about the Monet; what were the arrangements for the original and copy?"

"As we told you earlier, Julian, Aubrey Pinkerton dumped them both on us the Sunday before the concert at the Mill and collected them a week ago." Lucinda sounded more confident again. I decided to knock her off her perch.

"We know that he collected them from the Van Den Groot studio himself on 12th June which ties in with what you just confirmed but there was a woman driving the Volvo who had travelled over with him incognito on the previous night's ferry to Rotterdam. Was that you, Lucinda?" I asked abruptly.

She hesitated, just a moment too long before deciding that there was no harm in telling the truth. "How clever of you. Yes. I wanted to be sure that he wasn't going to run off with the original on his own account," she replied.

"And you've no idea where it is now. I suppose?"

There was no reply. Mallory resumed his questioning.

"About the Swiss bank account. Can you confirm the name and number of it for me? Then I'm just about done with my investigation for now. You'll both need to make formal statements in the morning before we decide whether charges may be brought?"

The Mansfield looked relieved. "May I bring the account details with me when we come to the police station in the morning?" Sir Percy asked.

"Better to get it for me now while we wait for Chief Inspector Cartwright to join us."

"Why is Cartwright coming? You said you had nearly finished your investigation."

"He wants to question you both about Aubrey Pinkerton's murder on your land last Friday evening."

Lucinda Mansfield looked up sharply. She had begun to relax but her expression tightened at the mention of the Chief Inspector's name and she looked uneasy again.

"The bank book is in the top right hand drawer of your desk, isn't it Percy?" she said. "I'll fetch it for you while you give these people a drink. Pour me one too, won't you." She stood up and moved towards the study.

"Will you go with her, please, Mrs Radclive - in case Lady Mansfield needs help in finding the bank book," said Mallory, more as an order than a request.

They left the room and Percy busied himself with glasses and an unopened bottle of Pinot Grigio on a side table at the back of the room. I could hear another car draw up in the courtyard and Detective Chief Inspector Cartwright with Sergeant Fellows entered from the direction of the kitchen. The Sergeant was carrying a shotgun which I recognized as one of Lucinda's Holland & Holland matched pair.

"Is your wife here? I'm here to talk to her rather than you, sir," the Chief Inspector asked Sir Percy.

"She's next door with Mrs. Radclive," Mallory answered for him and I nodded towards the study.

---oooOooo---

The next few minutes were like the dénouement in an episode of a well-loved TV detective series. Gaby emerged from the study looking bewildered. Propelling her forward with the muzzle of the Browning automatic pistol she had taken from Sir Percy's desk, Lucinda Mansfied advanced into the room. She motioned Gaby to join me on the sofa and pointed her gun at the Chief Inspector and his Sergeant.

"Sit down both of you," she commanded.

"I can see you know why we're here," said Cartwright sitting himself carefully on the edge of an upright chair with its back to a side wall.

"You think I killed Aubrey Pinkerton deliberately." Lucinda sounded almost normal - but not quite; her voice was that of an automaton.

"We've received the pathologist's report of the autopsy and it says that the shot which killed Mr. Pinkerton was fired from a 16 bore shotgun with unusually choked barrels. The county register of licences shows that you are the only recorded owner of such a weapon in this vicinity. Can you confirm that the gun Sergeant Fellows is holding which he found in your kitchen just now is your property."

"Of course, it's my gun," she snapped "but you've got it all wrong. It was self-defence. I only meant to scare him."

"Why don't you tell us what happened, Lady Mansfield," Cartwright encouraged her. "You have the right to remain silent but anything you say may be taken down and used in evidence against you. However, since you have already started you may prefer to go on."

"Last Thursday he came to collect the Monet copy so that it could be delivered to St. Winifred's, giving us more time to dispose of the original safely. Then, on Friday morning he telephoned us to say that he had taken the original instead and would keep it until we agreed a new deal to split the proceeds after a sale. I agreed to meet him that evening in the bottom field by the stream," she continued.

"You said earlier that Pinkerton collected both paintings: the original and the copy. Does that mean you still have the copy here?" Mallory asked.

"Very well. I misled you; the copy is upstairs under a spare room bed, but that has nothing to do with what happened next," Lucinda Mansfield replied impatiently. She maintained a firm grip on the Browning, no longer pointing it direct at the Chief Inspector but covering the five of us seated in front of her while she remained standing with her back to the fireplace. Percy remained at the drinks table.

"Inspector Mallory interrupted you. Please go on," Cartwright said.

"I took my shotgun with me when I went to meet him. He was a violent, unpredictable man and I felt at risk. He was upfront with his demands. He wanted my agreement to his taking the share of the pay-off that would have been Theodora's as well as his own. We haggled a bit and I offered to split it so that we each finished up with the same share on condition that he returned the original painting here. He agreed to the split but refused to bring the Monet back or tell me where he held it. So, I fired a shot over his head to prompt him and show that I was serious.

That jolted him; he said, with a smirk that it was in safe hands and that someone called Arsene Dupin would show me the way. I don't know anyone of that name but he said that Georgina Delahaye would introduce me. While I was considering what to do next, he rushed me and tried to grab the gun. I wouldn't let him take it off me and in the scuffle it went off again and he fell down dead. I bundled him into the stream hoping that the body would remain there for a few days while I made contact with this Mr. Dupin." She looked at the Chief Inspector with feigned innocence.

"I shall ask you to come with me now to continue assisting us with our inquiry, You will be able to make a written statement at the police station with your solicitor present," Cartwright responded politely rising to his feet.

Something appeared to snap inside her. Lucinda's gun came up again and her eyes blazed. "I'm not coming with you – now or in the morning," she screamed. "Percy, come and take this gun off me and keep them covered while I pack a case for us both. We're driving to the airport."

"Drop it, sister," came a new voice from the French windows as Georgina burst in. It had been raining again and water sparkled on her shiny black trench coat and sou'wester. The weapon she held two-handed with practised ease was unmistakable by its rectangular shape and light colour as a 9mm Glock 43.

---ooo0ooo---

Lucinda swung her gun towards Georgina, intending to shoot it out. Her reactions were hopelessly slow. A single shot from the Glock shattered her wrist and her own weapon fell to the floor. Gaby, who was nearest to her, scooped it up.

The tableau rearranged itself. Lucinda Mansfield sat in the chair vacated by Sergeant Fellows, nursing her wrist wrapped in a tea towel and in obvious pain. The Chief Inspector had telephoned for an ambulance, police cars and uniformed officers and now stood across from her holding her gun. Georgina swept the sou'wester off her head, shaking out her hair, discarded her trench coat and draped it over an upright chair by the door with the Glock stowed in a pocket. Mallory gripped Sir Percy firmly by an arm and led him to the sofa while Gaby and I went upstairs, retrieved the fake Monet from under a double bed and returned with it to the drawing room.

Cartwright resumed his questioning. "We'll come to you later, Mrs. Delahaye, but while Lady Mansfield is with us, perhaps we could talk a little about the two murders after the concert on June 21. Did you instruct Pinkerton to kill Theodora Pinkerton up at the lake?" he asked Lucinda.

"Hardly. He was stuck on Theodora. She had asked him to persuade me to abandon the plan for disposal of the Monet and return it to the College. I said I would discuss it with her after the concert and he informed her during the performance. What happened up at the lake was an accident," she said.

"Tell us about it," the Chief Inspector invited her.

"She was waiting for me when I arrived. We started to walk round the lake and I tried reasoning with her. She couldn't understand that with a £1 million or more share from the sale she could leave Oxford and live comfortably anywhere she liked in the world. After all, it wasn't as if she really loved Alexander. On the other side of the lake, we came to the place where the raft was moored; she attacked me and we struggled on the bank. One minute she had her hands round my neck choking me – the next she slipped and fell back hitting her head on the punt pole to which the raft was attached. I tried to revive her but she was dead."

"And on your way back, you encountered the waitress Molly Bennett?"

"There was a girl down at the bottom with one of the waiters at the back of the marquee but I didn't pay her any attention."

Georgina looked up as if about to say something but thought better of it and remained silent. The police arrived and Lucinda Mansfield was taken away in the ambulance with a policewoman accompanying her. Sir Percy was arrested and removed in a police car without the indignity of handcuffs. Sergeant Fellows was despatched to book them both, taking with him Lucinda's pair of 16 bore shotguns.

The rest of us regrouped to review the events of the past hour. Mallory poured us each a glass of the Pinot Grigio and we settled down. Ever a policeman, Cartwright opened the batting.

"Let's start with you Mrs. Delahaye. I assume that you have a licence for that handgun."

"Oh yes. When I left America the FBI fixed for me to be issued with a special licence on application from the Embassy. I was still at risk from the Mob and they have long tentacles over here," she answered.

"Why did you bring it with you tonight?" Gaby asked.

"I didn't. Normally, I keep the gun in the glove compartment of the Bentley but I took it into the house last weekend to clean and never returned it. I saw something here when we were setting up to make me think you might need some insurance when you arrived. You'll remember, Gaby, that when we were opening up the cases for the wine bottles we wanted scissors or a knife to cut the Sellotape and Lucinda produced a Stanley knife from her handbag? Well, that reminded me of poor Molly who had her throat slit. So, I drove home quickly to collect the Glock."

"If you're right, Molly's DNA may still be on the blade. I'll send it to forensics in the morning," said the Chief-

Inspector. "She probably did see the girl having a fag with her friend on her way up to the lake – not down."

"And the girl was alone at the bottom of the steps when she came down and had to be silenced permanently," Mallory finished for him.

"What do you think of her account of Theodora's death. Is it possible that it was an accident?" I asked.

"Highly unlikely, but we may not have a conclusive case; her Counsel might make something of it in Court. However, if the case against her for Molly's murder is open and shut, I don't see a jury believing her. Why would she have killed the girl, if it was an accident?" the Chief Inspector reasoned.

"That leaves Aubrey Pinkerton's shooting which is where we started this evening. Could it have been the outcome of a struggle?"

"The autopsy showed no powder burns on his clothing and the report concludes that he was shot at the same distance, probably about twenty feet, as the first shot at the tree behind him."

"You seem to have your murderer, Chief Inspector, but what about your investigation, Mr. Mallory?" Georgina enquired.

"Not quite there. One thing puzzles me. Before your timely arrival, Lady Mansfield told us that Pinkerton had said that someone called Arsene Lupin could show the way to the Monet original and that you would make the introduction. What did he mean?" Duncan replied.

Georgina and I looked at each other and laughed. She threw back her head and chuckled throatily. "Why, Arsene Lupin is indeed an old friend. He's Edgar Allan Poe's fictional private detective."

Enlightenment dawned in Gaby's face too and she almost spilt her drink with excitement.

"I know what you're both thinking and I've got it. '*The Purloined Letter*' must have inspired him," she said.

"Yes, we know now exactly where he put the canvas. We can collect it in the morning." I added.

"Good for Aubrey. Great to have shown a sense of humour at the time of his death," Georgina observed.

---ooo0ooo---

CHAPTER 27

July 27 to late October, around and about Oxford

"ISN'T THERE A RISK of it being sold?" Georgina had asked on our way to Little Clarendon Street the following morning. I couldn't answer her immediately. Now that we were grouped around the waist-high rack of suspension files loaded with paintings, prints and photographs in the basement of the Clarendon Gallery, I was better able to assess the risk.

Chief Inspector Cartwright had not joined us. He was busy at Kidlington police station supervising the taking of statements and engaging with the Director of Public Prosecution's office to frame the three murder charges against Lucinda Mansfield. The fraud charges against Sir Percy Mansfield were of less consequence and could wait. Sergeant Fellows had taken his written statement with a solicitor present and he had been released for the time being.

Those of us grouped in front of the unframed Claude Monet original included Valerie Wyngarde as well as the Digger, Georgina, Gaby and myself. I had extracted the canvas from its file and applied turpentine to the bottom right-hand corner to reveal the artist's signature. We admired the vibrant colours of sea and sky in the late Impressionist work of art.

"What's happened to the frame?" Georgina questioned me again.

"It's on the copy which we found under a bed at Eastwick Hall last night. Duncan has it back at the police station," Gaby said.

Most of the pictures and photographs in the files had price tickets on their backs. Only a few including the Monet had stickers with the initials P.O.A. - price on application. I was ready to now to answer Georgina's first question.

"You'll remember that in *The Purloined Letter* the thief conceals the stolen note by affixing his personal stamp to the envelope and placing it in the letter rack at his office where no-one will think of looking. Well, Pinkerton did something similar using the P.O.A. sticker. It wouldn't prevent someone off the street from picking out the Monet but if he or she wanted to buy it they would have to request whoever was serving to quote a price." I turned to Valerie and asked. "What would you do if that happened?"

She didn't hesitate. "I'd ask Aubrey. He selected everything for these files and always sets the pricing." Then, woefully "I really don't know what I shall do now."

"You've made your point, Julian. With a partner he didn't trust Pinkerton was taking only a minimal risk," Mallory said.

"Can we return the Monet to St. Winifred's this morning, Inspector?" Georgina asked him hopefully.

"I don't see why not, provided that the College signs a receipt. The fake copy with false signature is what I need as evidence and we already have that." He sat down and wrote out a formal receipt on a headed sheet that he took from his briefcase.

I helped Georgina take the Monet upstairs and outside to the Bentley parked on a yellow line. "I'll leave the receipt with Alexander's signature for Inspector Mallory at Kidlington police station on my way back, shall I?" she asked.

"I'll tell him not to expect it until the end of the day. I imagine that there'll be a degree of celebration between the two of you for the next few hours," I said.

She grinned wickedly and departed bearing gifts.

---ooo0ooo---

There was a lingering atmosphere of anti-climax over the weeks that followed. Both Chief Inspector Cartwright and Digger Mallory enjoyed their triumphs. For Cartwright, there was recognition that he had wiped the eye of Commander Wiggins and the Scotland Yard Murder Squad. He was rewarded with promotion to Superintendent and a wider Oxfordshire responsibility. Fellows passed his Inspector's exams and Cartwright took him on his team.

Duncan Mallory returned to London with a statement by Percy Mansfield which firmly identified Canning Kwok as a partner in the theft and disposal of paintings from Oxford colleges, enabling Harry Foung to arrest and charge him on his return to Hong Kong. Duncan's ability to achieve results by working effectively with international colleagues attracted attention from Interpol and he is being seconded to their Secretariat in Lyon with the rank of Chief Inspector. We plan to visit him there next year.

I fulfilled my promise to Charlie Dibbs. With Duncan's approval I gave him a full account of the art fraud which Aubrey Pinkerton had master-minded in partnership with Theodora Deakin and the Mansfields, including the sequence of steps in the investigation from Oxford to Amsterdam and back, then Hong Kong and finally back to the Gallery. I positioned Digger Mallory as the hero and played down my own role but gave him some attributable quotes. He did justice to the story, first as a headline news item which he sold to the national press and then in a longer article commissioned by a leading Sunday which specialises in investigative journalism. The feature article drew extensive public interest and has led to the offer of a permanent position as a staff journalist in Fleet Stret which Charlie is considering.

Lucinda Mansfield appeared at Oxford Crown Court on all three charges of murder in the second week of August.

The case against her was strengthened by a DNA match between the Stanley knife recovered from her handbag and the body of Molly Bennett. At a short preliminary hearing she was committed for trial at the Central Criminal Court and remanded in custody. She is held at Holloway women's prison and the trial is scheduled for the end of January.

Percy Mansfield denied any part in or prior knowledge of his wife's murder crimes and the DPP was content to leave it at charges of conspiracy to steal works of art and attempted fraud to which he pleaded guilty. At a preliminary hearing, he was granted unconditional bail and comes up for sentencing next month. Duncan expects him to serve time in an open prison with like offenders. Of course, his reputation is ruined but Schindler Lyne still want to publish his book and Robert has encouraged him to write an additional chapter about the criminal activities and graft committed by mainland Chinese officials living in Hong Kong. I've been to see Percy several times up at Eastwick Hall and continue to edit his manuscript as he sends the chapters through. He makes it difficult to be sympathetic by remaining as superior and conceited as ever. Perhaps denial is his protection against the humiliation which his appearance in Court and media attention will visit upon him.

Gaby and I remain pleased that we gave up living in London although life in Fullmere without drama will never be quite the same. My publishing projects abound and Robert has invited me to join the Board of Schindler Lyne. No extra money but it gives me a front seat in the enterprise. Gaby has persuaded Alexander Deakin not to close down the Clarendon Art Gallery and to take her in as a partner. It will take time to restore the Gallery's reputation but I am sure that she will. Valerie Wyngarde remains an employee and Christina Charteris has been told that the Gallery is no longer available as her private jewel box. I expect that she will want to sell her shares quite soon. Life has returned to normal for Fred who has found a black Labrador lady friend at The Old Rectory next door and enjoys his occasional lunches with Barry at the Eastwick Arms.

---oooOooo---

Last Thursday we dined on High Table at a St. Winifred's guest night. It was an evening dress occasion and most of those present in Hall were postgraduate students and graduate readers with a senior Common Room member at each end of table. They rose to their feet as Alexander Deakin led in the High Table party from the Common Room where we had been taking sherry. The other guests with us were a Congressman from Pennsylvania who had read law at St. Winifred's and his wife, a retired Anglican bishop and Georgina Delahaye. We were outnumbered by the eight St. Winifred's Fellows and wives who were exercising their entitlement to Hight Table attendance.

Gaby and Georgina eyed each other's dresses appreciatively: Gaby in midnight blue velvet and Georgina in restrained emerald green grosgrain, which offset perfectly her copper-coloured shoulder length hair. In the two months since we had last seen him Alexander had recovered his confidence and persona as Master. His cheeks had filled out and he had put on a little weight but it suited him. Tonight he was in ebullient mood enthusing about his recent trip to Hong Kong where he had trawled successfully among the local colleges of education and business leaders for next year's undergraduate intake. He had been accompanied by Georgina as his personal escort, paying her own airfare to avoid college criticism. His colleagues were generous in their thanks for her support in the recruitment drive. Alexander caught me by the arm and pointed at a blank space above the fireplace in which a log fire helped to keep off any autumn chill.

"That's where the Monet used to hang," he said. "I've moved it to the Fellows dining room where we'll take port and dessert later. The reason why it needed cleaning was the smoke from the fire over the years. We haven't decided yet what to put there in its place – probably some past St. Winifred's worthy, I expect."

The seating of guests at High Table had been predetermined by our host: to Alexander's right the Congressman, Frank Calloway, and then Georgina; to his left Gaby, then the Bishop and Nancy Calloway with myself beyond, flanked by the Senior Fellow's wife. We faced the body of the Hall opposite the various Fellows and their wives. I tried to keep the Congressman's wife involved in the largely parochial conversation at our end of the table but she was heavy going. The nasal twang of her Pennsylvania accent was unattractive and she displayed little enthusiasm for anything beyond life in Washington DC and no more than a passing interest in Oxford. At the other end of table Frank Calloway was holding forth on why Bill Clinton would not win a second term at the November Presidential election. I had formed an instant dislike of the man on meeting him before dinner; it was not just his inappropriate coloured bow tie which offended but the certainty with which he expressed his biased opinions. Georgina remained charming but I could see that patience was wearing thin among the rest of his audience.

In contrast to the company, the dinner was excellent. A coquille St. Jacques was followed by a half partridge each, crème brulee and angels on horseback as savoury. The food was accompanied by a Pouilly Fume and a Pichon Longueville which excelled. By the time we retired to the Fellows dining room most of us were feeling mellow; even Frank Galloway's brashness and Nancy's speech seemed less abrasive. The company rearranged itself to a different seating plan. Gaby was now on Alexander's right as he took his place at one end of the table and the two were soon in animated discussion about plans for the Gallery. On his left Nancy Calloway found common ground with the Senior Fellow who had just returned from a sabbatical as visiting lecturer at the Wharton School at Philadelphia University where she had taken a degree in social studies some years before. The bishop had been buttonholed by Frank Calloway who was telling him why American Evangelical Protestantism was superior to Anglicanism. Decanters of Port and Madeira were placed in front of the Master. The table was already set with a variety of fruit and nuts and with dessert plates and cutlery. I was pleased to find myself next to Georgina on her left at the other end of the table; it was the first time we had talked together since her liberation of the Monet from the Gallery.

"We've missed you in Fullmere. What have you been up to?" I asked.

"I've been a busy girl. Reorganising the business in London and spending time here in Oxford with Alexander at the weekends. We planned the Hong Kong recruitment trip carefully with entertaining every night for key players on the hit list and, as you've heard, it paid off."

"So, what now?"

"Well, I guess one thing leads to another, as they say." She lowered her voice and whispered in my ear. "Alexander has asked me to marry him. What do you think, Julian?"

"I'm delighted for you, Georgina – if that's what you want. How about the Wigmore Escort Agency? You won't be able to manage the business if you're the wife of the Master of St. Winifred's, will you?"

"I've taken care of that by making Gerald Marl a full partner and managing director. He's fully capable of taking it forward. I'll continue as non-executive Chairman and spend one day a week in London trying to extend the client base. Occasional use of Fullmere Mill for weekend house parties will be limited now to the most respectable longstanding clients. I'm trying hard to adapt to the life academic. How do you think I'm doing?" she asked, pouring herself a glass of port and passing the decanter to me.

"I'd say that you already have your feet under the High Table."

I poured myself a glass and raised it to her before passing the port decanter to my left. Georgina gave me her trademark wicked grin.

"Not bad for a broad from the Bronx," she said.

THE END

RITES OF SPRING

By
Jonathan Reuvid

When Julian Radclive joins the European office of a US multinational manufacturer in 1978 he doesn't expect to be involved in a possible murder on arrival at its recently acquired factory in a small German village, nor in the mysterious contraband traffic with a sister company in Brazil. And nobody told him that he would encounter murderous former Nazis in Germany or be dealing with a Gestapo war criminal when he visits Rio.

Avoiding the perils of corporate politics he enlists the uncertain support of British intelligence. Julian sets about rescuing his company from the threat of a looming public relations disaster. Playing amateur detective may be a game, but when he and his wife Gaby become targets for assassins the fun is soon over.

New Generation Publishing   ISBN 978-1-80369-047-6

Printed in Great Britain
by Amazon